# WHEN CROCS FLY

# WHEN CROCS FLY

Stephan T. Pastis

**Andrews McMeel**
**Publishing®**

a division of Andrews McMeel Universal

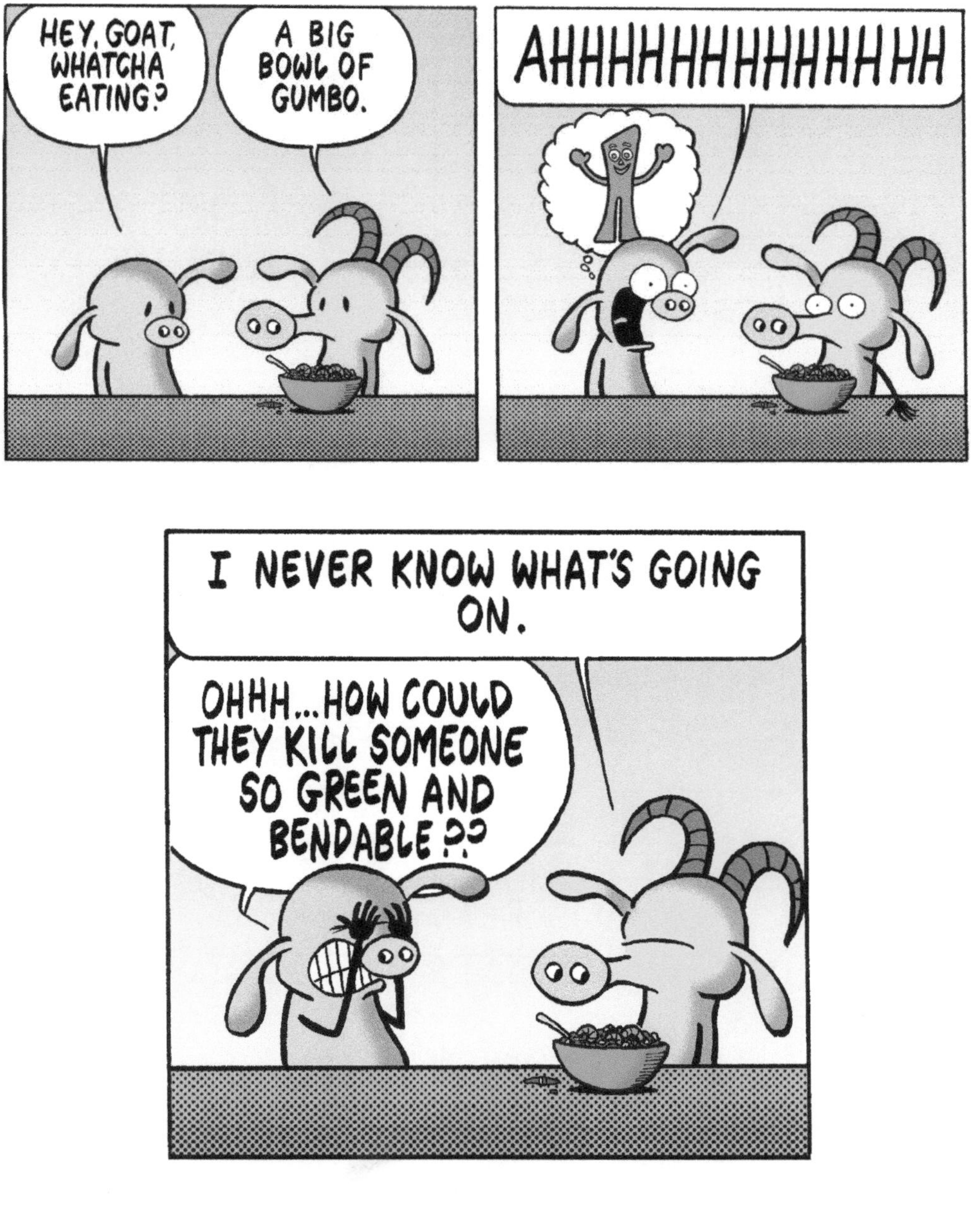
HEY, GOAT, WHATCHA EATING?
A BIG BOWL OF GUMBO.
AHHHHHHHHHHHHHH
I NEVER KNOW WHAT'S GOING ON.
OHHH...HOW COULD THEY KILL SOMEONE SO GREEN AND BENDABLE??

Zeeba neighba...Come heres.
WHAT DO YOU WANT.?
Time geev up. Crocs find you mail slot.

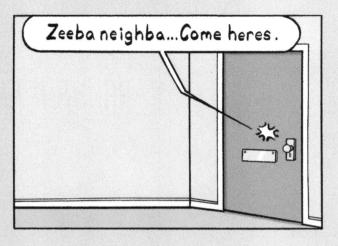

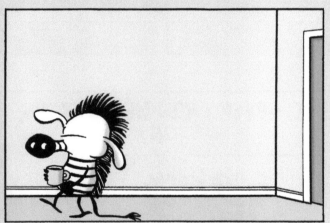

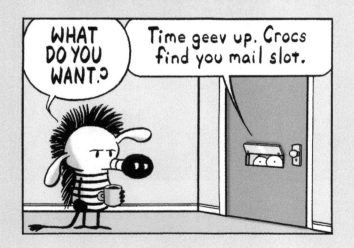

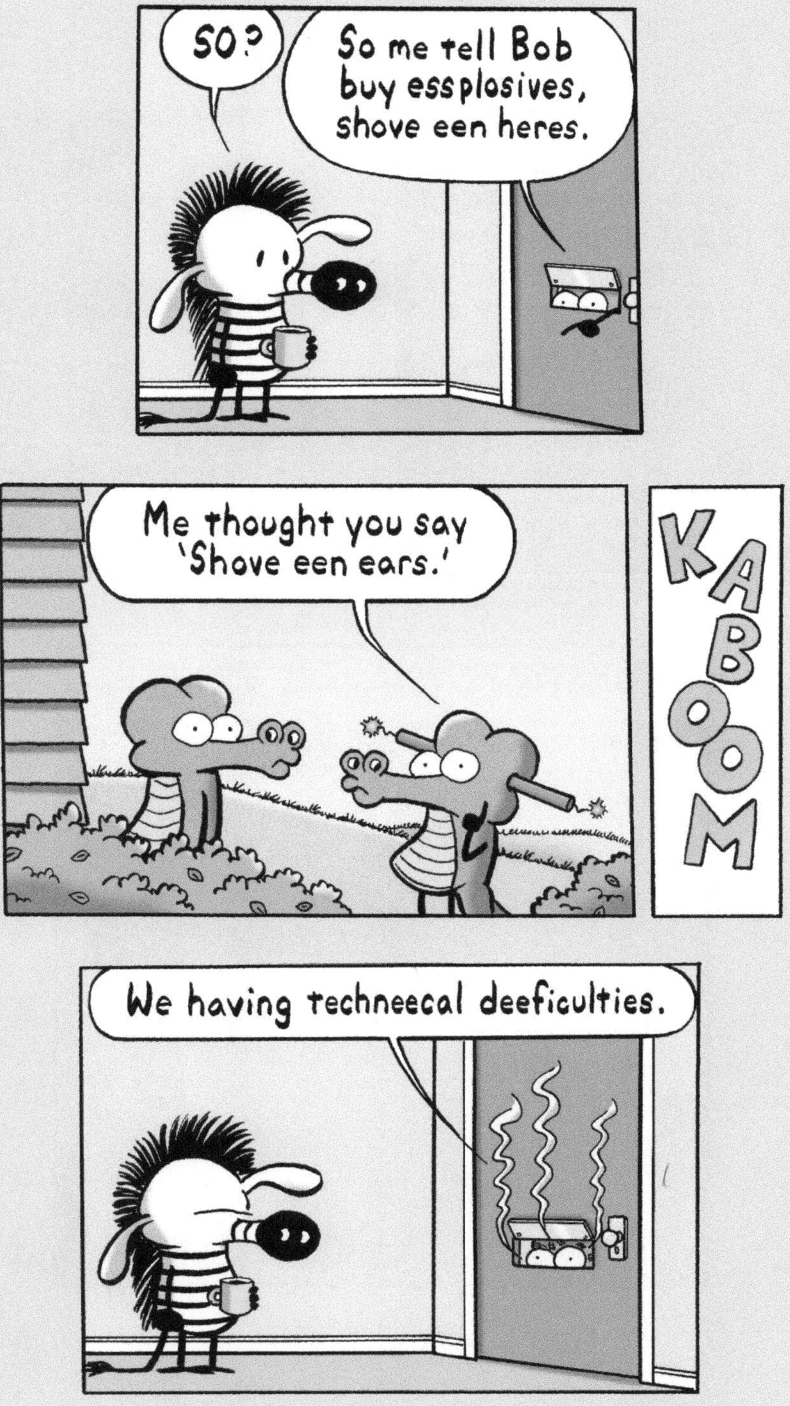
SO?
So me tell Bob buy essplosives, shove een heres.
Me thought you say 'Shove een ears.'
KABOOM
We having techneecal deeficulties.

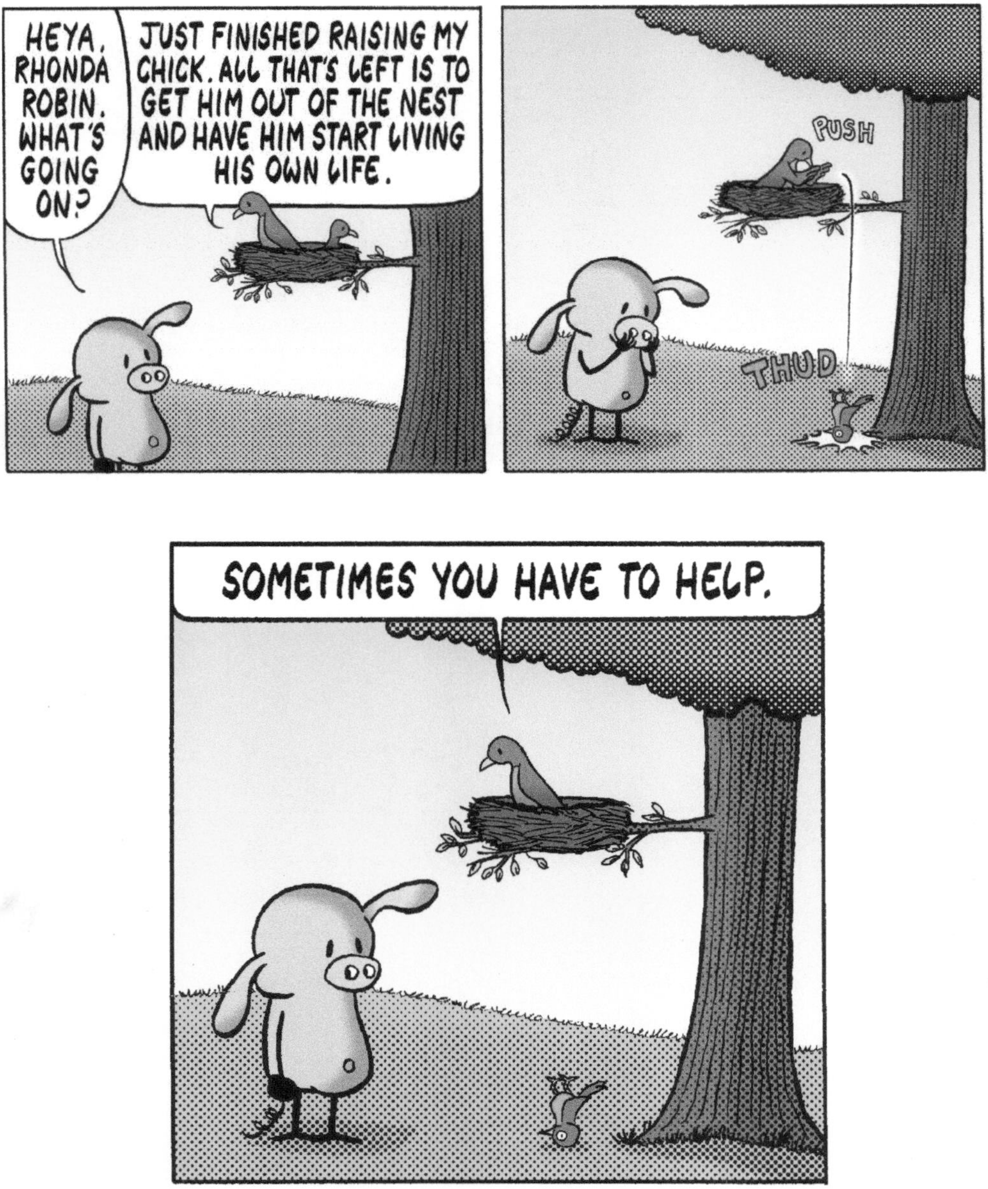
HEYA, RHONDA ROBIN. WHAT'S GOING ON?
JUST FINISHED RAISING MY CHICK. ALL THAT'S LEFT IS TO GET HIM OUT OF THE NEST AND HAVE HIM START LIVING HIS OWN LIFE.
PUSH
THUD
SOMETIMES YOU HAVE TO HELP.

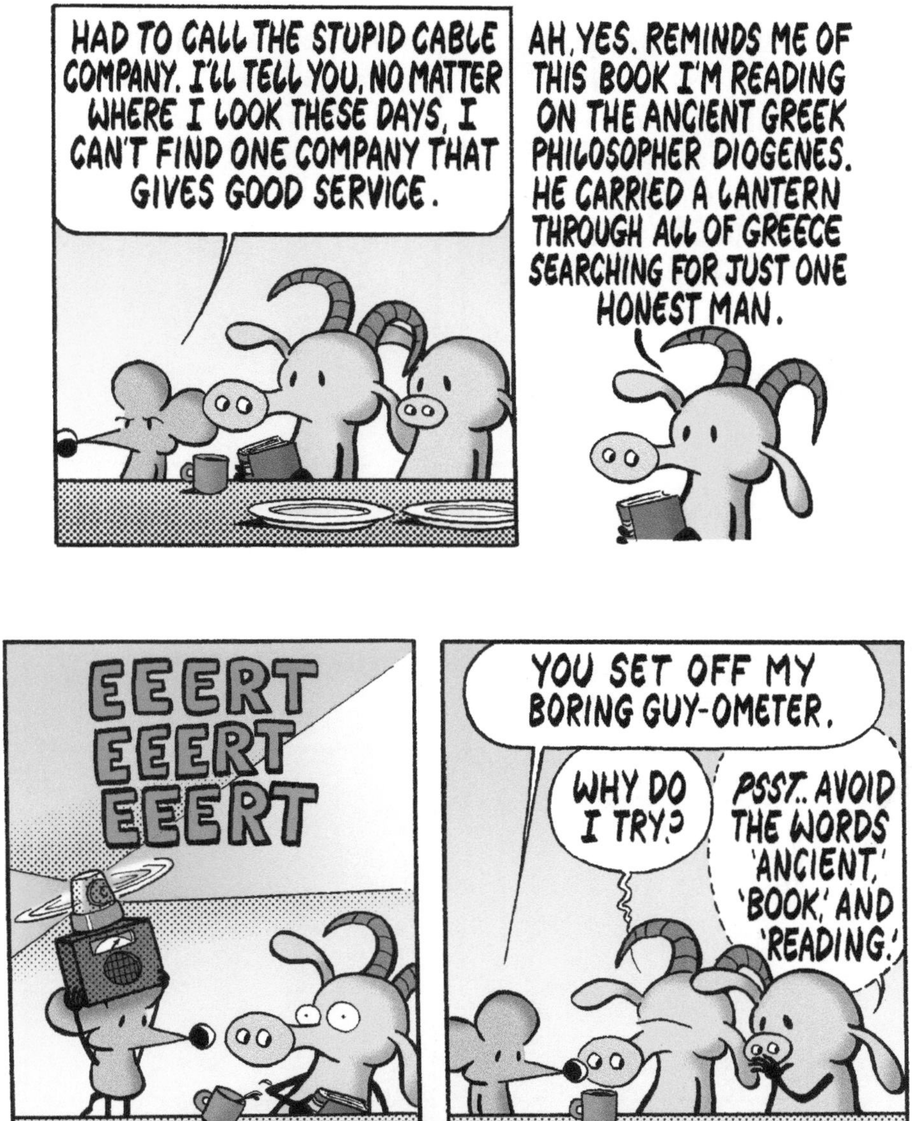
HAD TO CALL THE STUPID CABLE COMPANY. I'LL TELL YOU, NO MATTER WHERE I LOOK THESE DAYS, I CAN'T FIND ONE COMPANY THAT GIVES GOOD SERVICE.
AH, YES. REMINDS ME OF THIS BOOK I'M READING ON THE ANCIENT GREEK PHILOSOPHER DIOGENES. HE CARRIED A LANTERN THROUGH ALL OF GREECE SEARCHING FOR JUST ONE HONEST MAN.
EEERT
EEERT
EEERT
YOU SET OFF MY BORING GUY-OMETER.
WHY DO I TRY?
PSST.. AVOID THE WORDS 'ANCIENT,' 'BOOK,' AND 'READING.'

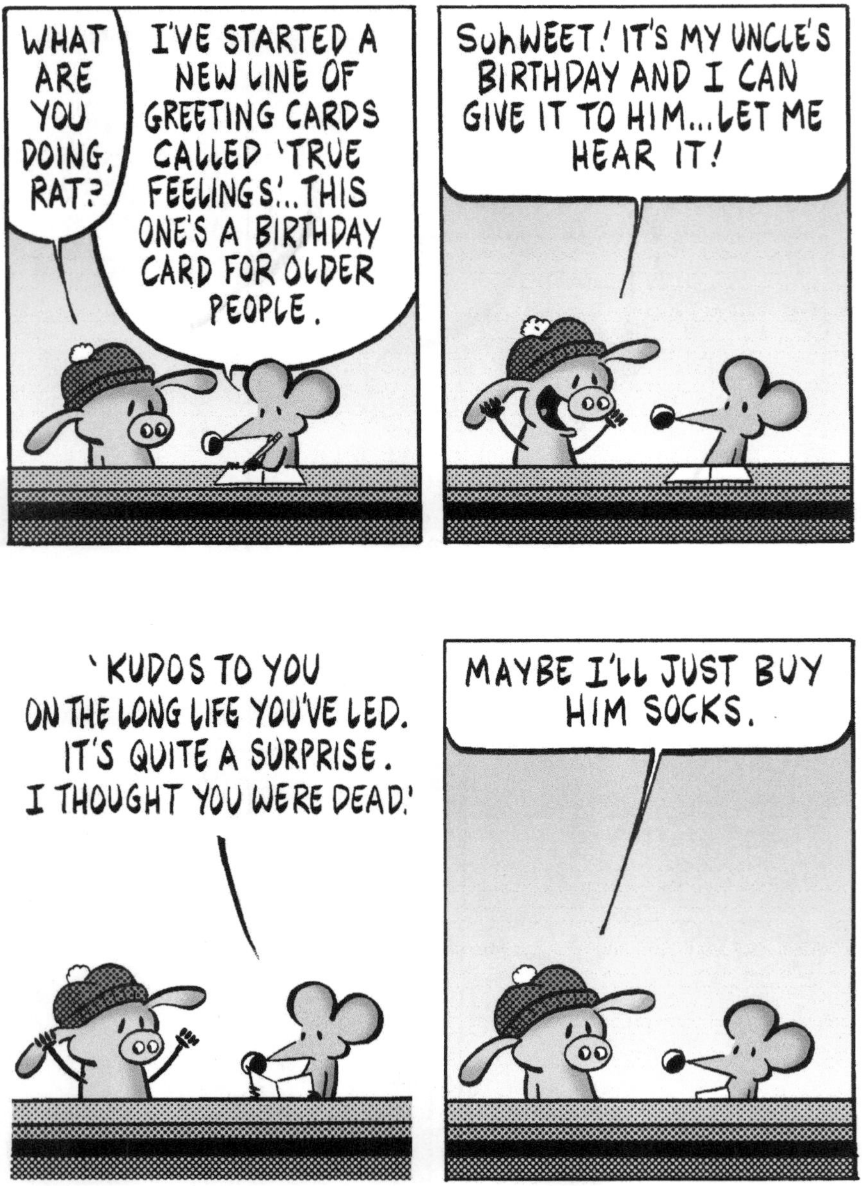
WHAT ARE YOU DOING, RAT?
I'VE STARTED A NEW LINE OF GREETING CARDS CALLED 'TRUE FEELINGS'...THIS ONE'S A BIRTHDAY CARD FOR OLDER PEOPLE.
SUHWEET! IT'S MY UNCLE'S BIRTHDAY AND I CAN GIVE IT TO HIM...LET ME HEAR IT!
'KUDOS TO YOU ON THE LONG LIFE YOU'VE LED. IT'S QUITE A SURPRISE. I THOUGHT YOU WERE DEAD.'
MAYBE I'LL JUST BUY HIM SOCKS.

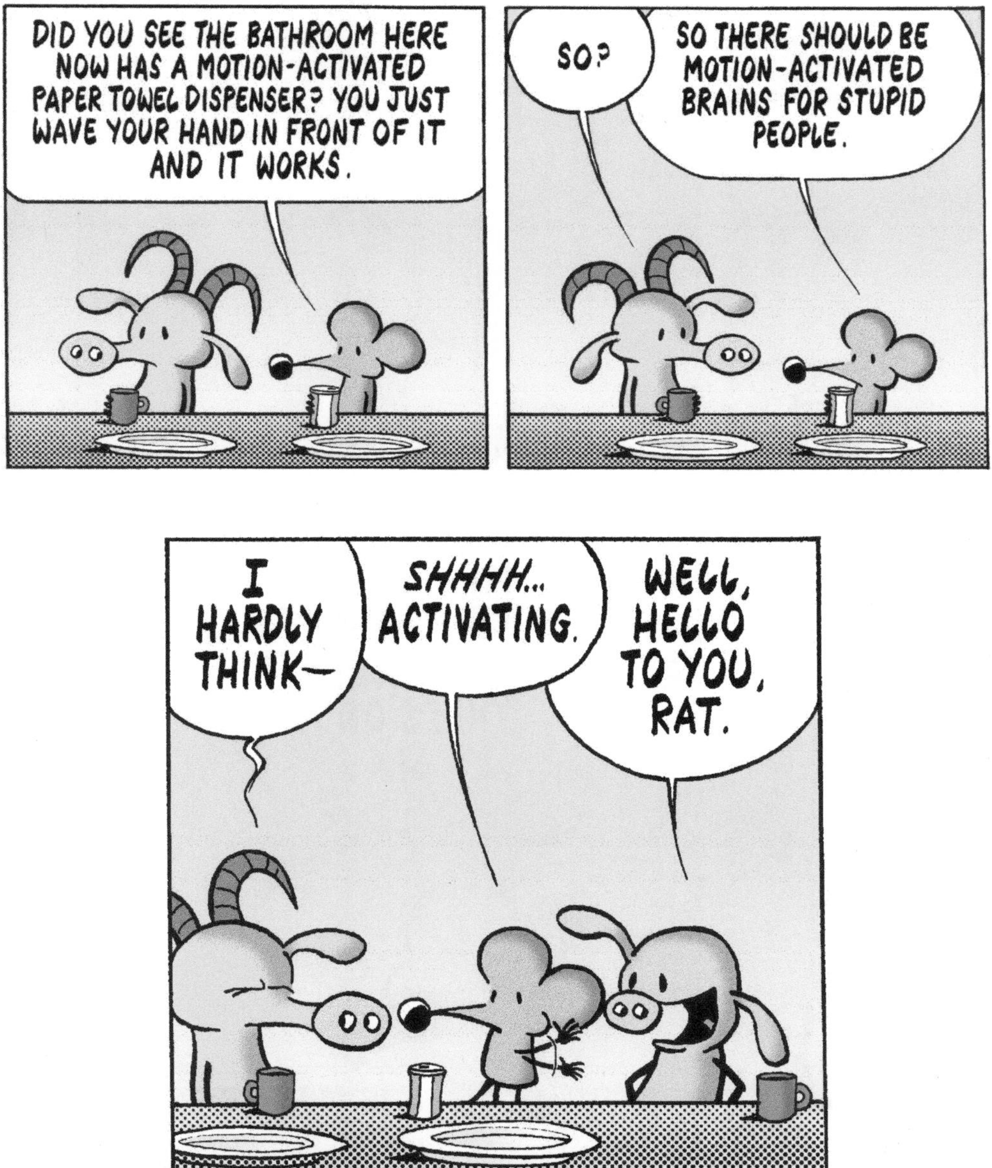
DID YOU SEE THE BATHROOM HERE NOW HAS A MOTION-ACTIVATED PAPER TOWEL DISPENSER? YOU JUST WAVE YOUR HAND IN FRONT OF IT AND IT WORKS.
SO?
SO THERE SHOULD BE MOTION-ACTIVATED BRAINS FOR STUPID PEOPLE.
I HARDLY THINK—
SHHHH... ACTIVATING.
WELL, HELLO TO YOU, RAT.

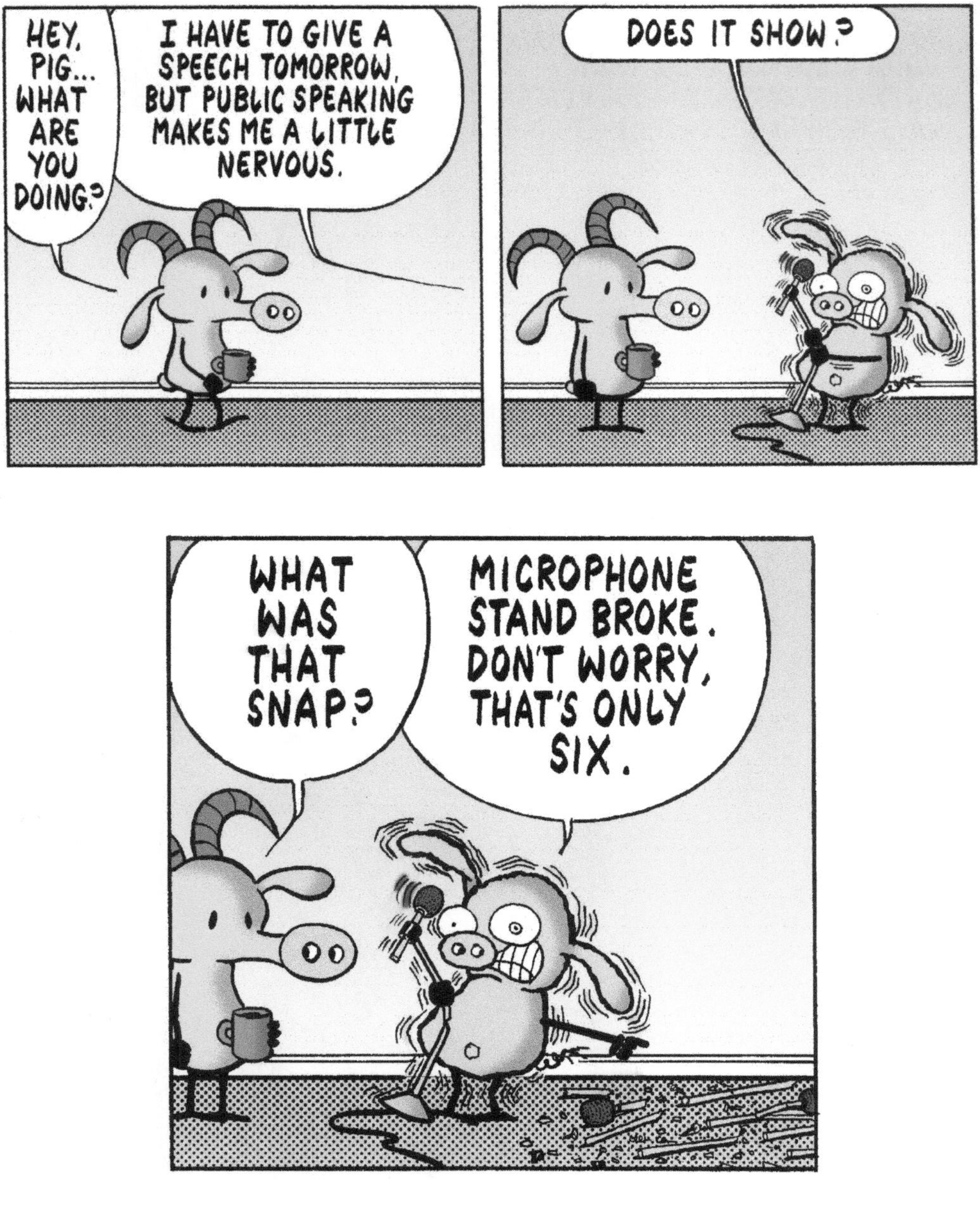
HEY, PIG... WHAT ARE YOU DOING?
I HAVE TO GIVE A SPEECH TOMORROW, BUT PUBLIC SPEAKING MAKES ME A LITTLE NERVOUS.
DOES IT SHOW?
WHAT WAS THAT SNAP?
MICROPHONE STAND BROKE. DON'T WORRY, THAT'S ONLY SIX.

HEY, RAT. WHATCHA WATCHING ?
THE START OF THE SUPER BOWL. THE PLAYERS RUN OUT OF THEIR LOCKER ROOMS AND DOWN THIS TUNNEL, THEN EMERGE FROM THIS CLOUD OF SMOKE ONTO THE FIELD.
THE LOCKER ROOM'S ON FIRE! THE LOCKER ROOM'S ON FIRE!

I SEE THE PRE-GAME SHOW HAS CONFUSED YOU.
RUN FASTER, FAT MEN, FASTER!!

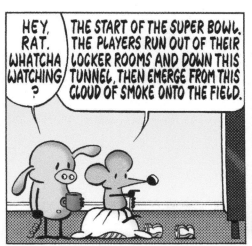

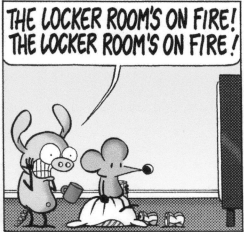

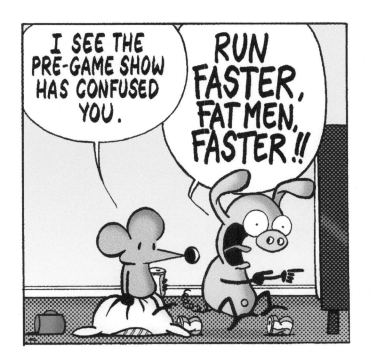

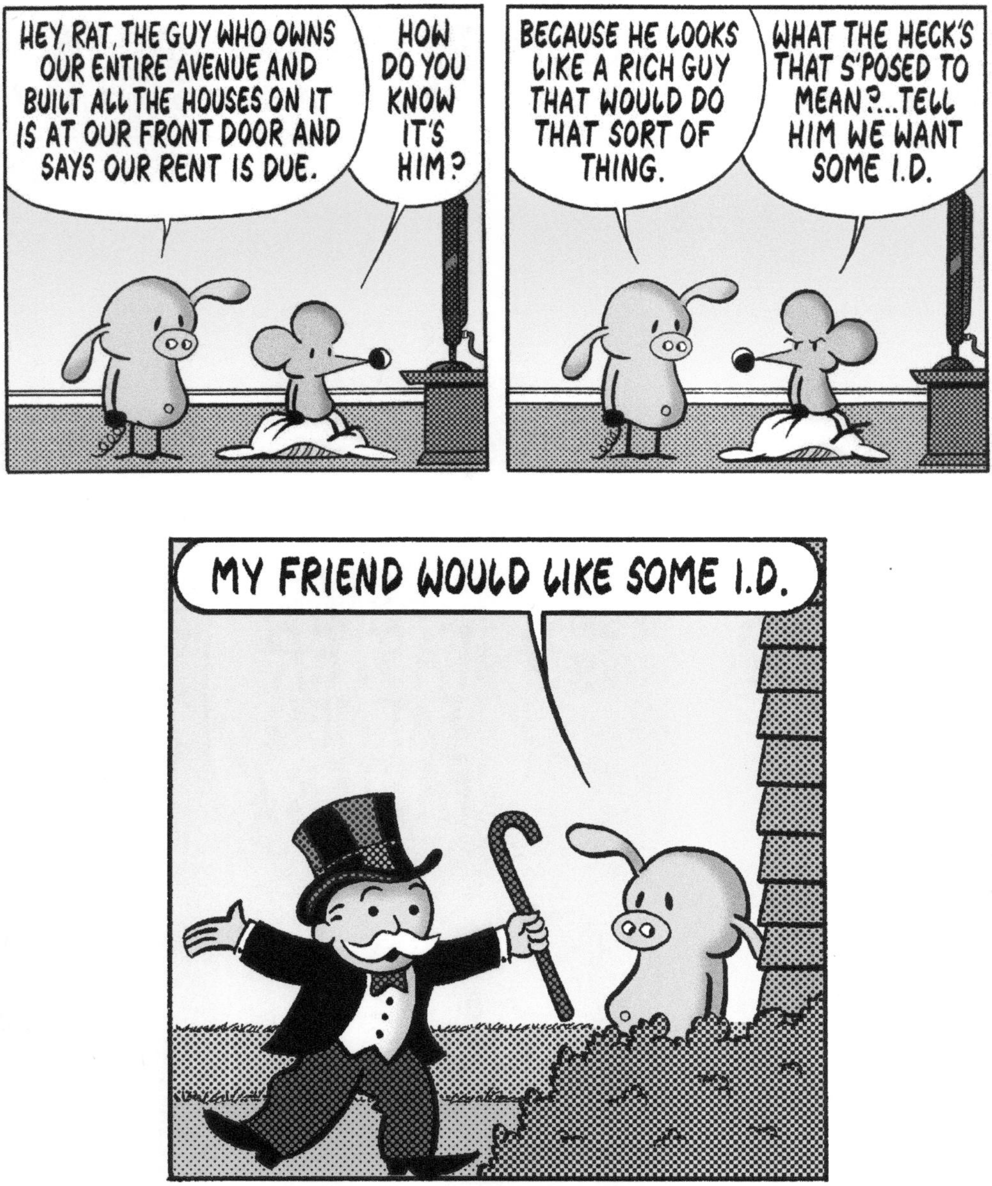
HEY, RAT, THE GUY WHO OWNS OUR ENTIRE AVENUE AND BUILT ALL THE HOUSES ON IT IS AT OUR FRONT DOOR AND SAYS OUR RENT IS DUE.
HOW DO YOU KNOW IT'S HIM?
BECAUSE HE LOOKS LIKE A RICH GUY THAT WOULD DO THAT SORT OF THING.
WHAT THE HECK'S THAT S'POSED TO MEAN?...TELL HIM WE WANT SOME I.D.
MY FRIEND WOULD LIKE SOME I.D.

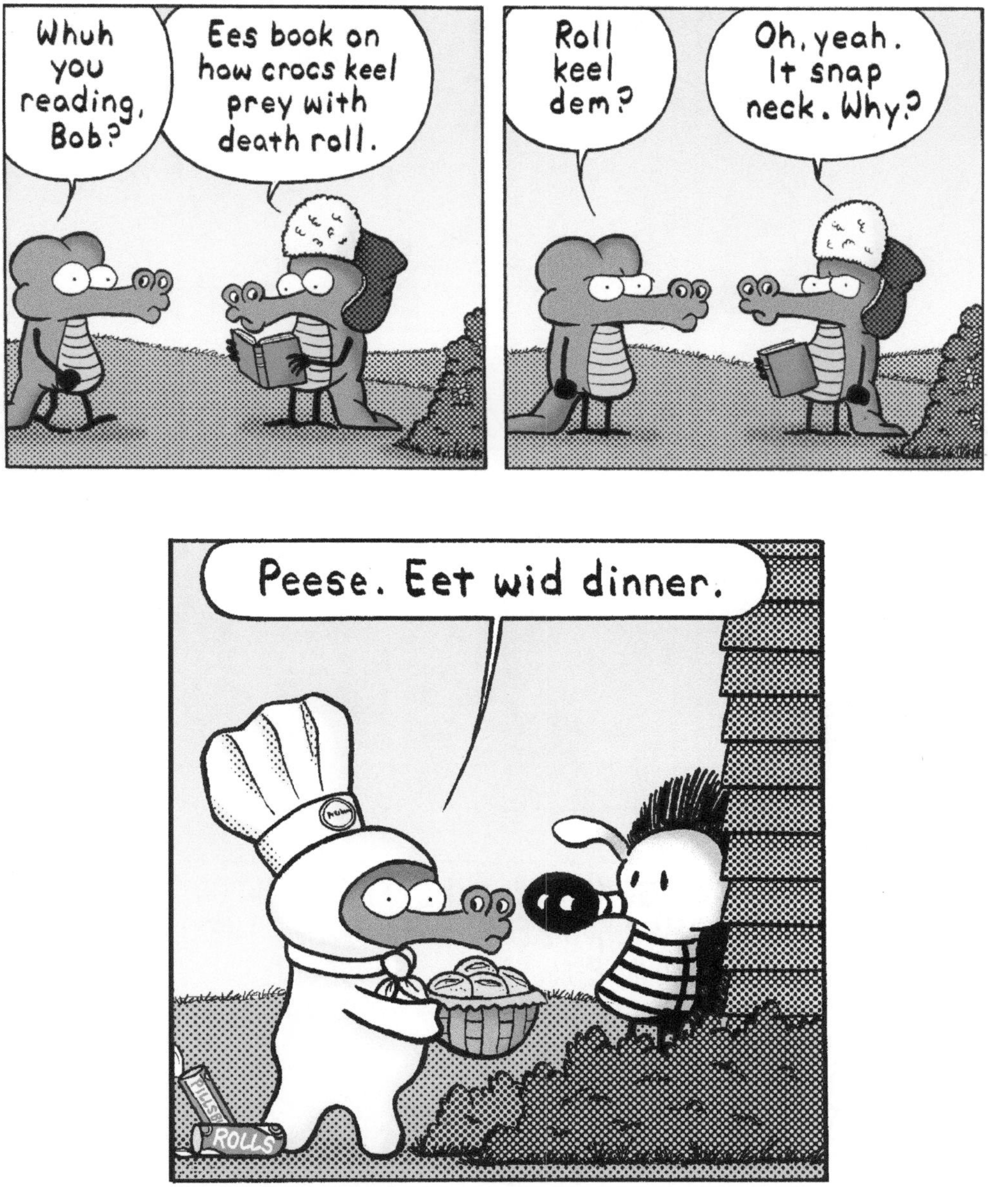
Whuh you reading, Bob?
Ees book on how crocs keel prey with death roll.
Roll keel dem?
Oh, yeah. It snap neck. Why?
Peese. Eet wid dinner.
ROLLS

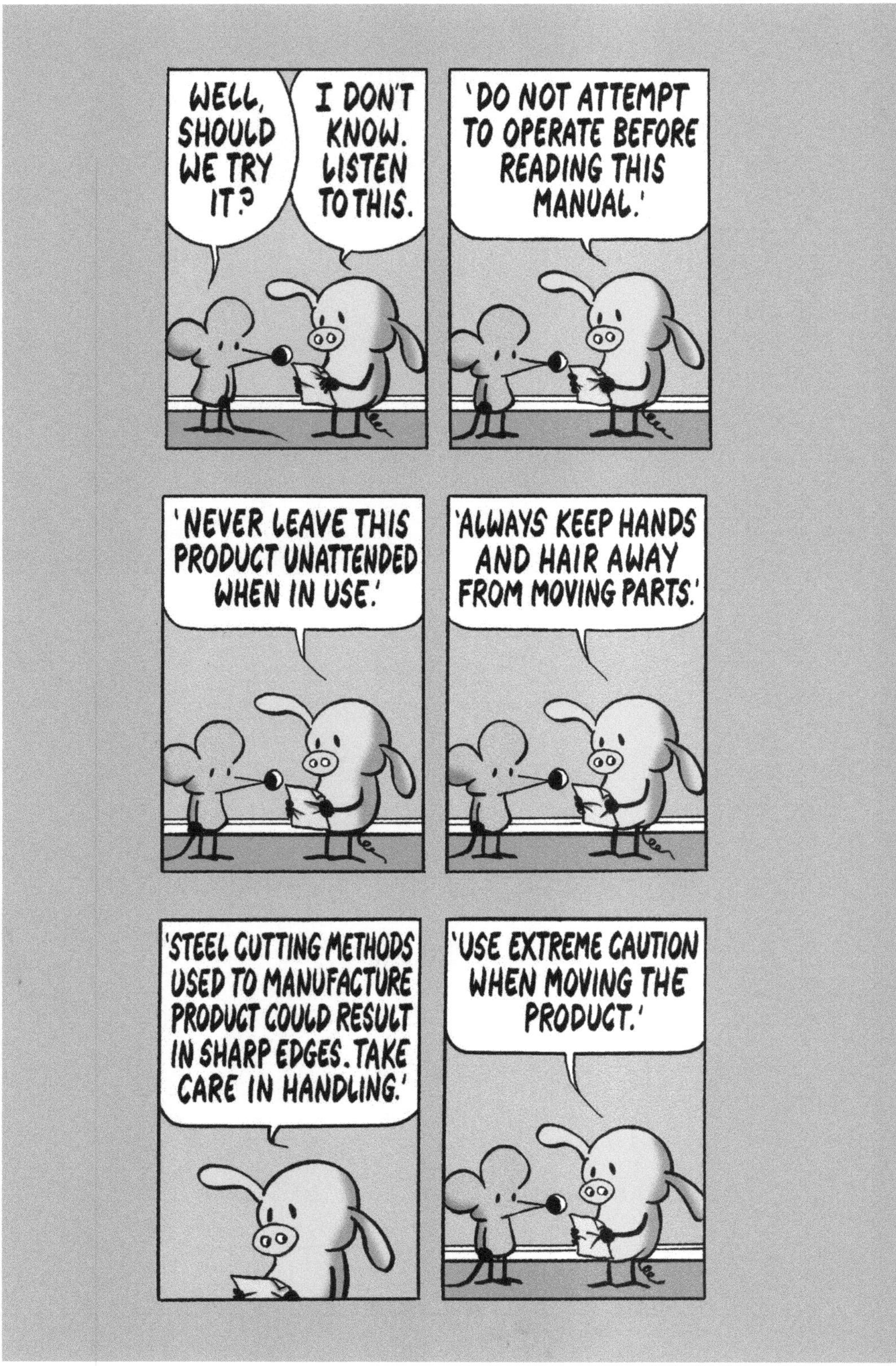
WELL, SHOULD WE TRY IT?
I DON'T KNOW. LISTEN TO THIS.
'DO NOT ATTEMPT TO OPERATE BEFORE READING THIS MANUAL.'
'NEVER LEAVE THIS PRODUCT UNATTENDED WHEN IN USE.'
'ALWAYS KEEP HANDS AND HAIR AWAY FROM MOVING PARTS.'
'STEEL CUTTING METHODS USED TO MANUFACTURE PRODUCT COULD RESULT IN SHARP EDGES. TAKE CARE IN HANDLING.'
'USE EXTREME CAUTION WHEN MOVING THE PRODUCT.'

'VERY HIGH TEMPERATURES ARE REACHED DURING USE. TAKE EXTREME CARE WHEN PRODUCT IS IN USE.'
'DO NOT OPERATE NEAR DRAPES, CURTAINS, OR WALLS, AS FIRE AND SUBSTANTIAL PROPERTY DAMAGE MAY RESULT.'
'FAILURE ON THE PART OF THE USER TO ADHERE TO THESE WARNINGS COULD RESULT IN SERIOUS INJURY OR DEATH OF THE USER.'
TOASTER
I'VE NEVER BEEN SO AFRAID OF A TOASTER.

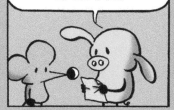

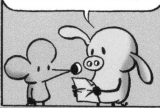

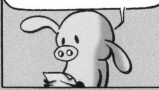

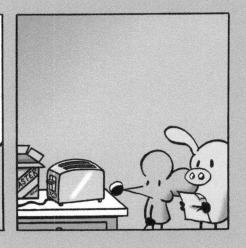

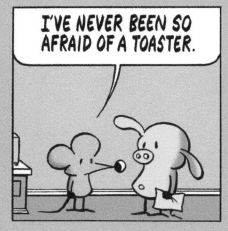

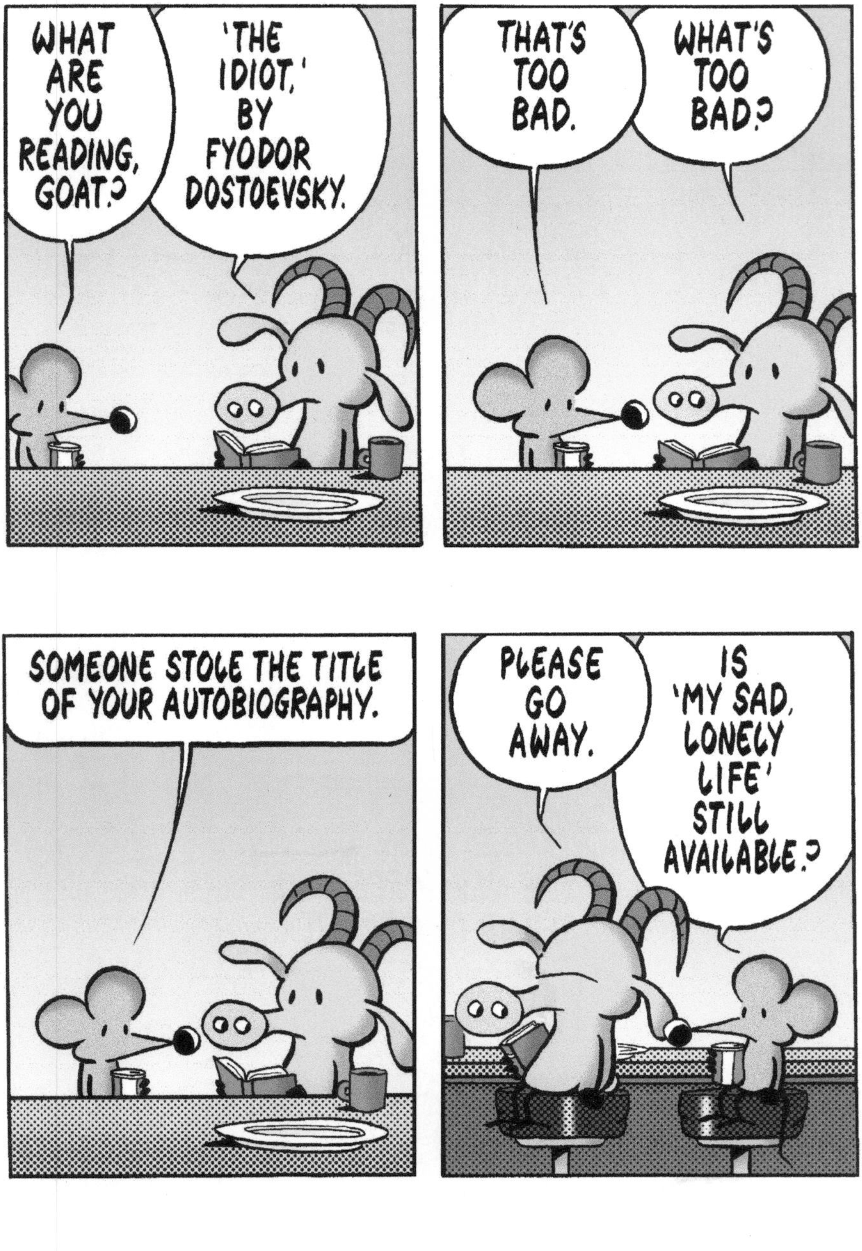
WHAT ARE YOU READING, GOAT?
'THE IDIOT,' BY FYODOR DOSTOEVSKY.
THAT'S TOO BAD.
WHAT'S TOO BAD?
SOMEONE STOLE THE TITLE OF YOUR AUTOBIOGRAPHY.
PLEASE GO AWAY.
IS 'MY SAD, LONELY LIFE' STILL AVAILABLE?

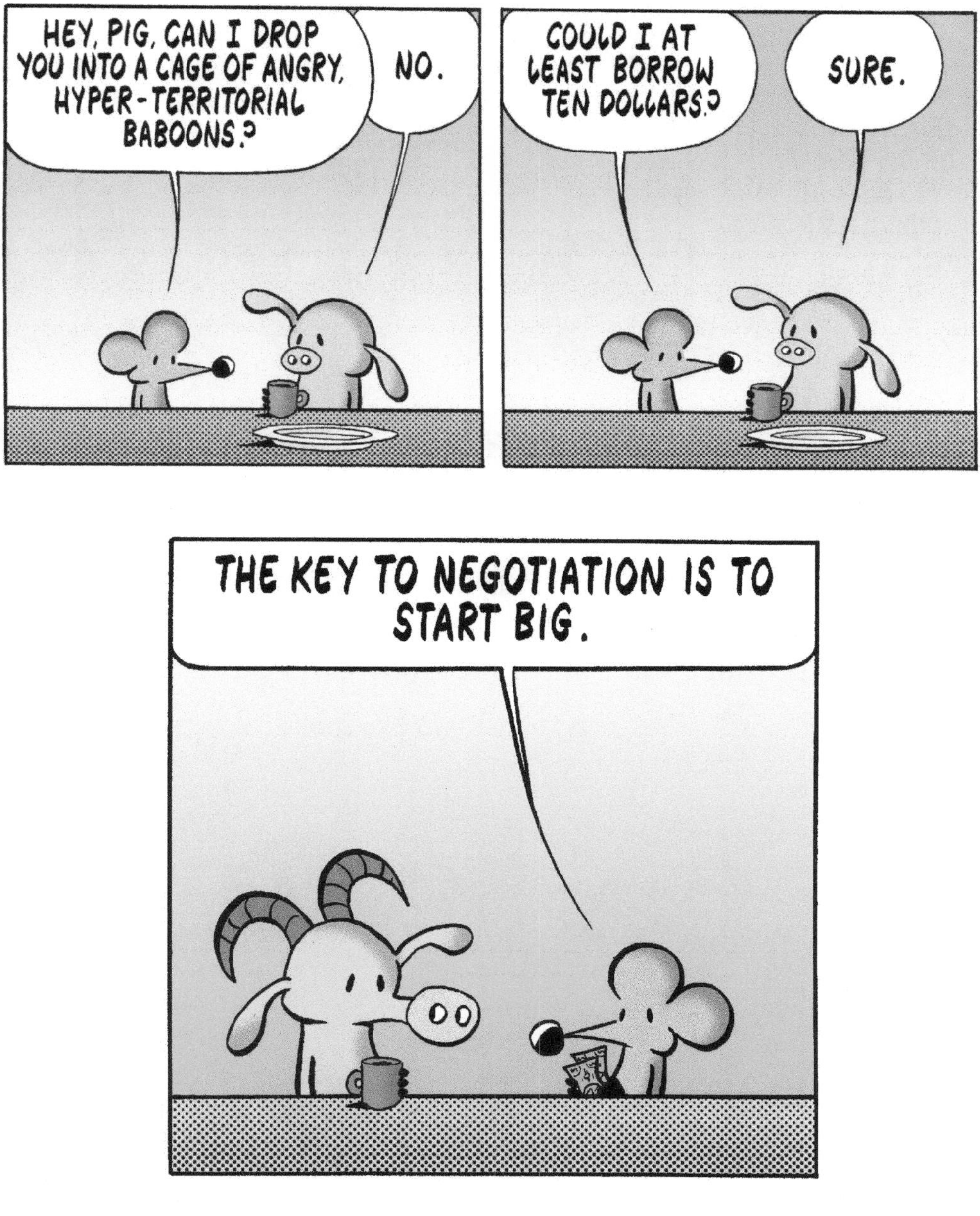
HEY, PIG, CAN I DROP YOU INTO A CAGE OF ANGRY, HYPER-TERRITORIAL BABOONS?
NO.
COULD I AT LEAST BORROW TEN DOLLARS?
SURE.
THE KEY TO NEGOTIATION IS TO START BIG.

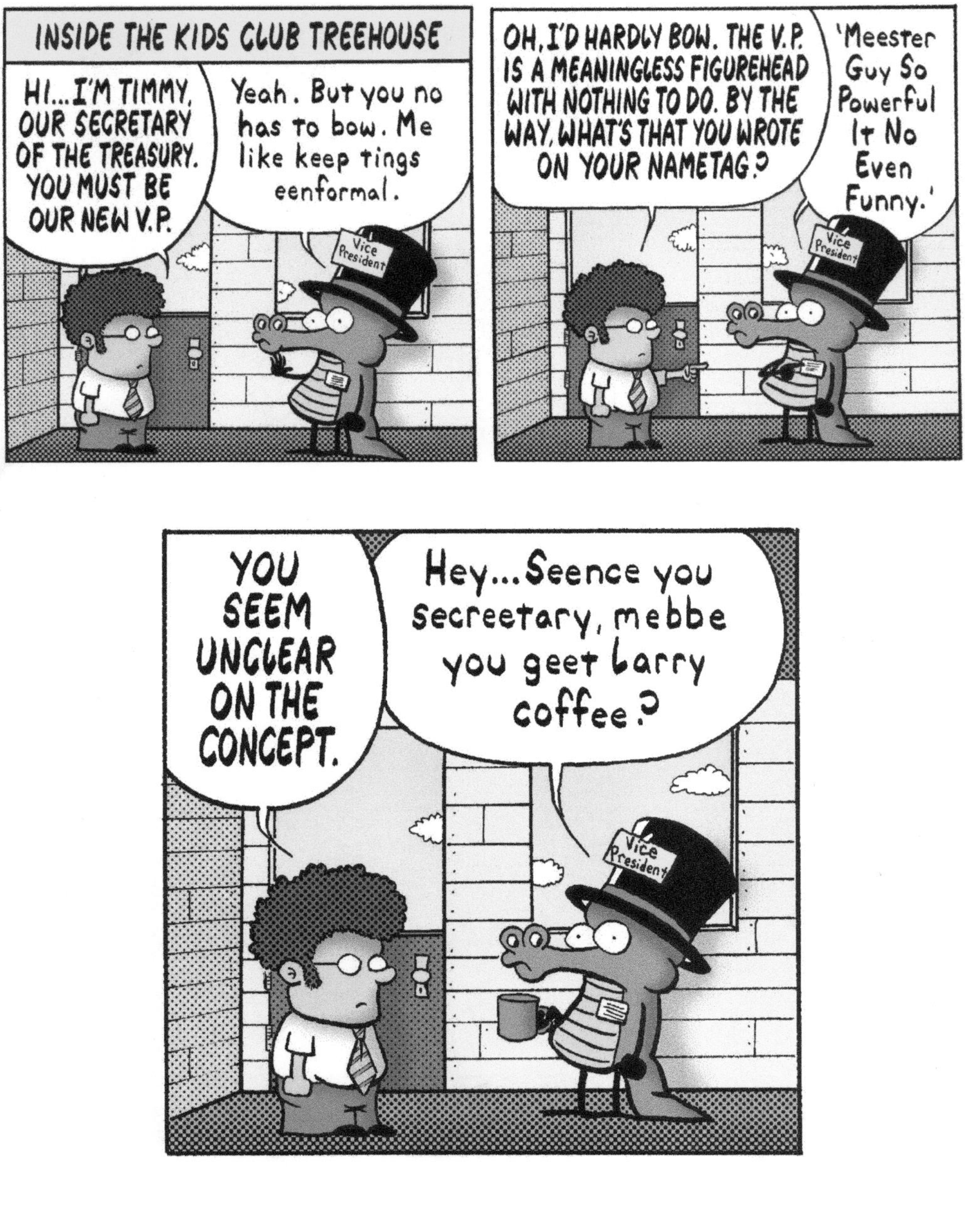
INSIDE THE KIDS CLUB TREEHOUSE
HI...I'M TIMMY, OUR SECRETARY OF THE TREASURY. YOU MUST BE OUR NEW V.P.
Yeah. But you no has to bow. Me like keep tings eenformal.
Vice President
OH, I'D HARDLY BOW. THE V.P. IS A MEANINGLESS FIGUREHEAD WITH NOTHING TO DO. BY THE WAY, WHAT'S THAT YOU WROTE ON YOUR NAMETAG?
'Meester Guy So Powerful It No Even Funny.'
YOU SEEM UNCLEAR ON THE CONCEPT.
Hey...Seence you secreetary, mebbe you geet Larry coffee?

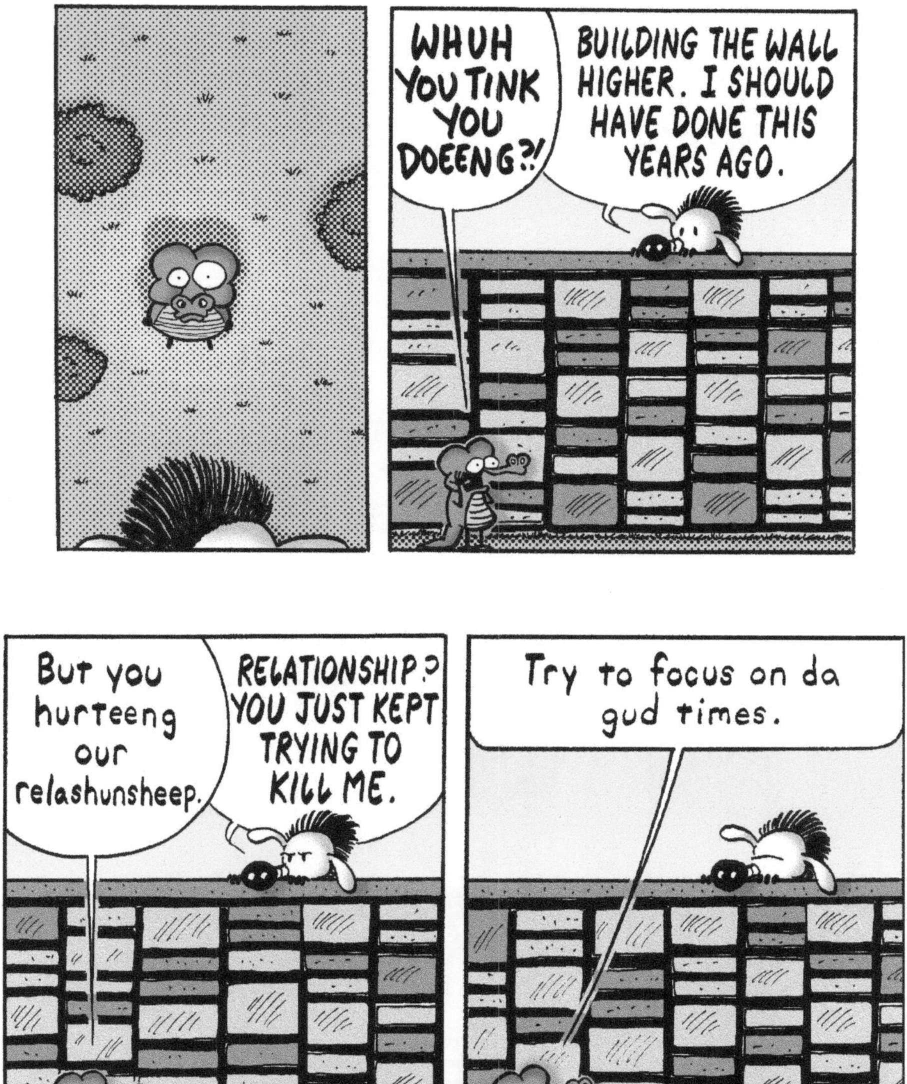
WHUH YOU TINK YOU DOEENG?!
BUILDING THE WALL HIGHER. I SHOULD HAVE DONE THIS YEARS AGO.
But you hurteeng our relashunsheep.
RELATIONSHIP? YOU JUST KEPT TRYING TO KILL ME.
Try to focus on da gud times.

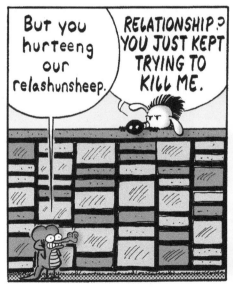

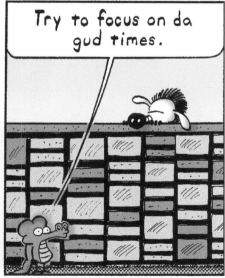

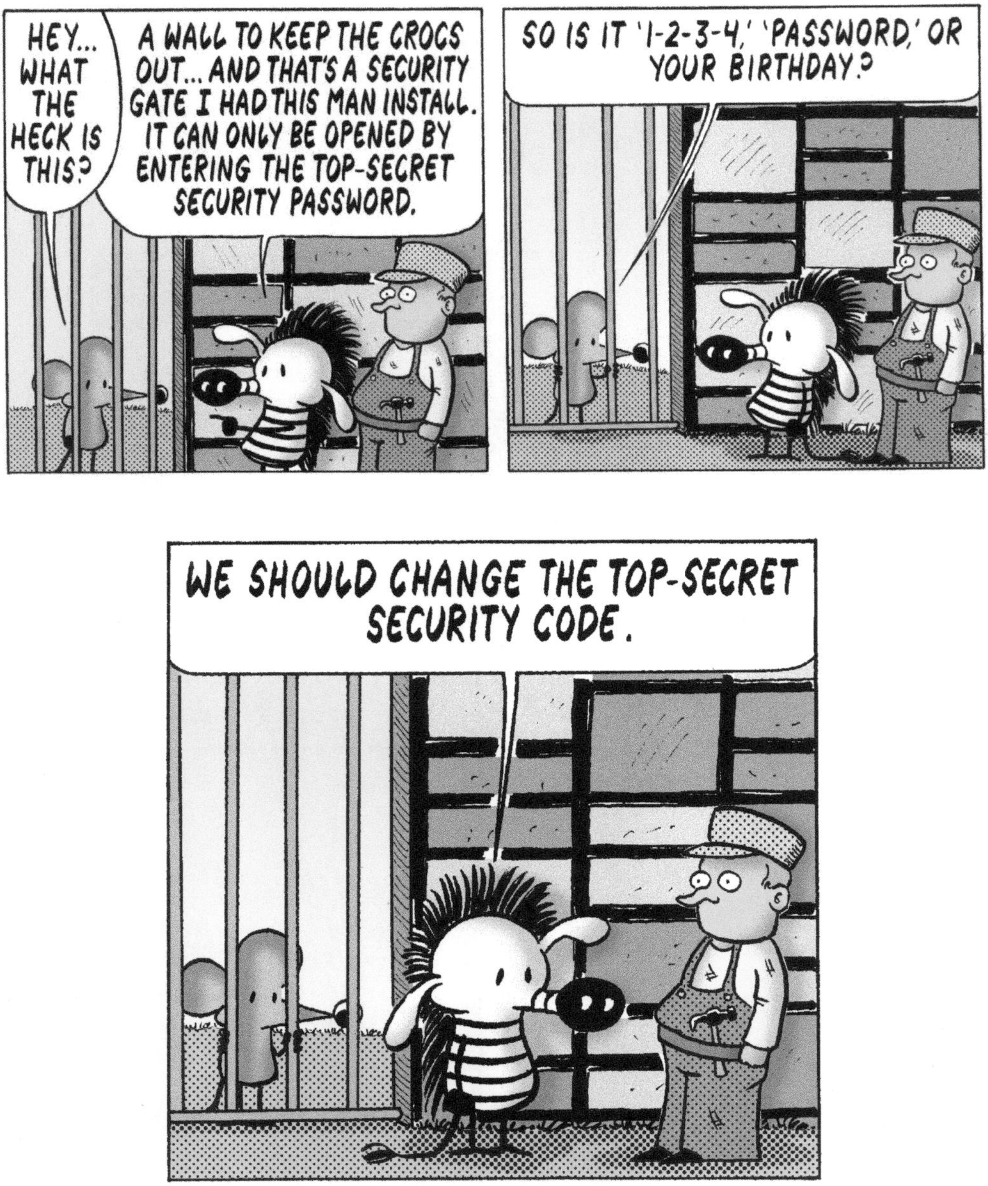
HEY... WHAT THE HECK IS THIS?
A WALL TO KEEP THE CROCS OUT... AND THAT'S A SECURITY GATE I HAD THIS MAN INSTALL. IT CAN ONLY BE OPENED BY ENTERING THE TOP-SECRET SECURITY PASSWORD.
SO IS IT '1-2-3-4,' 'PASSWORD,' OR YOUR BIRTHDAY?
WE SHOULD CHANGE THE TOP-SECRET SECURITY CODE.

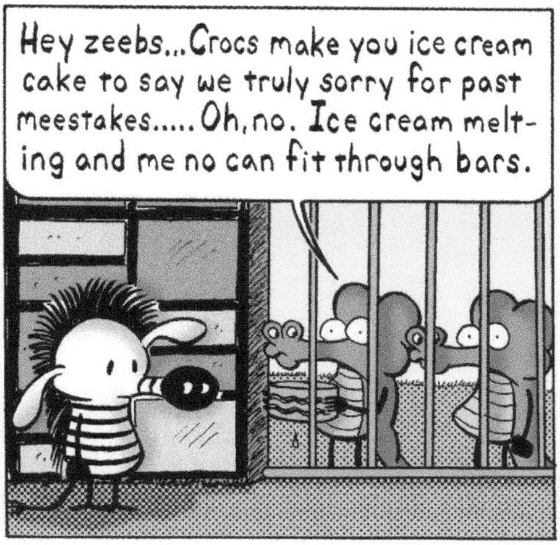
Hey zeebs...Crocs make you ice cream cake to say we truly sorry for past meestakes.....Oh, no. Ice cream melting and me no can fit through bars.

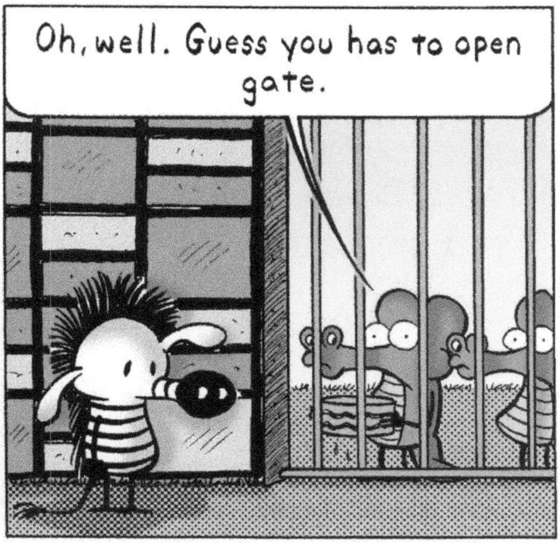
Oh, well. Guess you has to open gate.

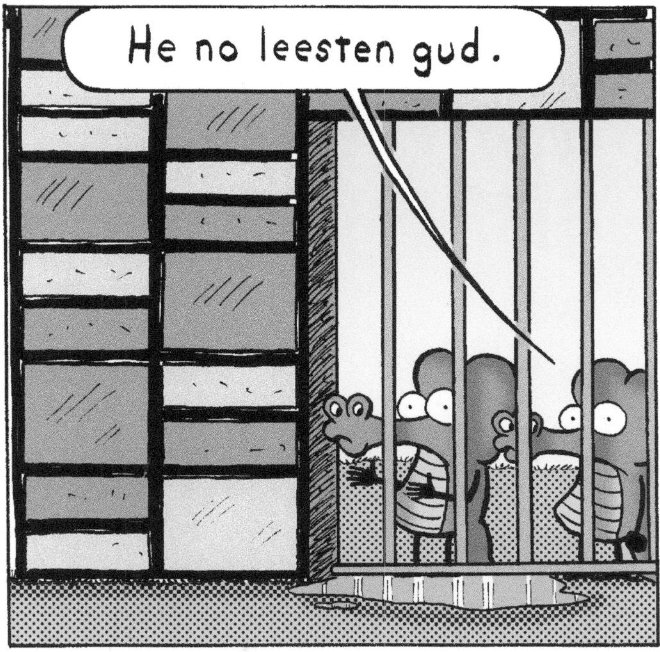
He no leesten gud.

NOW THAT YOU HAVE THIS BIG WALL AROUND YOUR PROPERTY, AREN'T YOU WORRIED YOU COULD LOSE THE KEY TO THE GATE?
NO. I HAVE A SPARE THAT I KEEP IN A SAFE PLACE.
SAFE ENOUGH THAT YOU DON'T THINK THE CROCS CAN GET TO IT?
YEP.

Reech for it, Bob.
You reech for it, Burt.

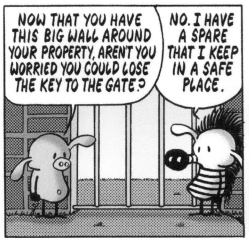

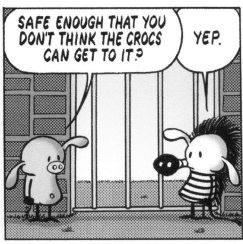

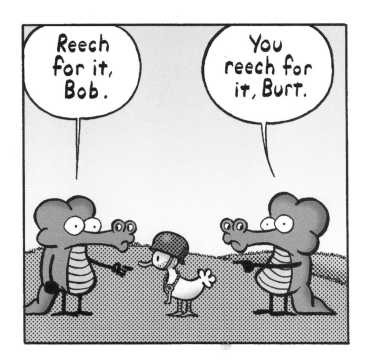

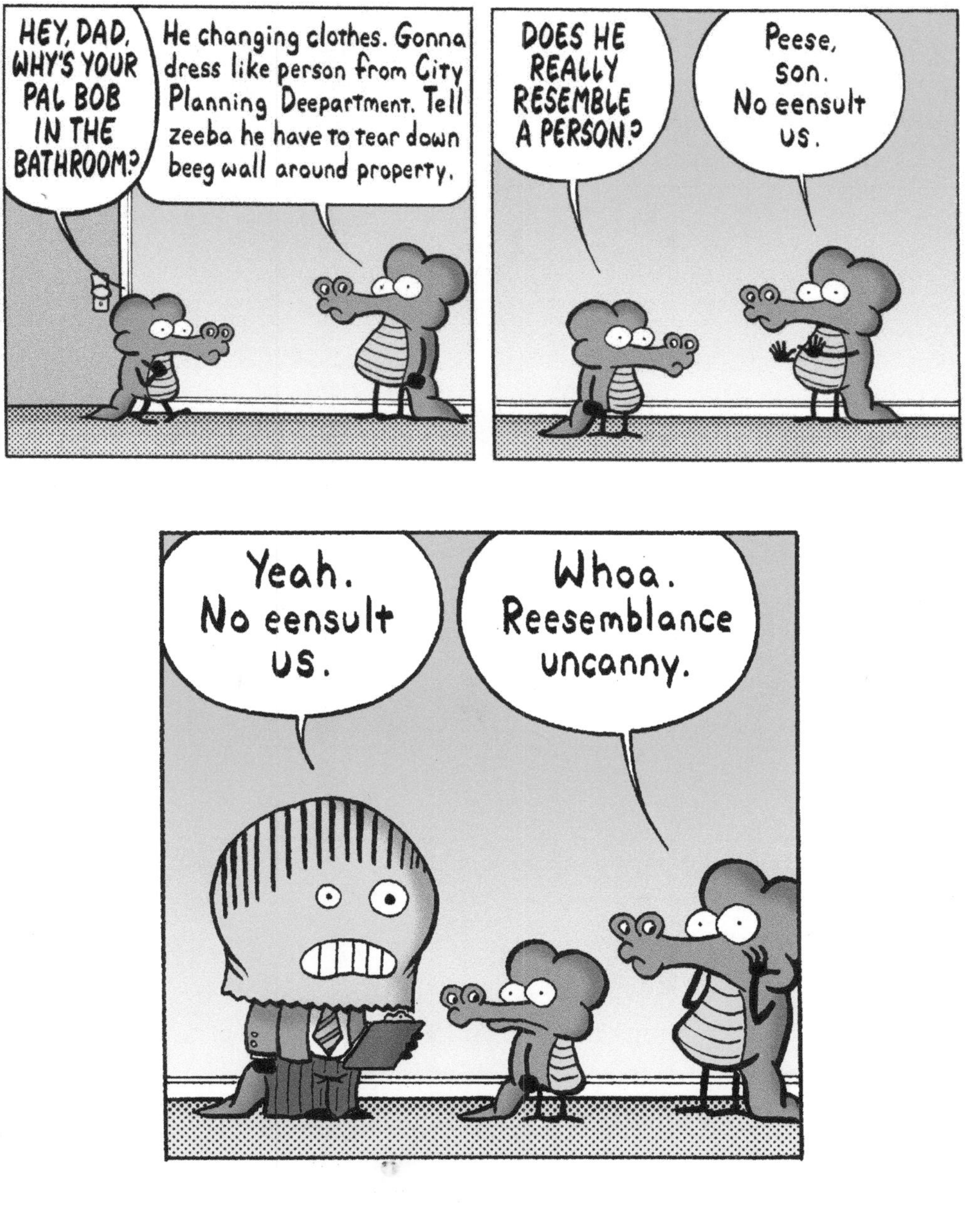
HEY, DAD, WHY'S YOUR PAL BOB IN THE BATHROOM?
He changing clothes. Gonna dress like person from City Planning Deepartment. Tell zeeba he have to tear down beeg wall around property.
DOES HE REALLY RESEMBLE A PERSON?
Peese, son. No eensult us.
Yeah. No eensult us.
Whoa. Reesemblance uncanny.

HI, MS. JONES. HAVE YOU MET MY NEIGHBOR BOB'S SON, JOJO? HE'S LEARNING KAZOO. HE'S HOPING IT WILL ONE DAY BE A NICE EXTRACURRICULAR ACTIVITY THAT COULD BEEF UP HIS COLLEGE APPLICATION.

SHOW HER, JOJO.

TOOT.

THAT'S NICE. THIS IS MY SON, PHILLIP. HE PLAYS VIOLIN.

HE'S ALSO PRESIDENT OF THE STUDENT BODY, THE DEBATE TEAM, AND THE DRAMA CLUB.

WHICH HASN'T STOPPED HIM FROM GETTING A 4.6 G.P.A. AND THE HIGHEST S.A.T. SCORE IN HIS SCHOOL'S HISTORY.

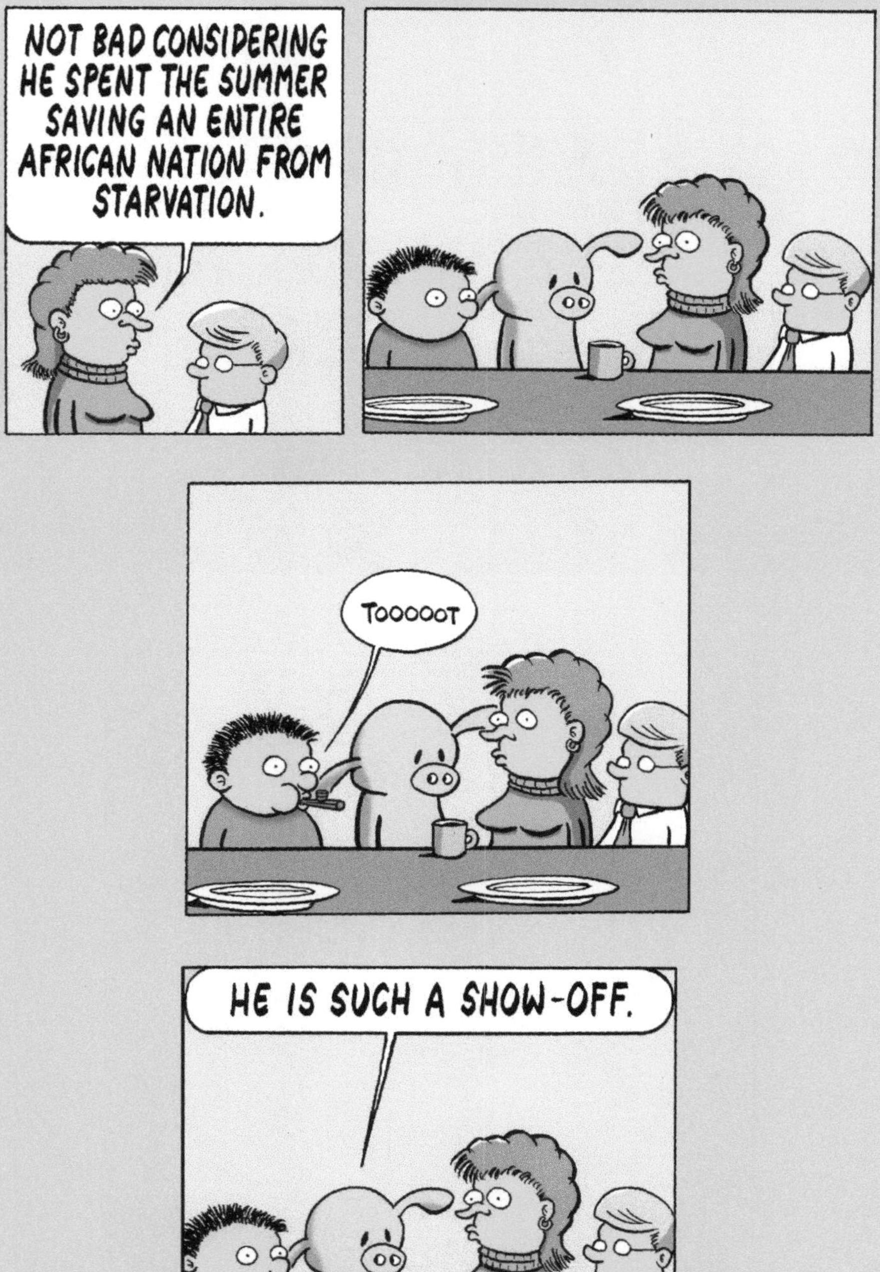
NOT BAD CONSIDERING HE SPENT THE SUMMER SAVING AN ENTIRE AFRICAN NATION FROM STARVATION.
TOOOOOT
HE IS SUCH A SHOW-OFF.

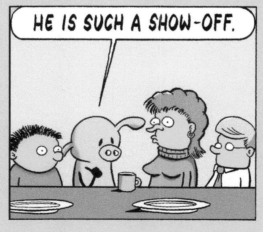

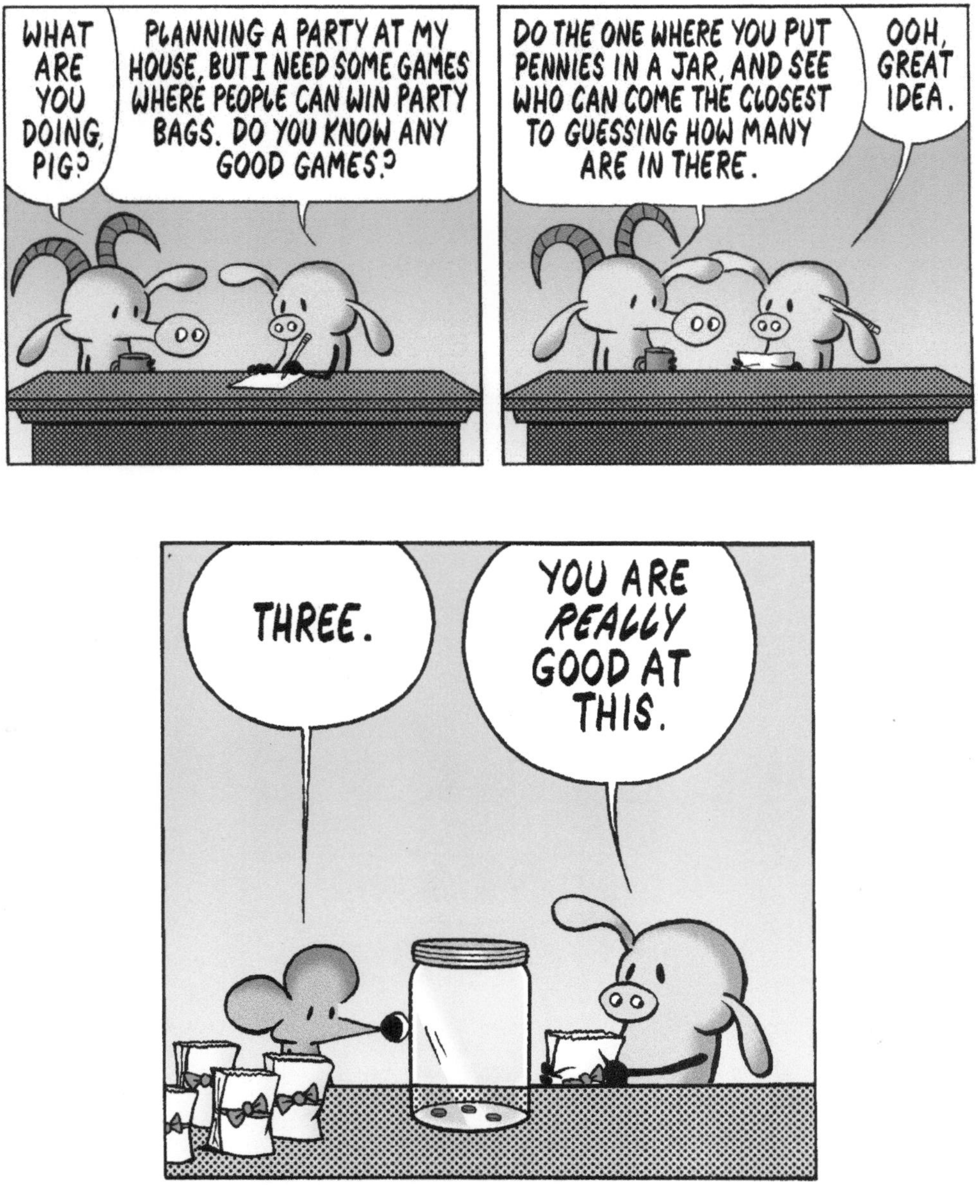
WHAT ARE YOU DOING, PIG?
PLANNING A PARTY AT MY HOUSE, BUT I NEED SOME GAMES WHERE PEOPLE CAN WIN PARTY BAGS. DO YOU KNOW ANY GOOD GAMES?
DO THE ONE WHERE YOU PUT PENNIES IN A JAR, AND SEE WHO CAN COME THE CLOSEST TO GUESSING HOW MANY ARE IN THERE.
OOH, GREAT IDEA.
THREE.
YOU ARE *REALLY* GOOD AT THIS.

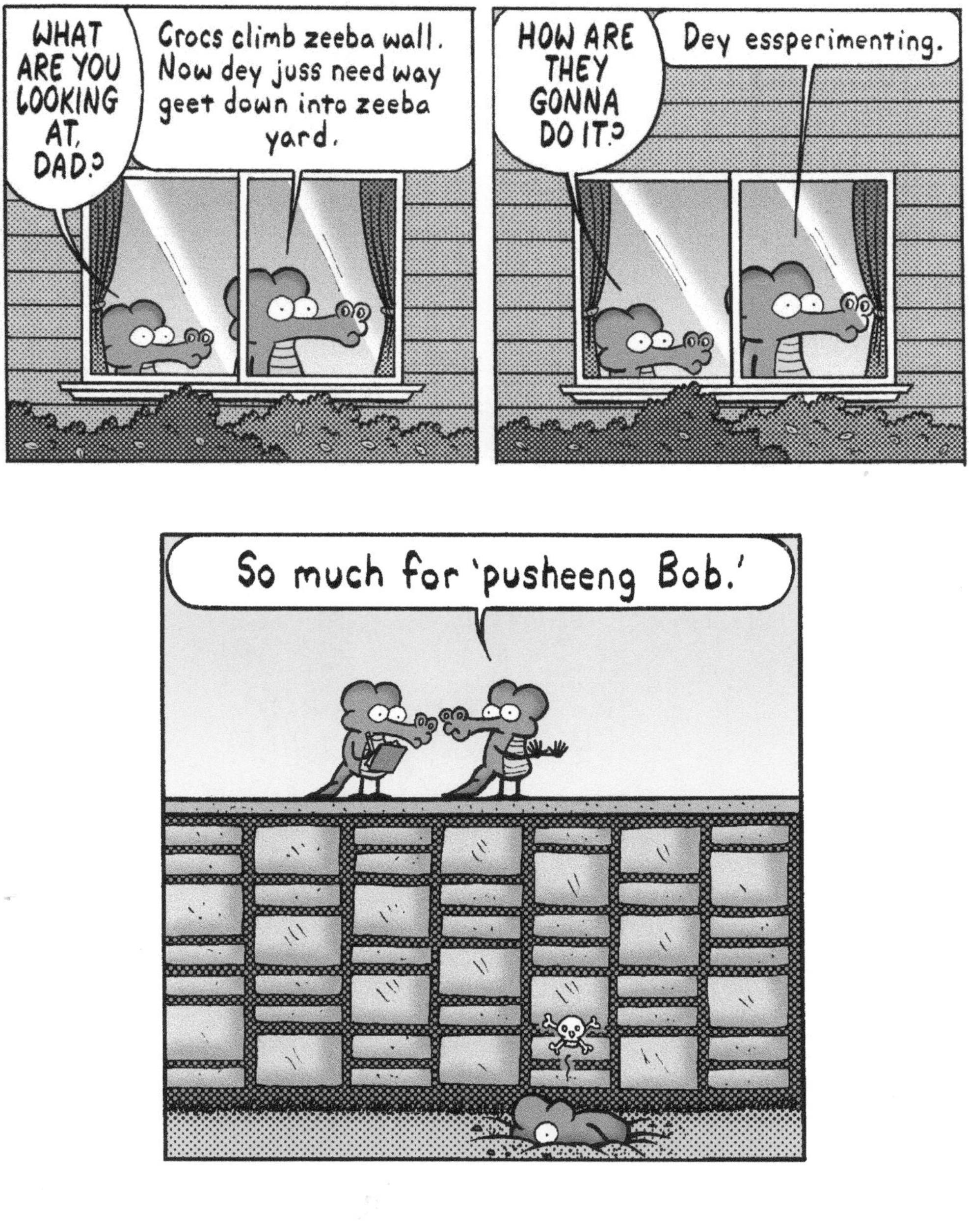
WHAT ARE YOU LOOKING AT, DAD?
Crocs climb zeeba wall. Now dey juss need way geet down into zeeba yard.
HOW ARE THEY GONNA DO IT?
Dey essperimenting.
So much for 'pusheeng Bob.'

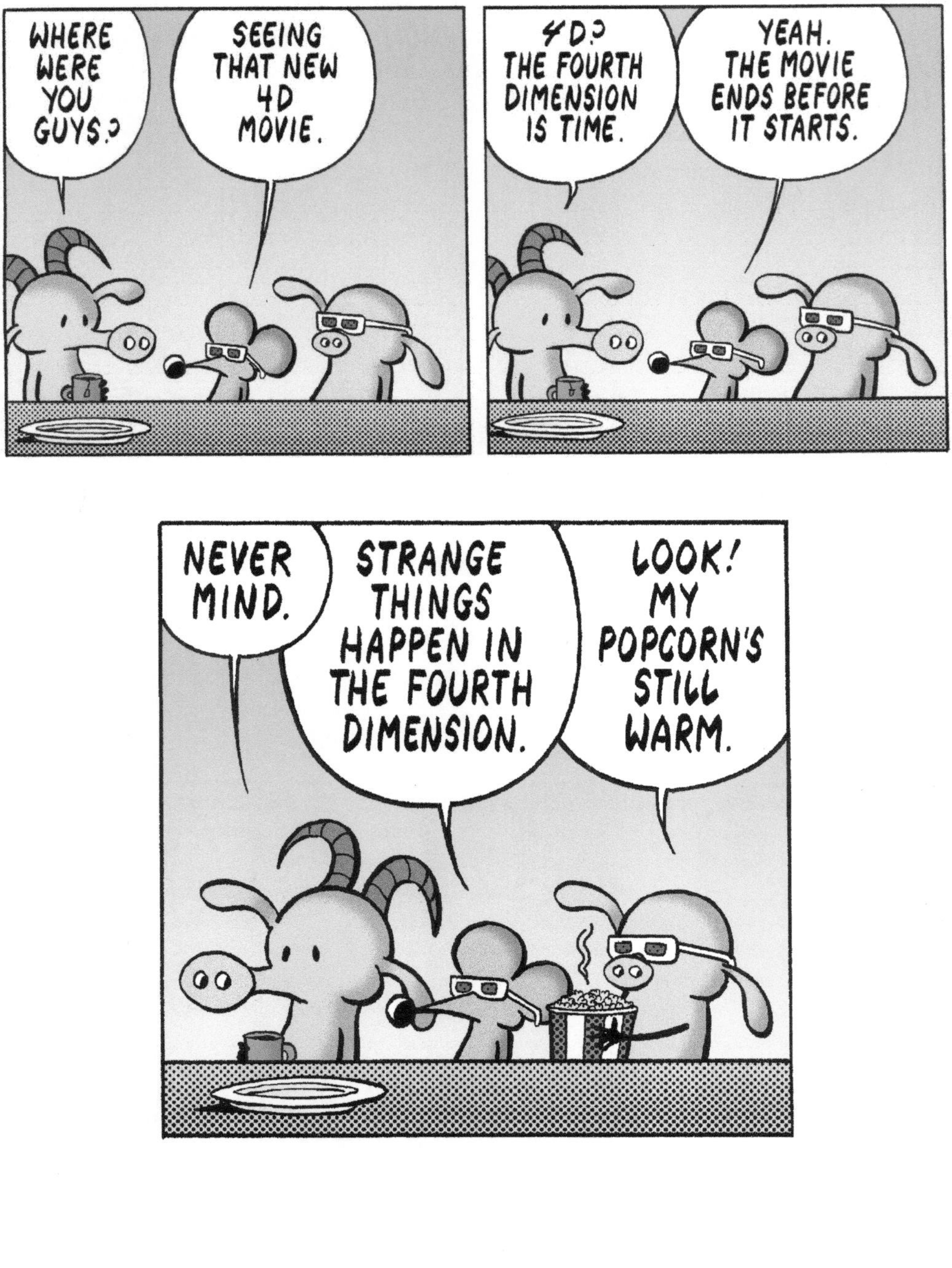
WHERE WERE YOU GUYS?
SEEING THAT NEW 4D MOVIE.
4D? THE FOURTH DIMENSION IS TIME.
YEAH. THE MOVIE ENDS BEFORE IT STARTS.
NEVER MIND.
STRANGE THINGS HAPPEN IN THE FOURTH DIMENSION.
LOOK! MY POPCORN'S STILL WARM.

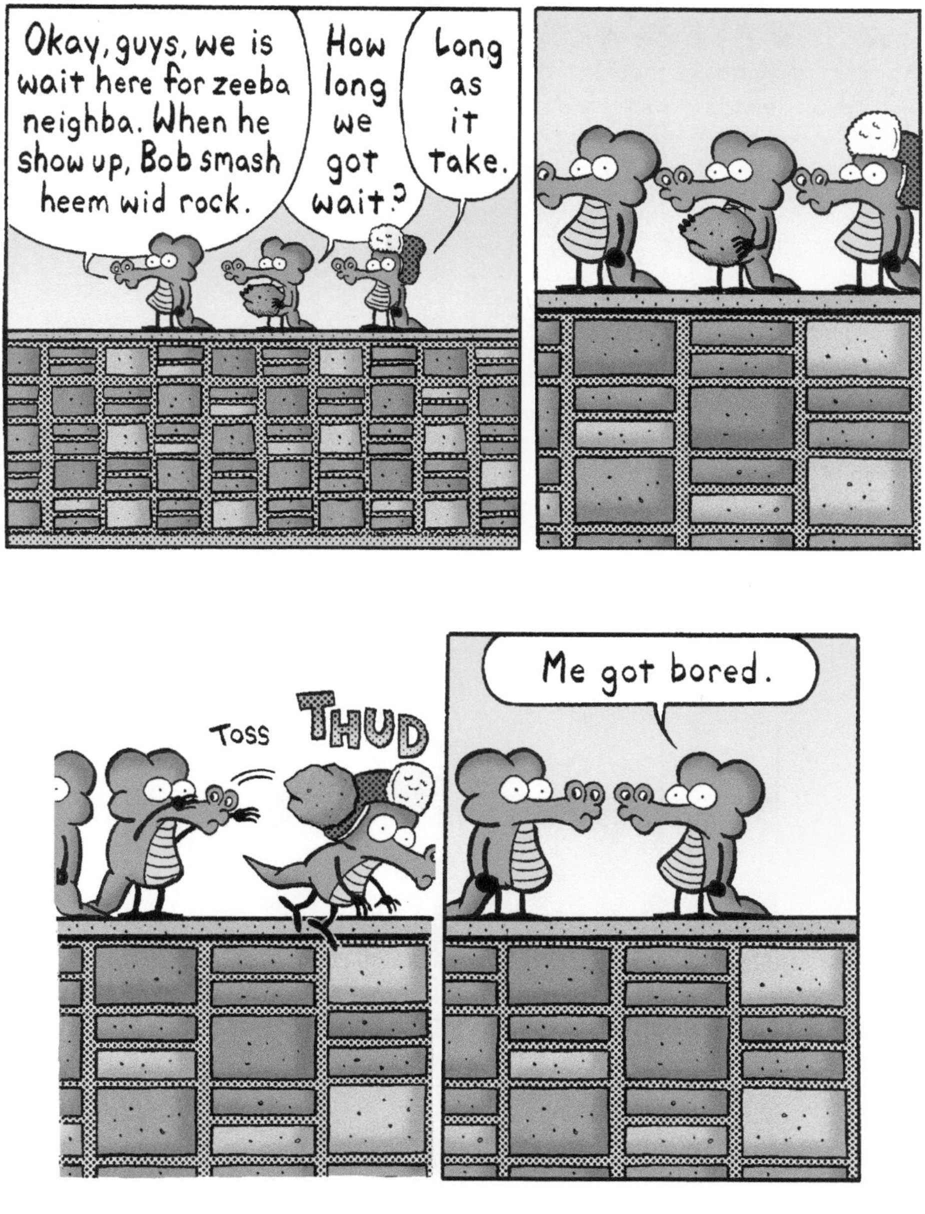
Okay, guys, we is wait here for zeeba neighba. When he show up, Bob smash heem wid rock.
How long we got wait?
Long as it take.
Toss
THUD
Me got bored.

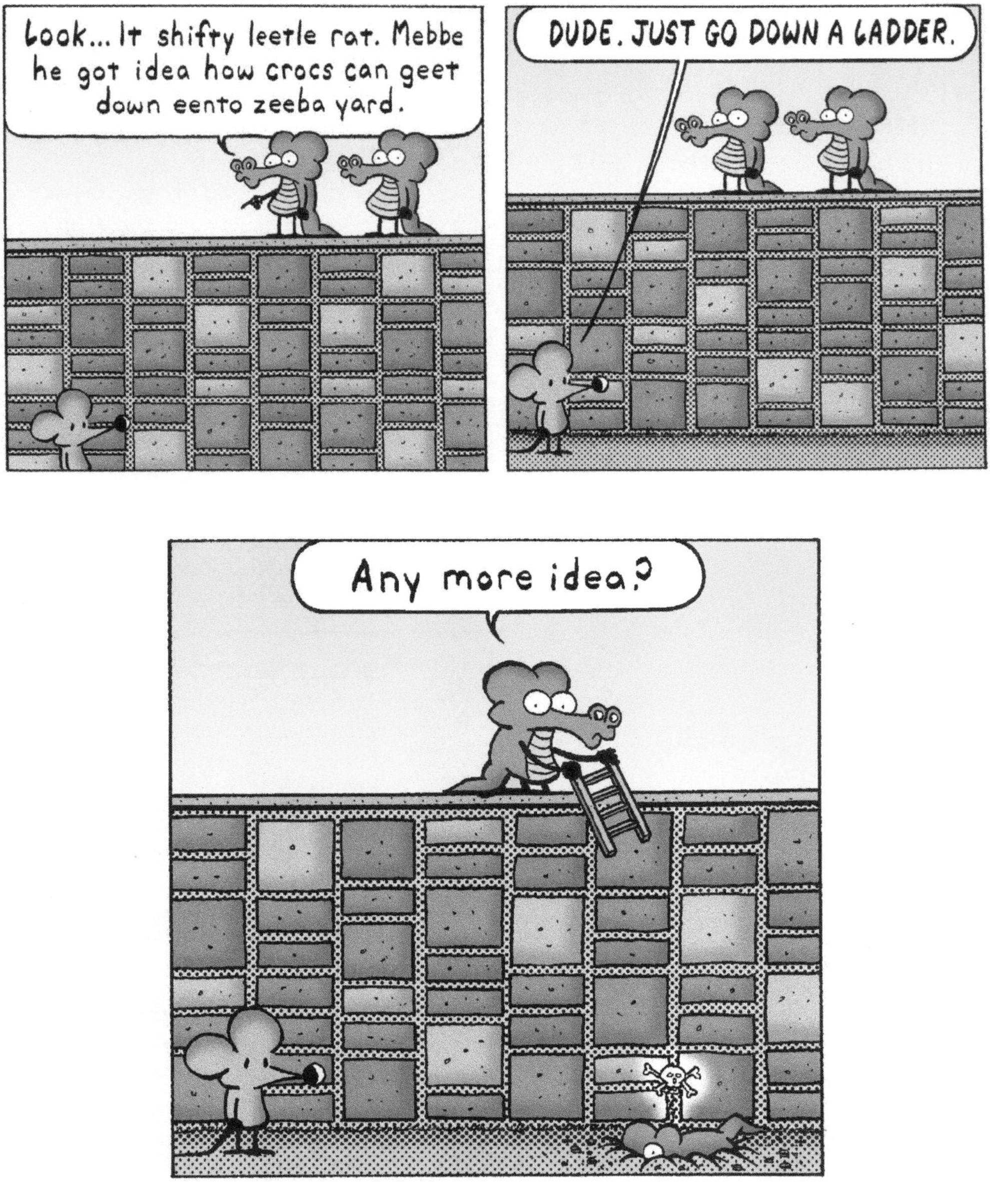
Look... It shifty leetle rat. Mebbe he got idea how crocs can geet down eento zeeba yard.
DUDE. JUST GO DOWN A LADDER.
Any more idea?

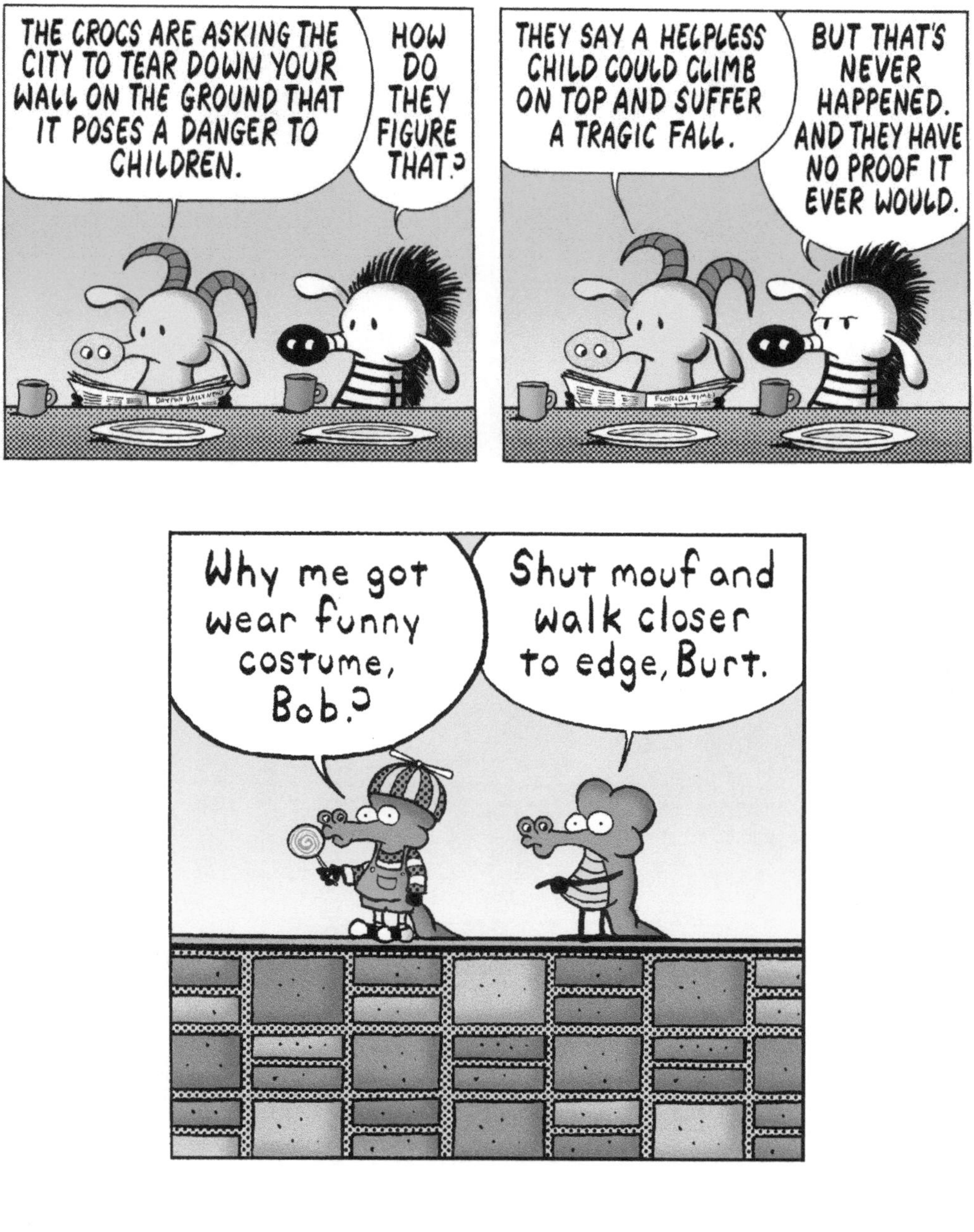
THE CROCS ARE ASKING THE CITY TO TEAR DOWN YOUR WALL ON THE GROUND THAT IT POSES A DANGER TO CHILDREN.
HOW DO THEY FIGURE THAT?
THEY SAY A HELPLESS CHILD COULD CLIMB ON TOP AND SUFFER A TRAGIC FALL.
BUT THAT'S NEVER HAPPENED. AND THEY HAVE NO PROOF IT EVER WOULD.
Why me got wear funny costume, Bob?
Shut mouf and walk closer to edge, Burt.

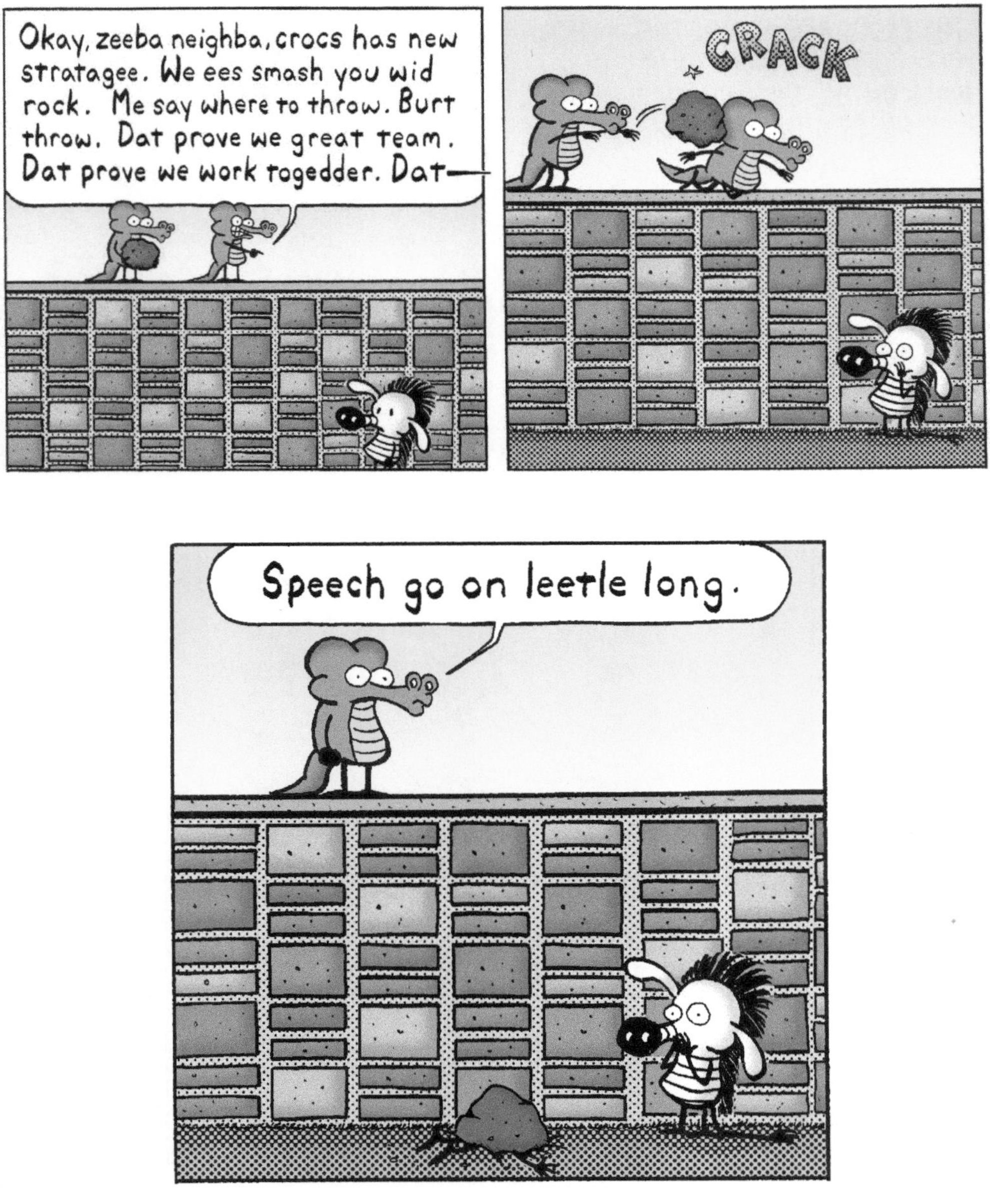
Okay, zeeba neighba, crocs has new stratagee. We ees smash you wid rock. Me say where to throw. Burt throw. Dat prove we great team. Dat prove we work togedder. Dat—
CRACK
Speech go on leetle long.

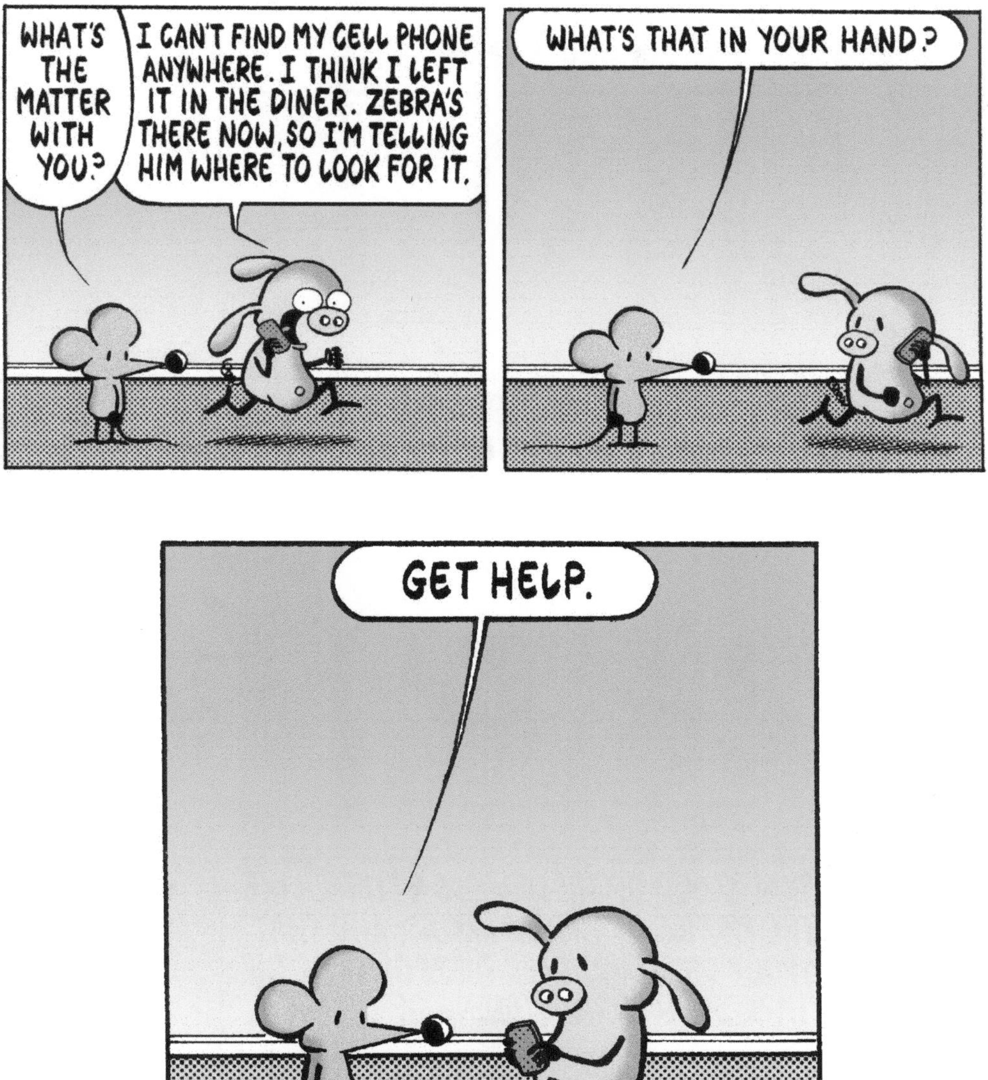
WHAT'S THE MATTER WITH YOU?
I CAN'T FIND MY CELL PHONE ANYWHERE. I THINK I LEFT IT IN THE DINER. ZEBRA'S THERE NOW, SO I'M TELLING HIM WHERE TO LOOK FOR IT.
WHAT'S THAT IN YOUR HAND?
GET HELP.

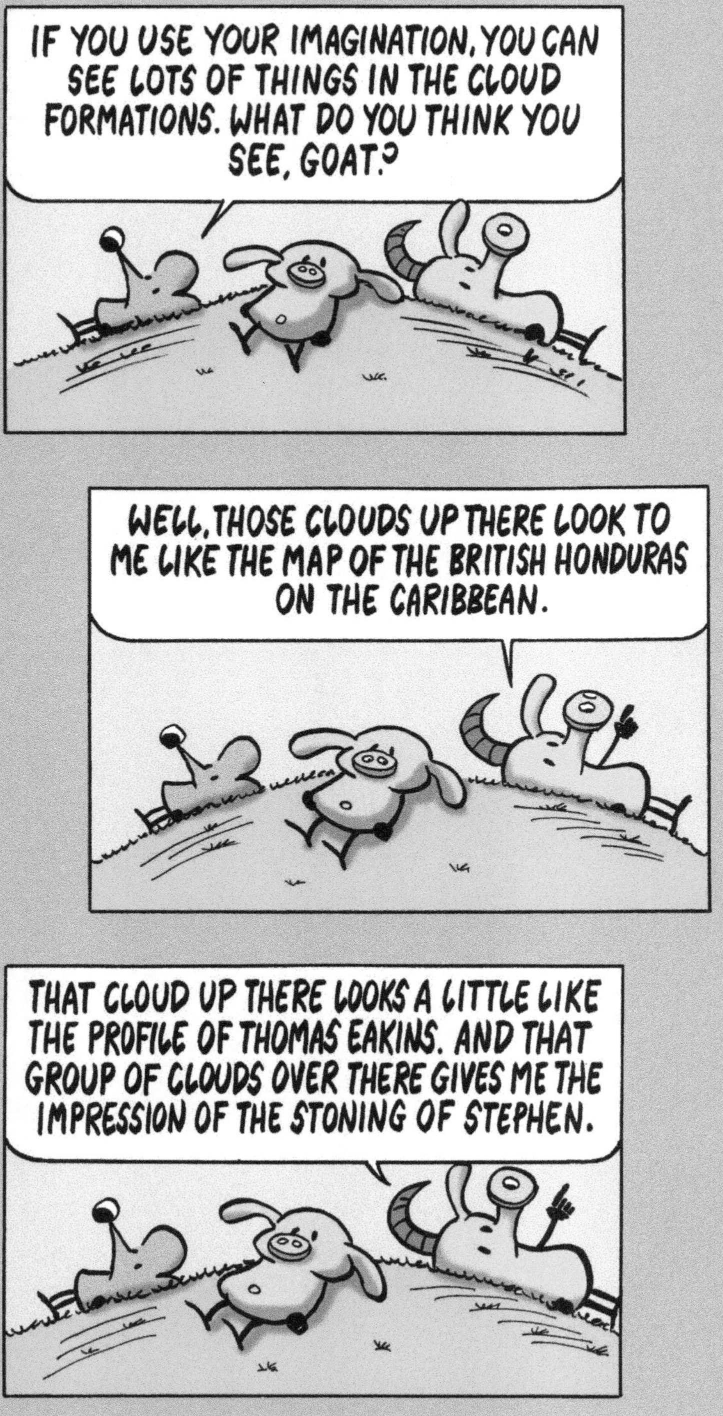
IF YOU USE YOUR IMAGINATION, YOU CAN SEE LOTS OF THINGS IN THE CLOUD FORMATIONS. WHAT DO YOU THINK YOU SEE, GOAT?
WELL, THOSE CLOUDS UP THERE LOOK TO ME LIKE THE MAP OF THE BRITISH HONDURAS ON THE CARIBBEAN.
THAT CLOUD UP THERE LOOKS A LITTLE LIKE THE PROFILE OF THOMAS EAKINS. AND THAT GROUP OF CLOUDS OVER THERE GIVES ME THE IMPRESSION OF THE STONING OF STEPHEN.

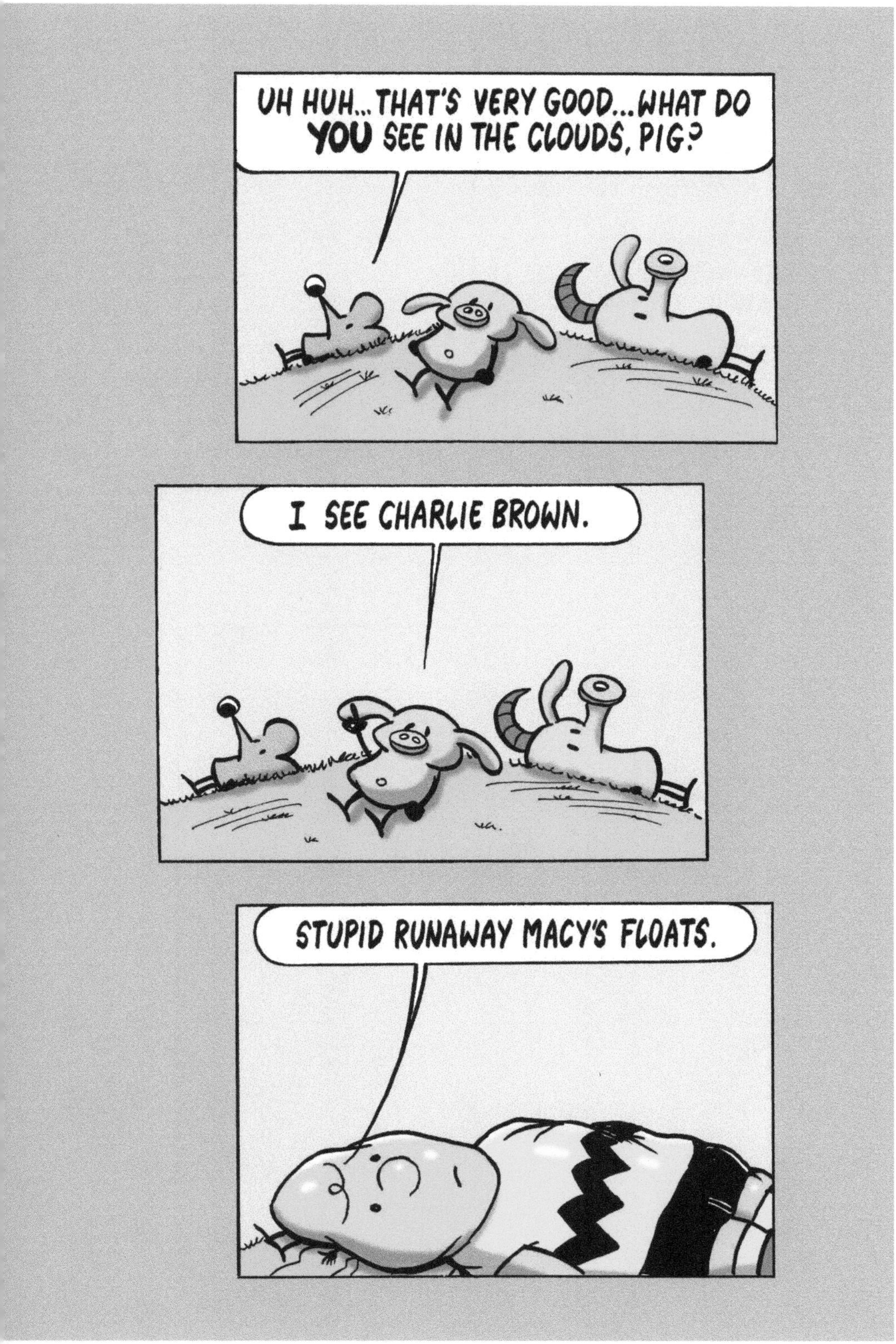
UH HUH... THAT'S VERY GOOD... WHAT DO YOU SEE IN THE CLOUDS, PIG?
I SEE CHARLIE BROWN.
STUPID RUNAWAY MACY'S FLOATS.

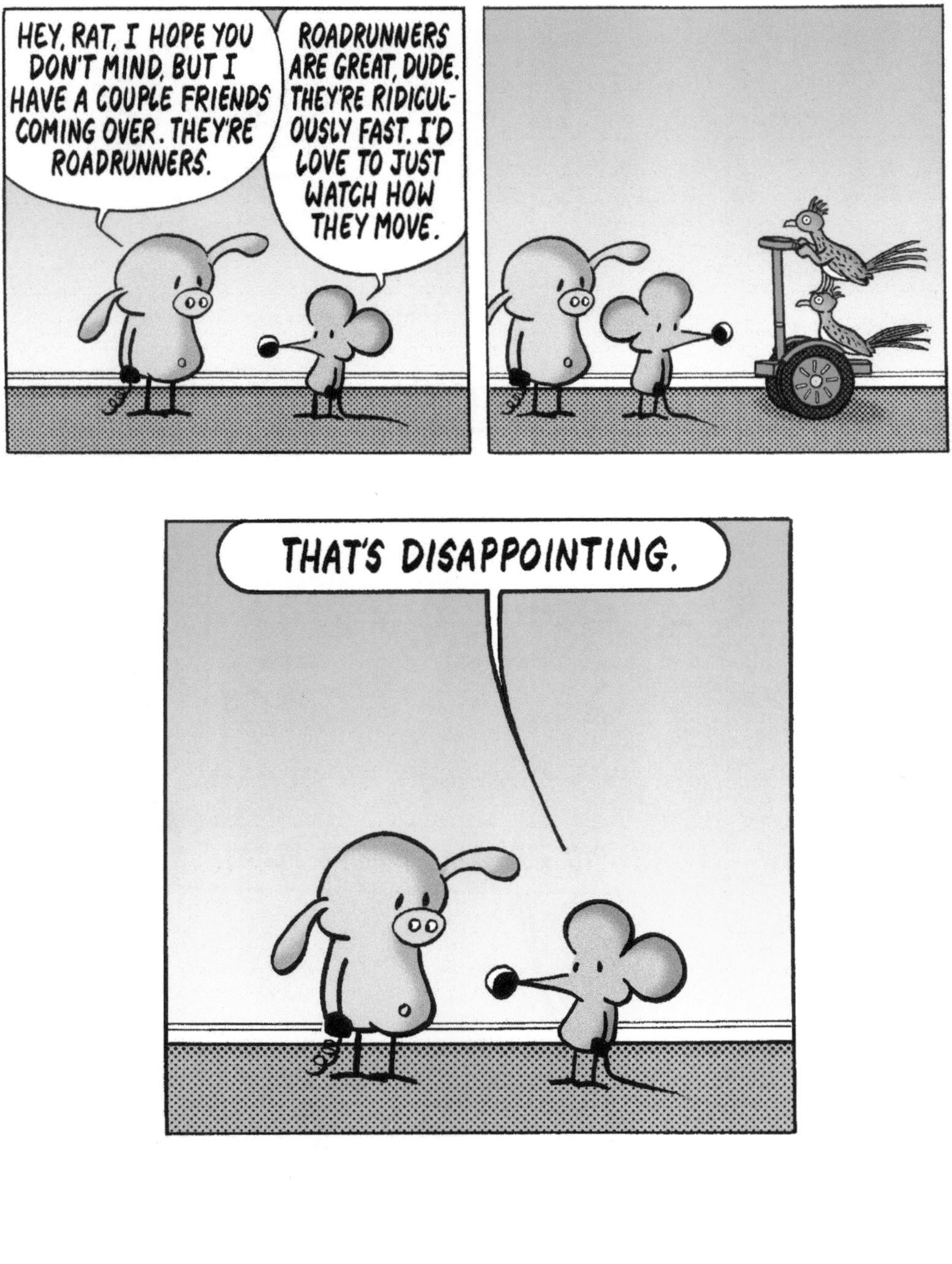
HEY, RAT, I HOPE YOU DON'T MIND, BUT I HAVE A COUPLE FRIENDS COMING OVER. THEY'RE ROADRUNNERS.
ROADRUNNERS ARE GREAT, DUDE. THEY'RE RIDICULOUSLY FAST. I'D LOVE TO JUST WATCH HOW THEY MOVE.
THAT'S DISAPPOINTING.

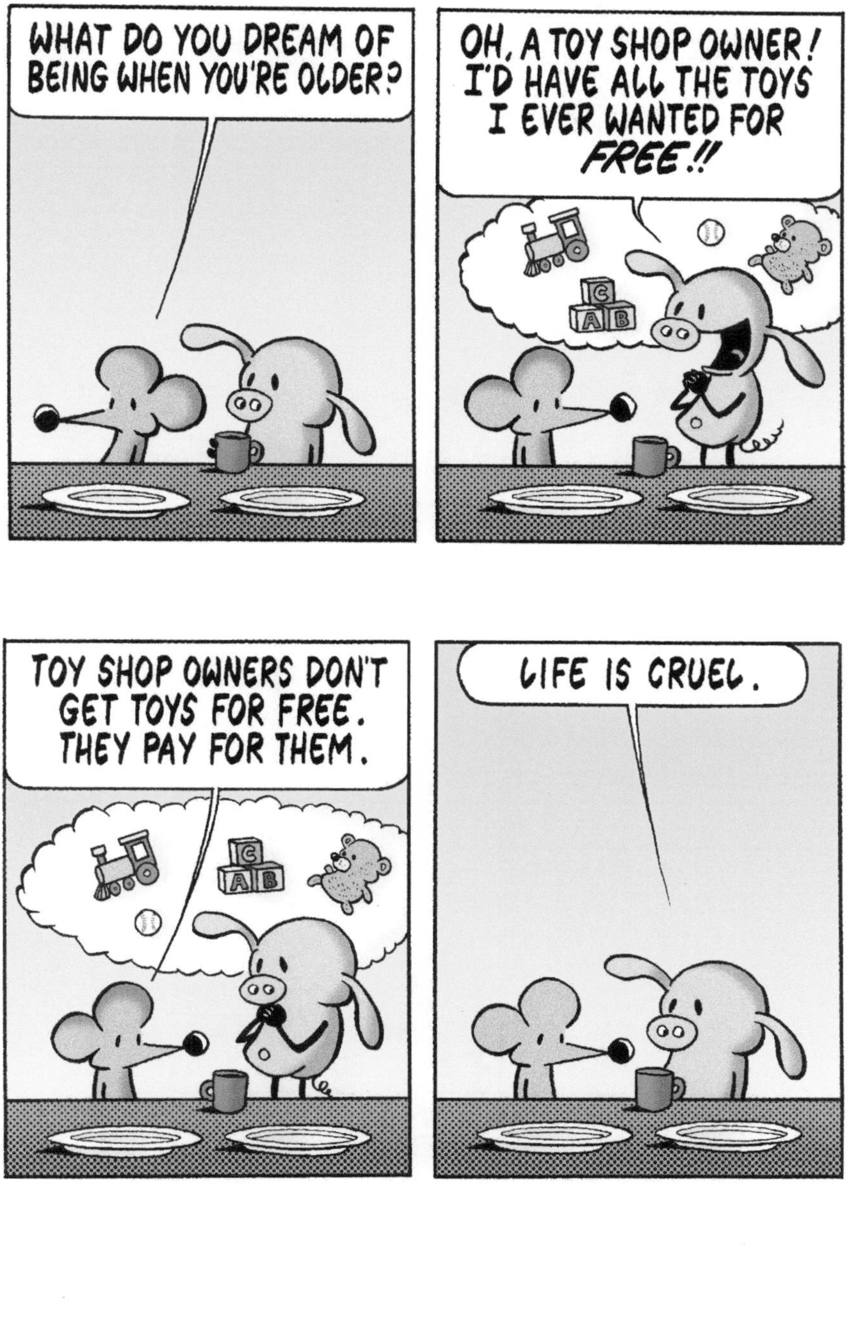
WHAT DO YOU DREAM OF BEING WHEN YOU'RE OLDER?
OH, A TOY SHOP OWNER! I'D HAVE ALL THE TOYS I EVER WANTED FOR *FREE!!*
TOY SHOP OWNERS DON'T GET TOYS FOR FREE. THEY PAY FOR THEM.
LIFE IS CRUEL.

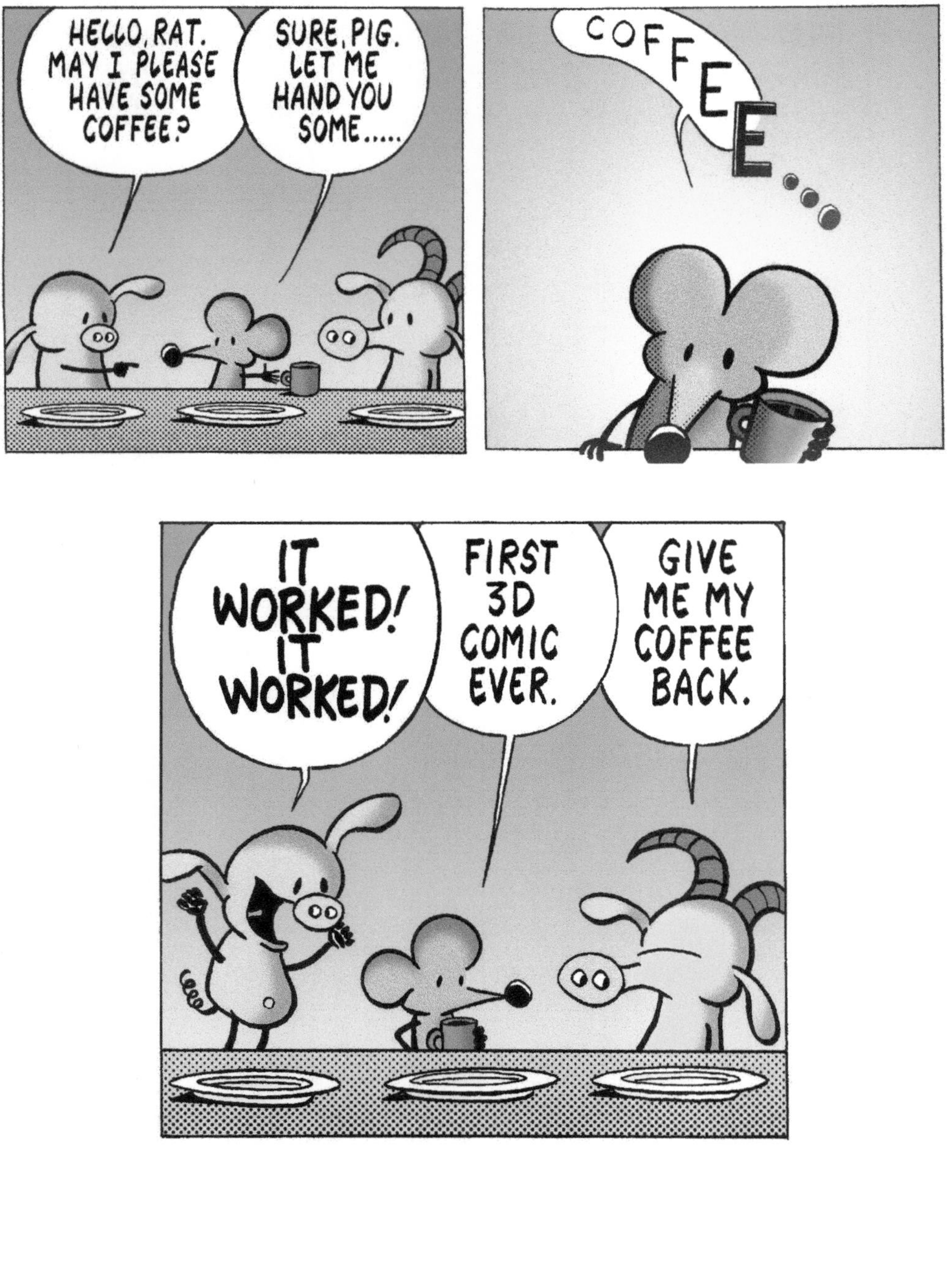
HELLO, RAT. MAY I PLEASE HAVE SOME COFFEE?
SURE, PIG. LET ME HAND YOU SOME.....
COFFEE...
IT WORKED! IT WORKED!
FIRST 3D COMIC EVER.
GIVE ME MY COFFEE BACK.

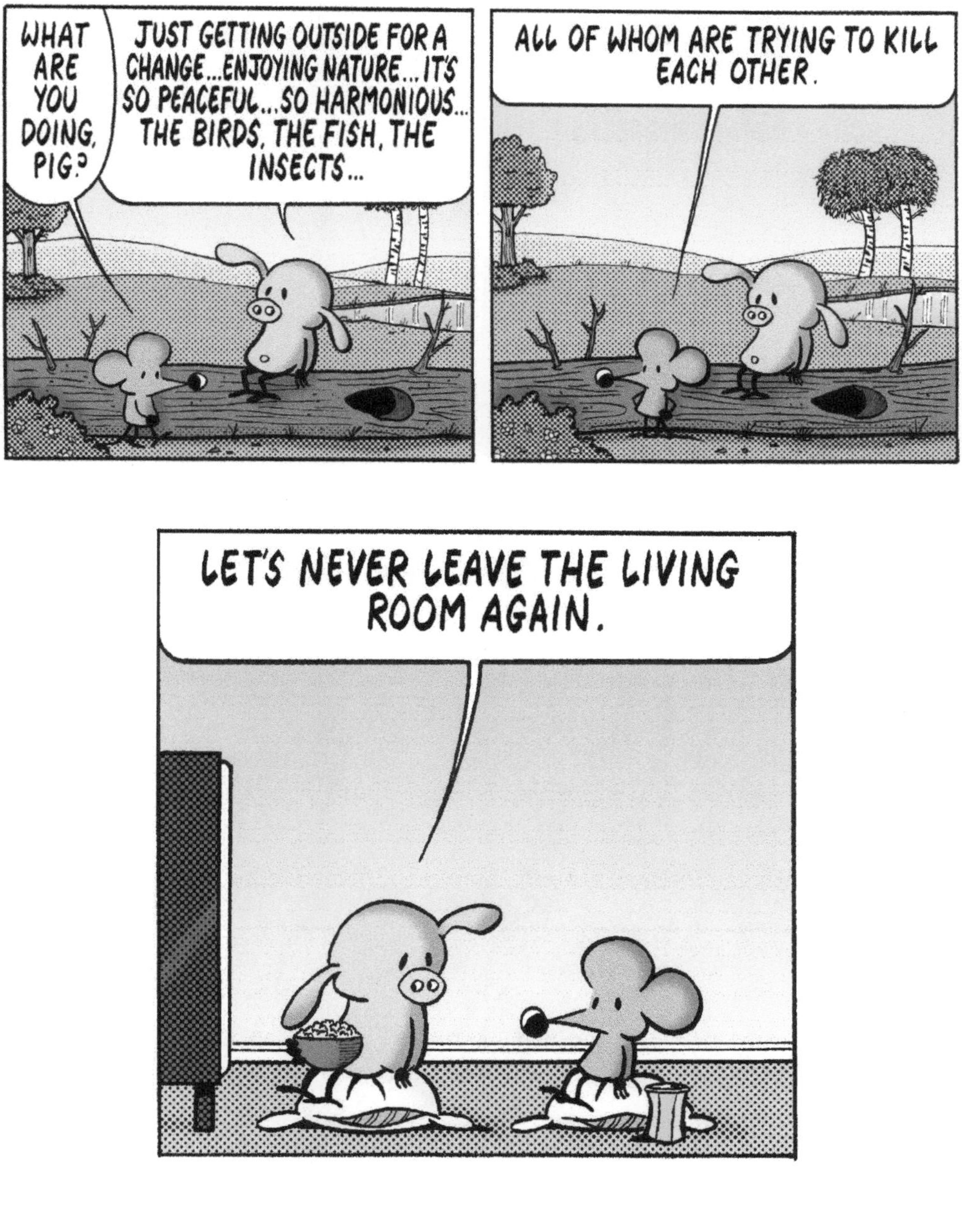
WHAT ARE YOU DOING, PIG?
JUST GETTING OUTSIDE FOR A CHANGE...ENJOYING NATURE...IT'S SO PEACEFUL...SO HARMONIOUS... THE BIRDS, THE FISH, THE INSECTS...
ALL OF WHOM ARE TRYING TO KILL EACH OTHER.
LET'S NEVER LEAVE THE LIVING ROOM AGAIN.

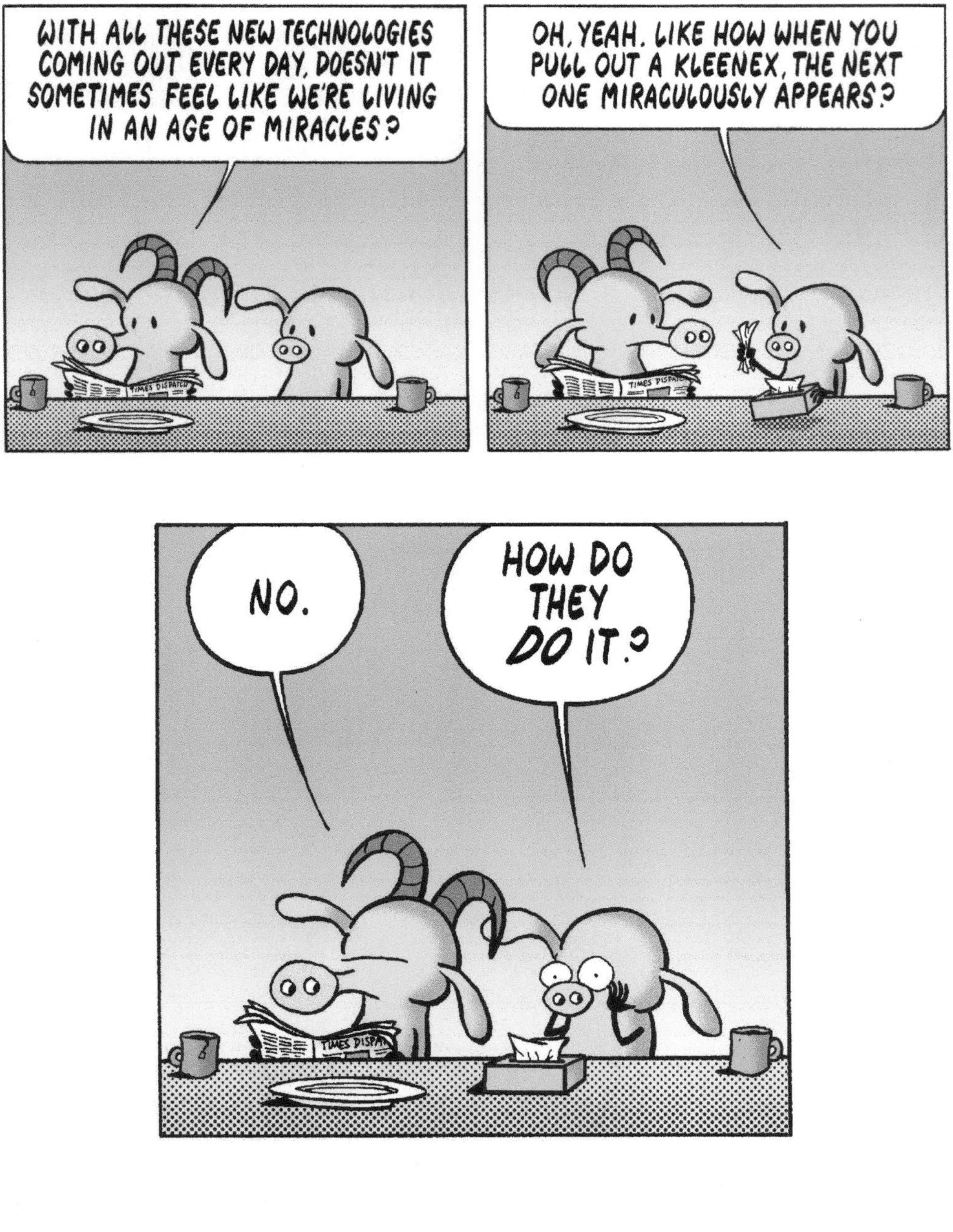
WITH ALL THESE NEW TECHNOLOGIES COMING OUT EVERY DAY, DOESN'T IT SOMETIMES FEEL LIKE WE'RE LIVING IN AN AGE OF MIRACLES?
TIMES DISPATCH
OH, YEAH. LIKE HOW WHEN YOU PULL OUT A KLEENEX, THE NEXT ONE MIRACULOUSLY APPEARS?
TIMES DISPATCH
NO.
HOW DO THEY *DO* IT?
TIMES DISPA

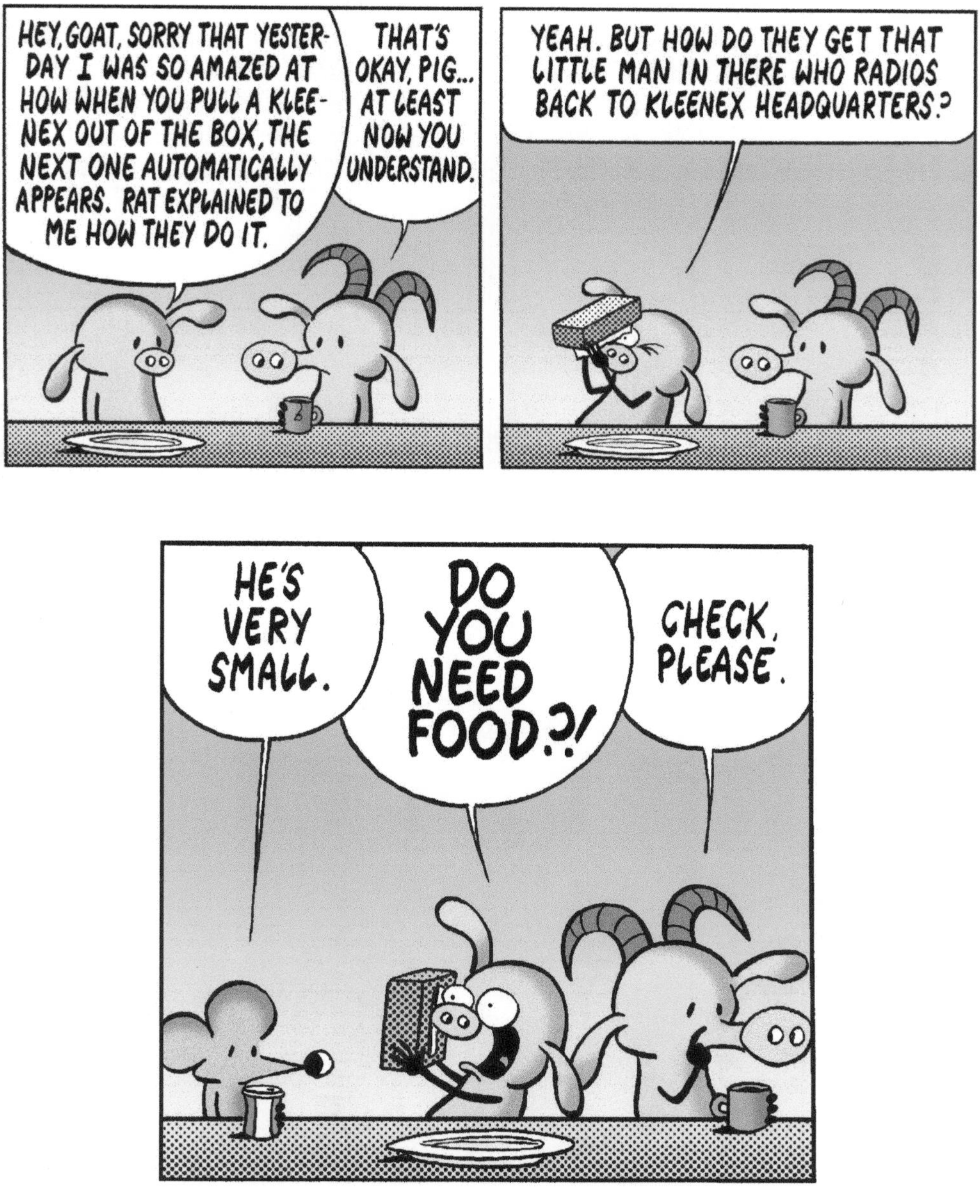
HEY, GOAT, SORRY THAT YESTERDAY I WAS SO AMAZED AT HOW WHEN YOU PULL A KLEENEX OUT OF THE BOX, THE NEXT ONE AUTOMATICALLY APPEARS. RAT EXPLAINED TO ME HOW THEY DO IT.
THAT'S OKAY, PIG... AT LEAST NOW YOU UNDERSTAND.
YEAH. BUT HOW DO THEY GET THAT LITTLE MAN IN THERE WHO RADIOS BACK TO KLEENEX HEADQUARTERS?
HE'S VERY SMALL.
DO YOU NEED FOOD?!
CHECK, PLEASE.

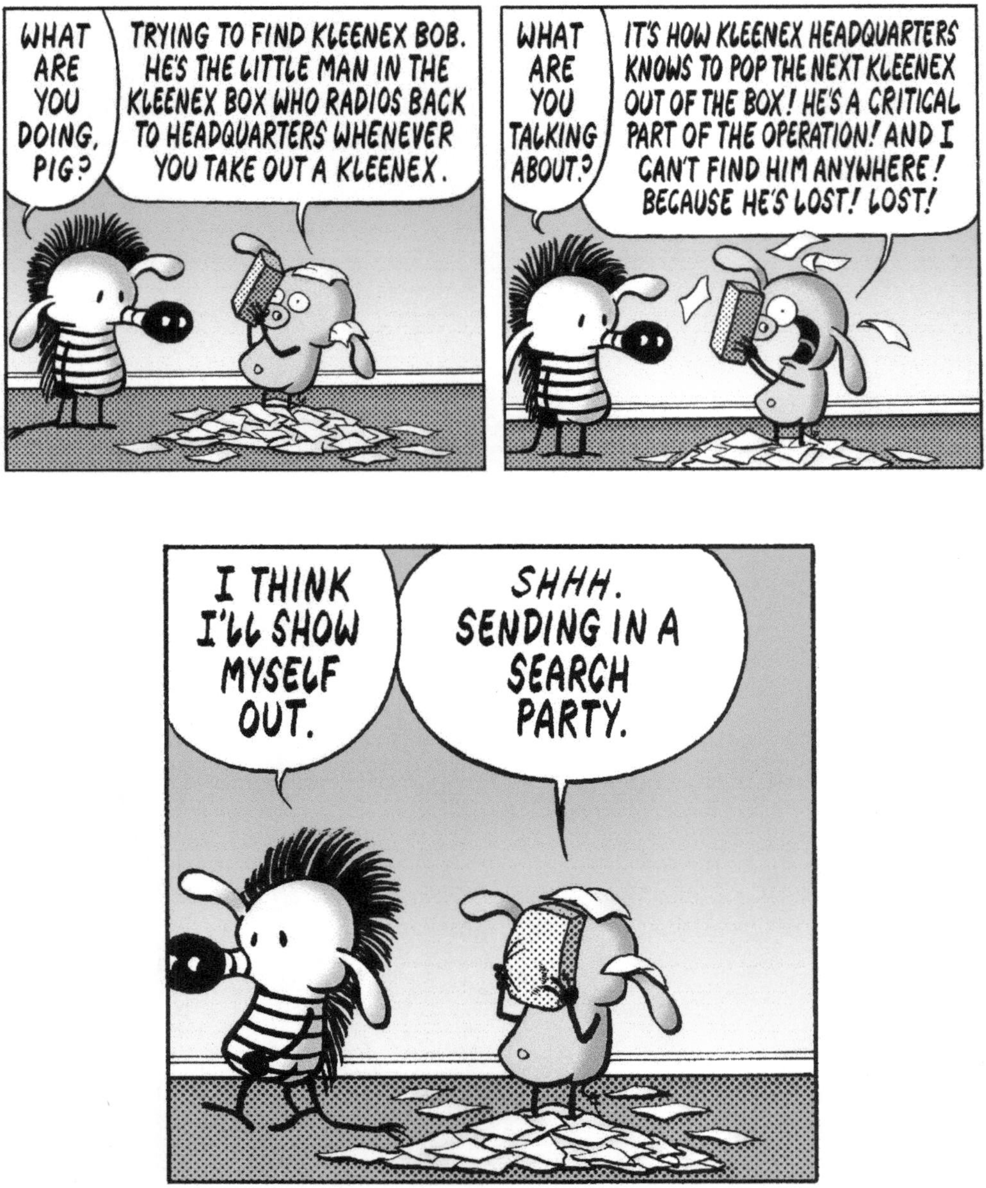
WHAT ARE YOU DOING, PIG?
TRYING TO FIND KLEENEX BOB. HE'S THE LITTLE MAN IN THE KLEENEX BOX WHO RADIOS BACK TO HEADQUARTERS WHENEVER YOU TAKE OUT A KLEENEX.
WHAT ARE YOU TALKING ABOUT?
IT'S HOW KLEENEX HEADQUARTERS KNOWS TO POP THE NEXT KLEENEX OUT OF THE BOX! HE'S A CRITICAL PART OF THE OPERATION! AND I CAN'T FIND HIM ANYWHERE! BECAUSE HE'S LOST! LOST!
I THINK I'LL SHOW MYSELF OUT.
SHHH. SENDING IN A SEARCH PARTY.

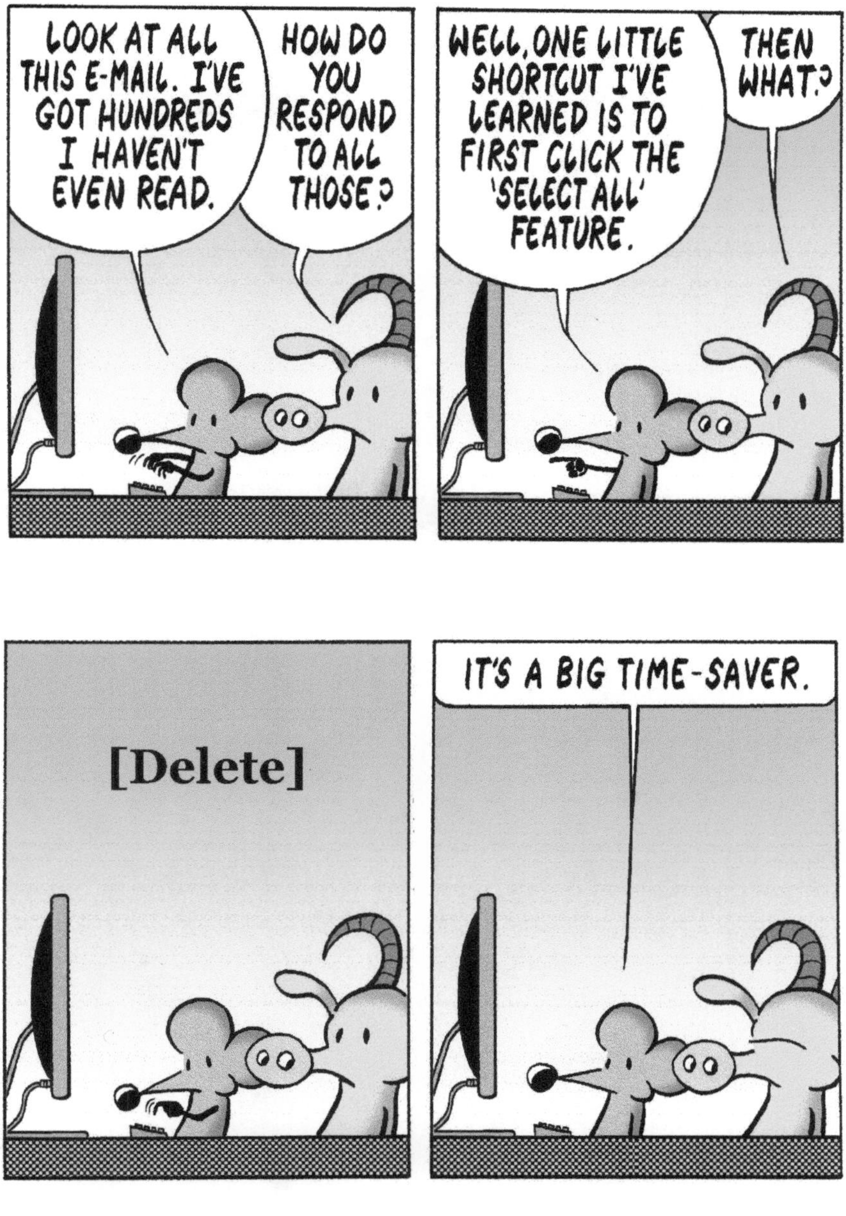
LOOK AT ALL THIS E-MAIL. I'VE GOT HUNDREDS I HAVEN'T EVEN READ.
HOW DO YOU RESPOND TO ALL THOSE?
WELL, ONE LITTLE SHORTCUT I'VE LEARNED IS TO FIRST CLICK THE 'SELECT ALL' FEATURE.
THEN WHAT?
[Delete]
IT'S A BIG TIME-SAVER.

LOOKS LIKE ONE OF YOUR NEIGHBORS GOT HIMSELF APPOINTED TO THE CITY PLANNING COMMISSION.
TRIBUNE
WHAT'S THAT?
THEY'RE THE GUYS WHO ISSUE PERMITS FOR ANY CONSTRUCTION YOU WANT TO DO.
TRIBUNE
THEY DON'T BY CHANCE HAVE THE RIGHT TO TEAR DOWN STUFF YOU BUILD WITHOUT A PERMIT, DO THEY?

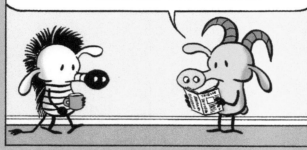

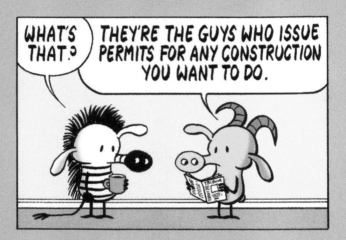

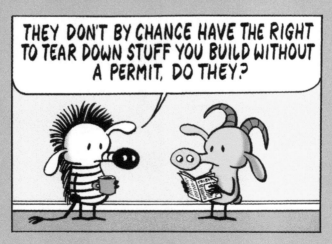

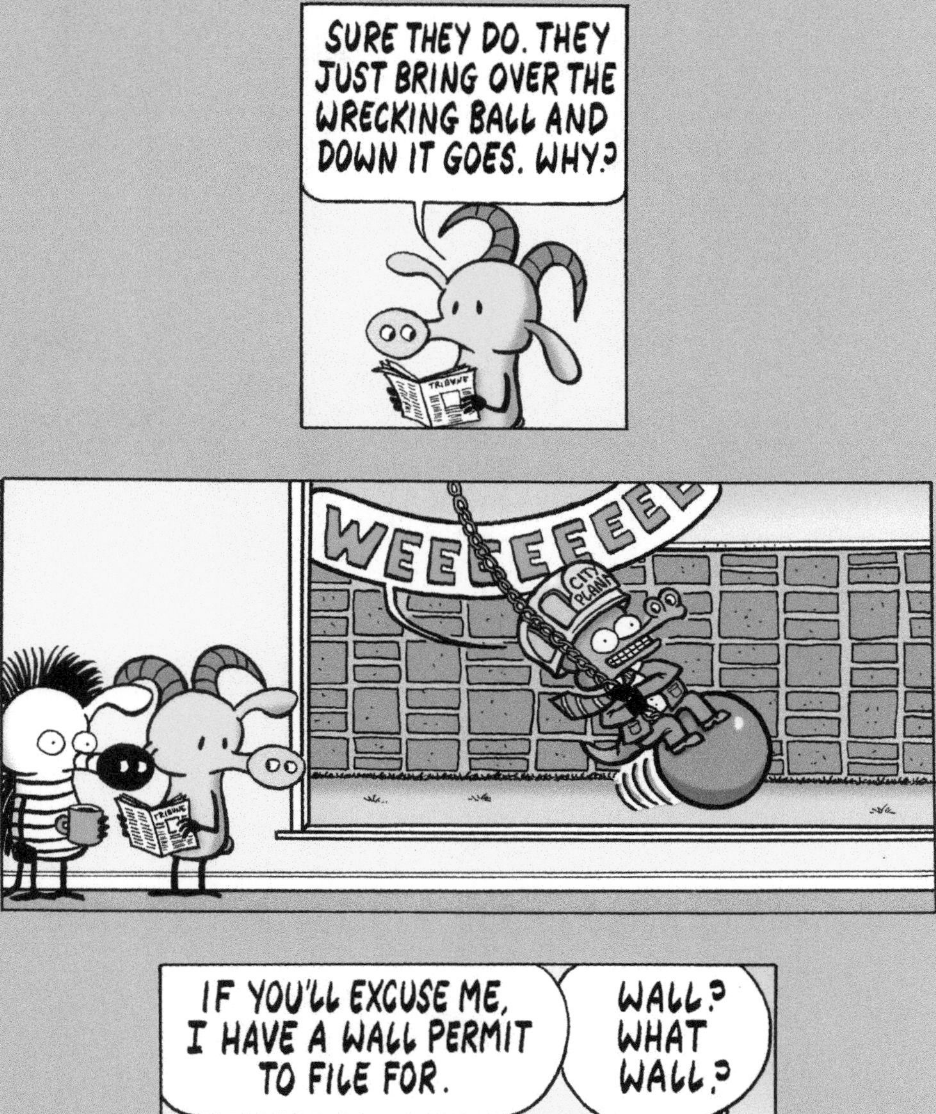
SURE THEY DO. THEY JUST BRING OVER THE WRECKING BALL AND DOWN IT GOES. WHY?
WEEEEEEEE
IF YOU'LL EXCUSE ME, I HAVE A WALL PERMIT TO FILE FOR.
WALL? WHAT WALL?

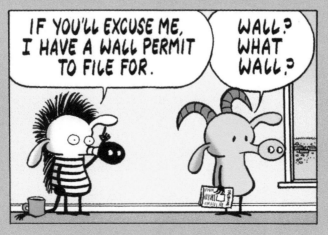

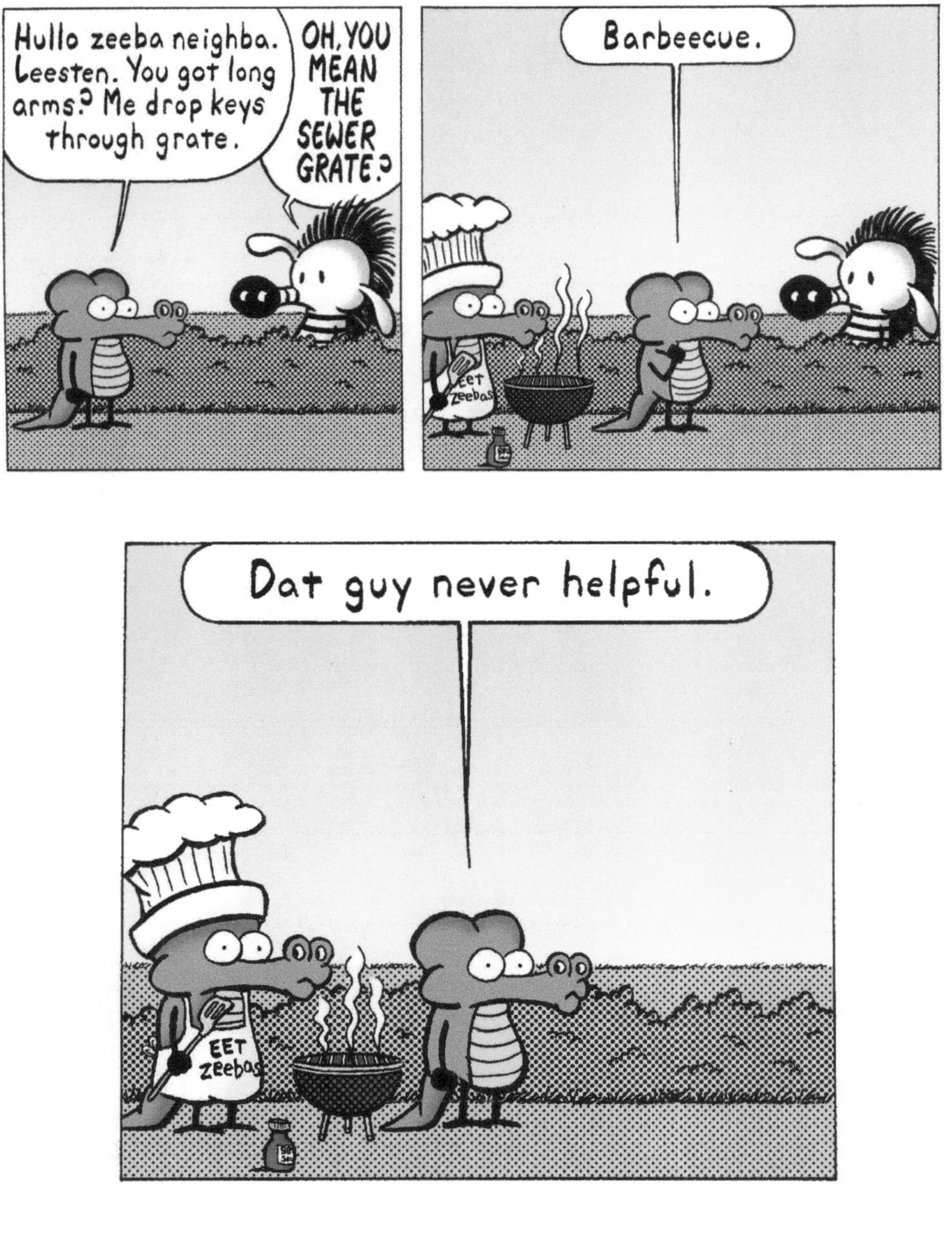
Hullo zeeba neighba. Leesten. You got long arms? Me drop keys through grate.
OH, YOU MEAN THE SEWER GRATE?
Barbeecue.
EET zeebas
Dat guy never helpful.
EET zeebas

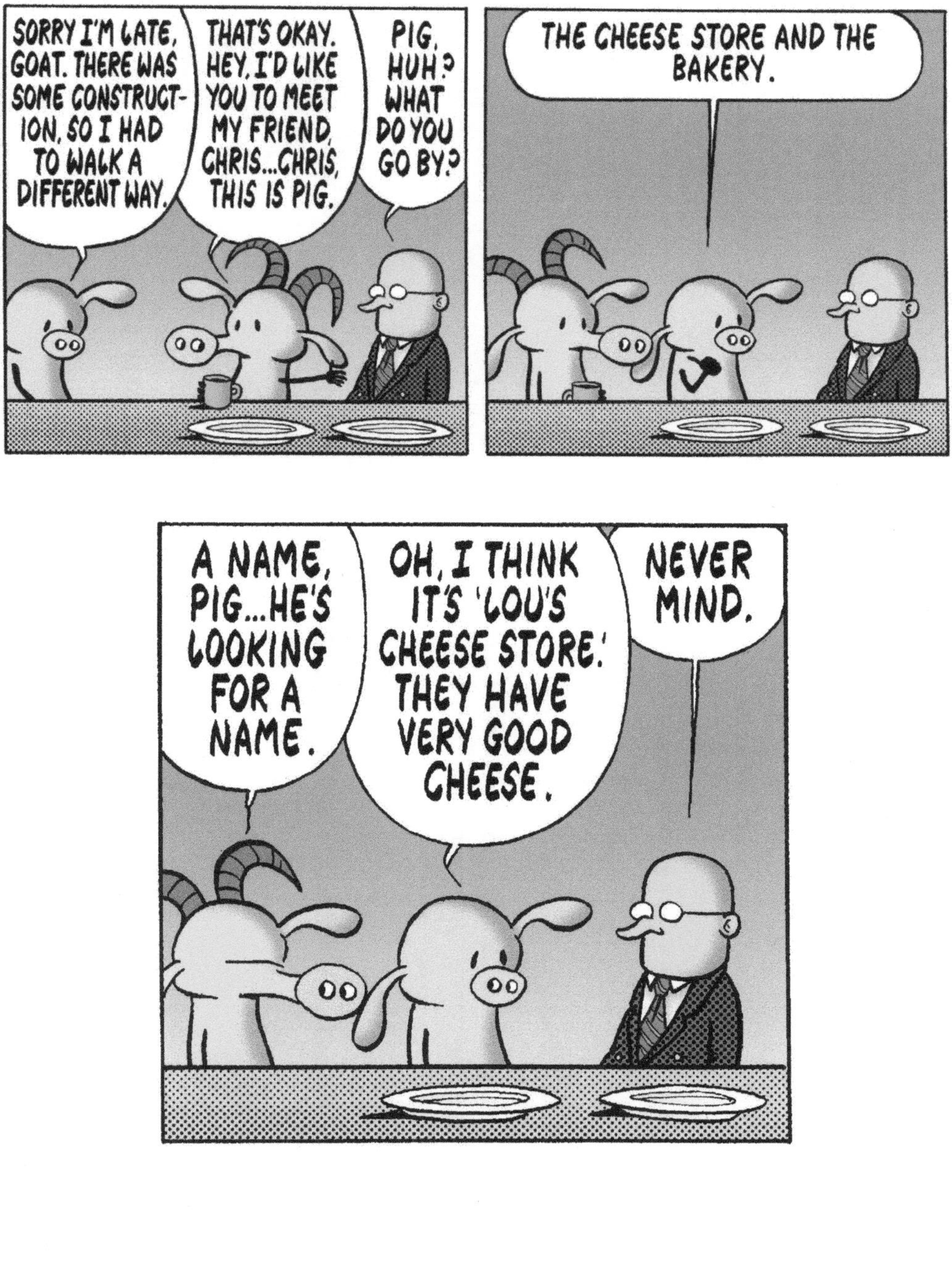
SORRY I'M LATE, GOAT. THERE WAS SOME CONSTRUCTION, SO I HAD TO WALK A DIFFERENT WAY.
THAT'S OKAY. HEY, I'D LIKE YOU TO MEET MY FRIEND, CHRIS...CHRIS, THIS IS PIG.
PIG, HUH? WHAT DO YOU GO BY?
THE CHEESE STORE AND THE BAKERY.
A NAME, PIG...HE'S LOOKING FOR A NAME.
OH, I THINK IT'S 'LOU'S CHEESE STORE.' THEY HAVE VERY GOOD CHEESE.
NEVER MIND.

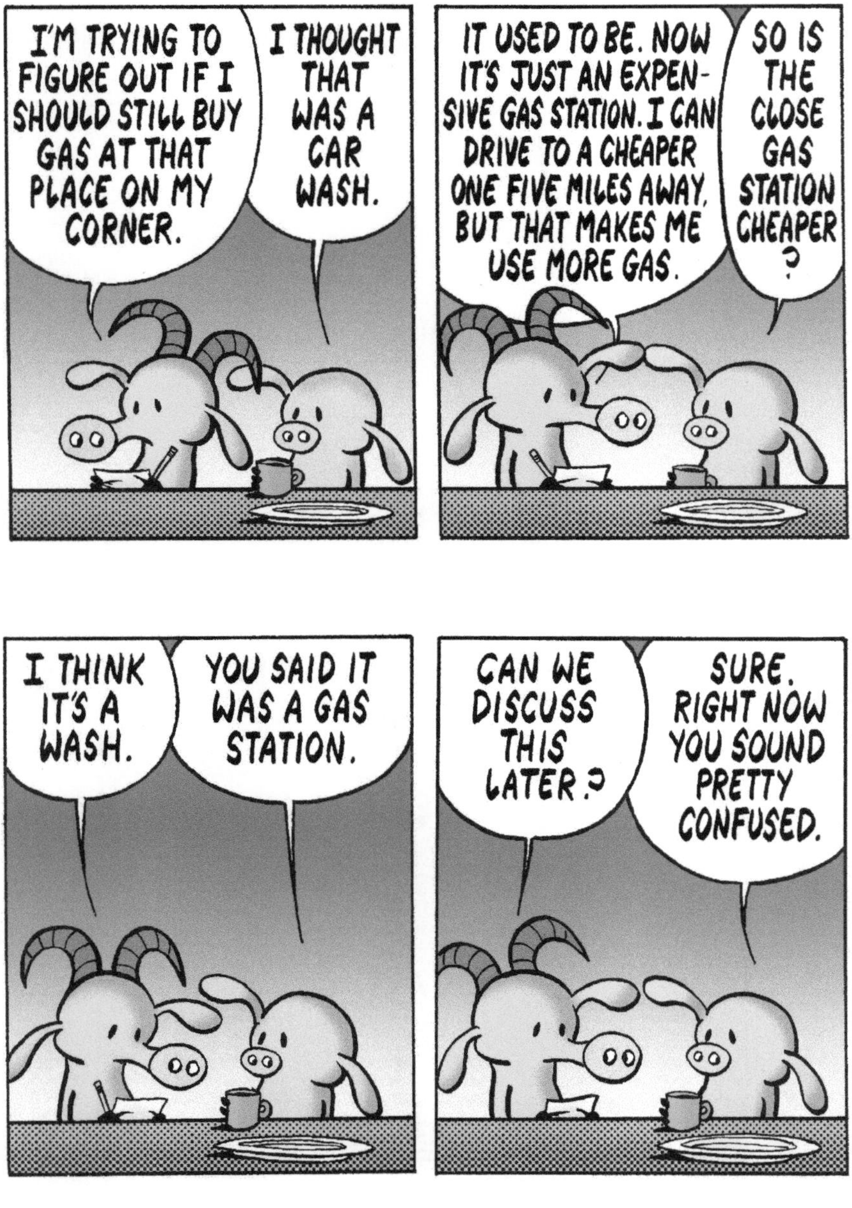
I'M TRYING TO FIGURE OUT IF I SHOULD STILL BUY GAS AT THAT PLACE ON MY CORNER.
I THOUGHT THAT WAS A CAR WASH.
IT USED TO BE. NOW IT'S JUST AN EXPENSIVE GAS STATION. I CAN DRIVE TO A CHEAPER ONE FIVE MILES AWAY, BUT THAT MAKES ME USE MORE GAS.
SO IS THE CLOSE GAS STATION CHEAPER?
I THINK IT'S A WASH.
YOU SAID IT WAS A GAS STATION.
CAN WE DISCUSS THIS LATER?
SURE. RIGHT NOW YOU SOUND PRETTY CONFUSED.

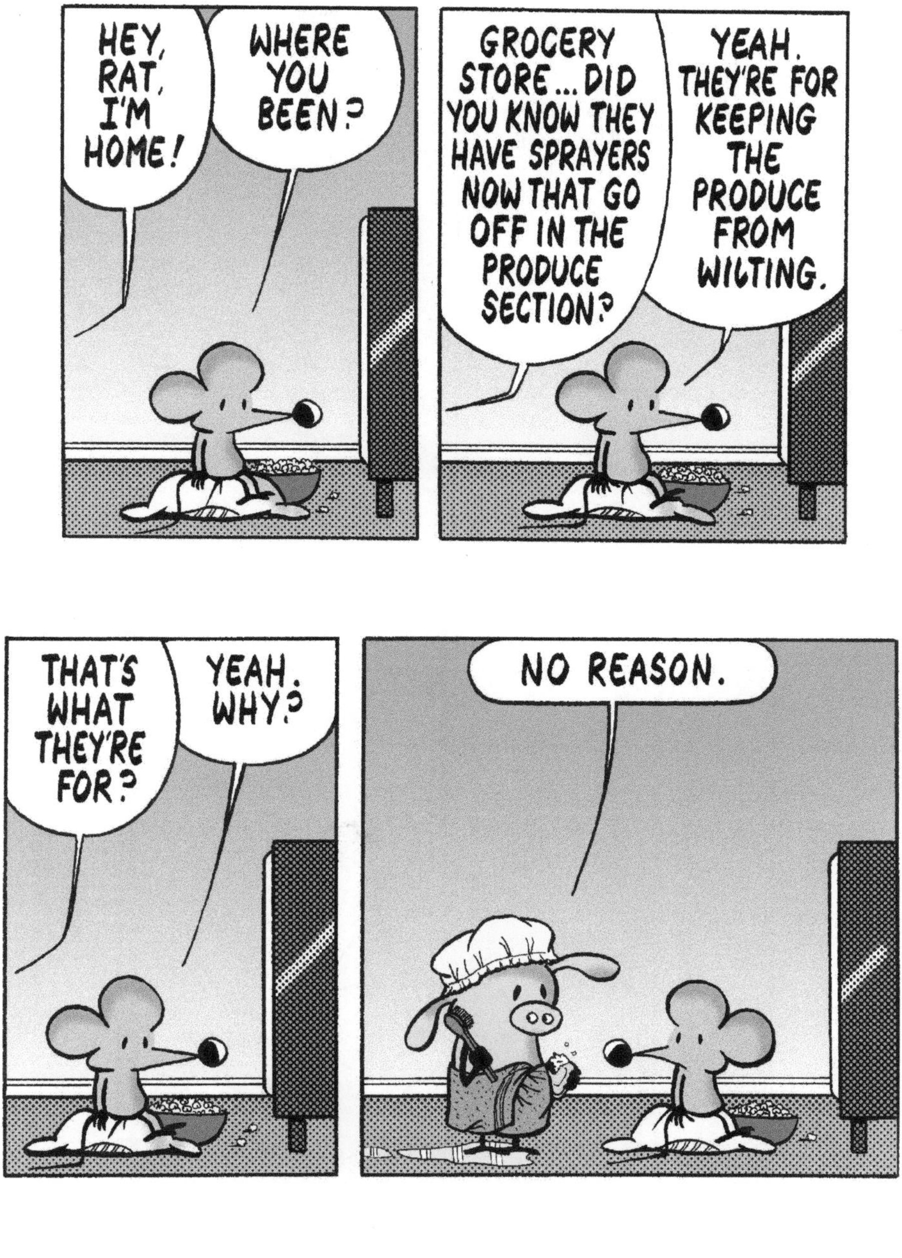
HEY, RAT, I'M HOME!
WHERE YOU BEEN?
GROCERY STORE... DID YOU KNOW THEY HAVE SPRAYERS NOW THAT GO OFF IN THE PRODUCE SECTION?
YEAH. THEY'RE FOR KEEPING THE PRODUCE FROM WILTING.
THAT'S WHAT THEY'RE FOR?
YEAH. WHY?
NO REASON.

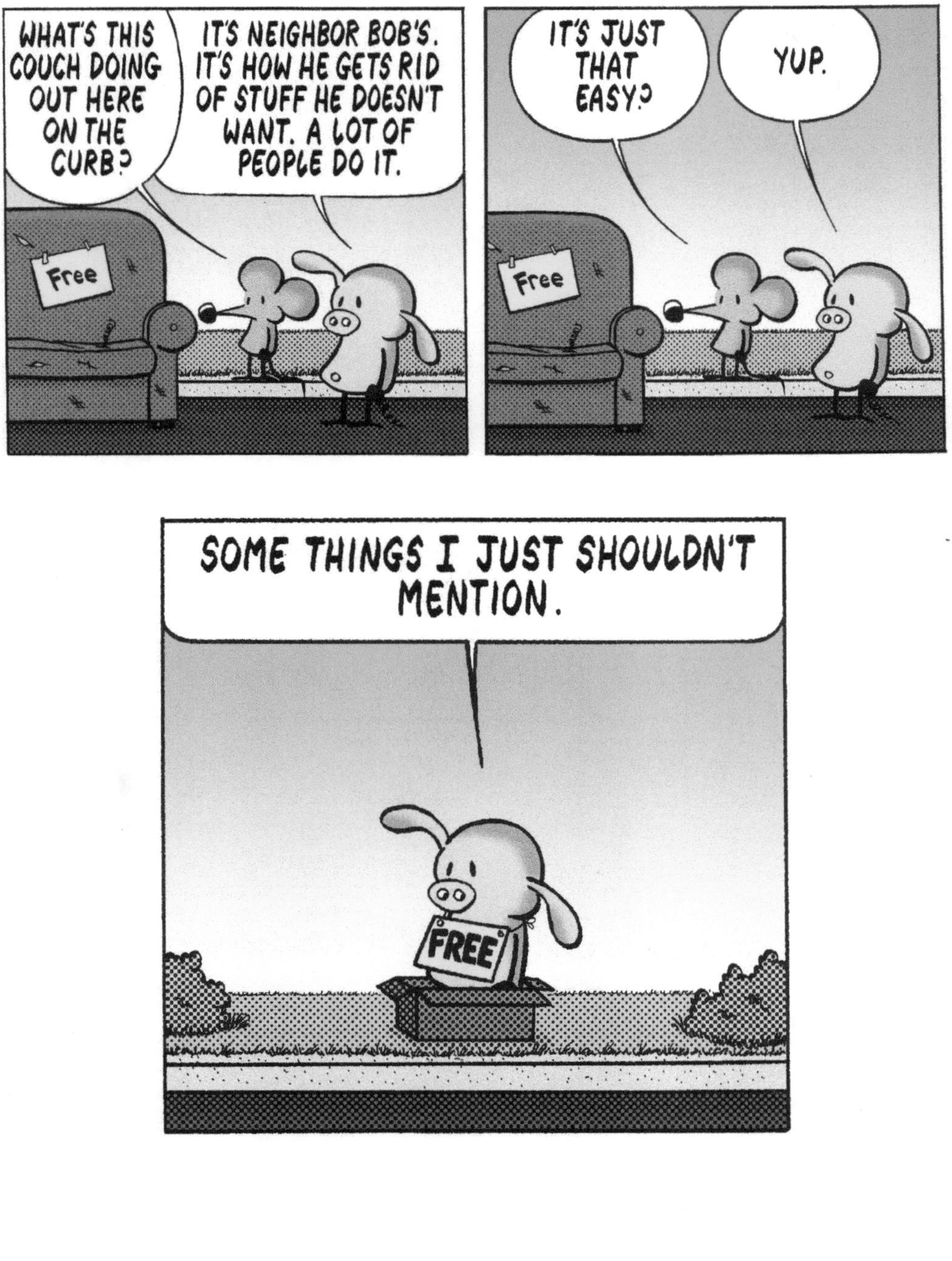
WHAT'S THIS COUCH DOING OUT HERE ON THE CURB?
IT'S NEIGHBOR BOB'S. IT'S HOW HE GETS RID OF STUFF HE DOESN'T WANT. A LOT OF PEOPLE DO IT.
Free
IT'S JUST THAT EASY?
YUP.
Free
SOME THINGS I JUST SHOULDN'T MENTION.
FREE

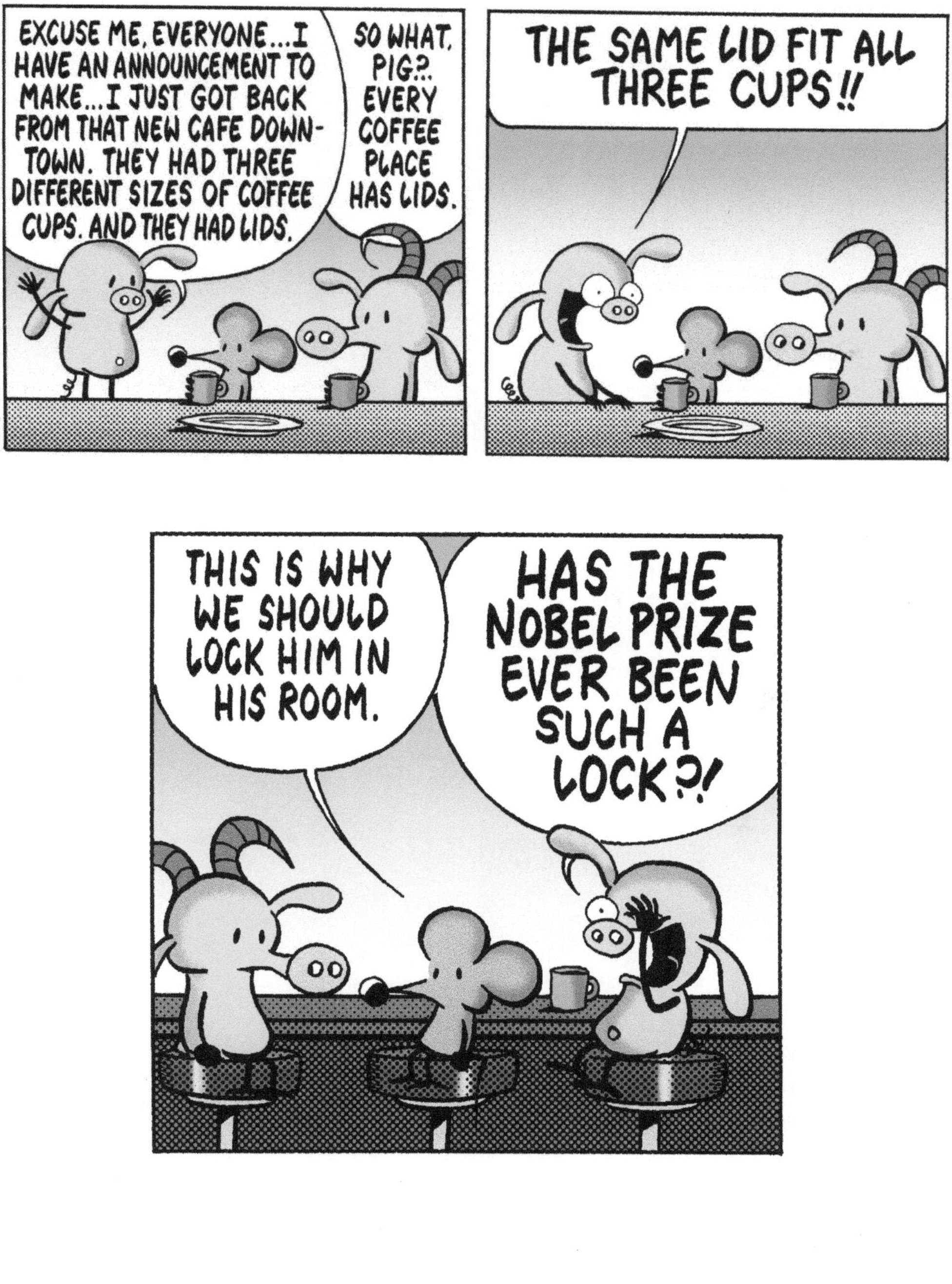
EXCUSE ME, EVERYONE...I HAVE AN ANNOUNCEMENT TO MAKE...I JUST GOT BACK FROM THAT NEW CAFE DOWNTOWN. THEY HAD THREE DIFFERENT SIZES OF COFFEE CUPS. AND THEY HAD LIDS.
SO WHAT, PIG?.. EVERY COFFEE PLACE HAS LIDS.
THE SAME LID FIT ALL THREE CUPS!!
THIS IS WHY WE SHOULD LOCK HIM IN HIS ROOM.
HAS THE NOBEL PRIZE EVER BEEN SUCH A LOCK?!

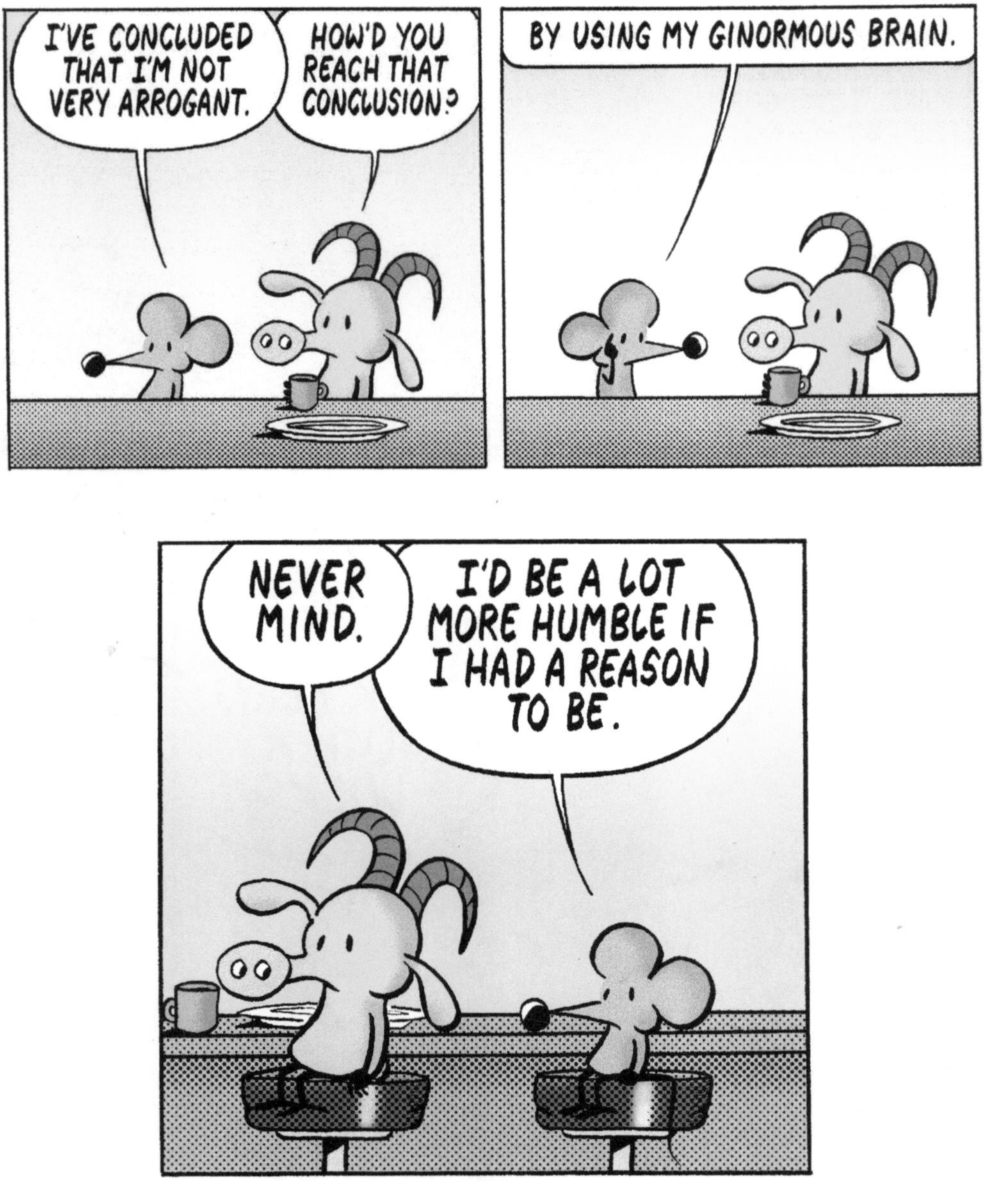
I'VE CONCLUDED THAT I'M NOT VERY ARROGANT.
HOW'D YOU REACH THAT CONCLUSION?
BY USING MY GINORMOUS BRAIN.
NEVER MIND.
I'D BE A LOT MORE HUMBLE IF I HAD A REASON TO BE.

Hey, Rat...Didja see the funny YouTube video me and Goat emailed you?

I did.
TOO LOL.

TOO LOL?

The
Opposite
Of
Laugh
Out
Loud

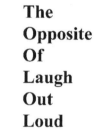

THAT HURTS.

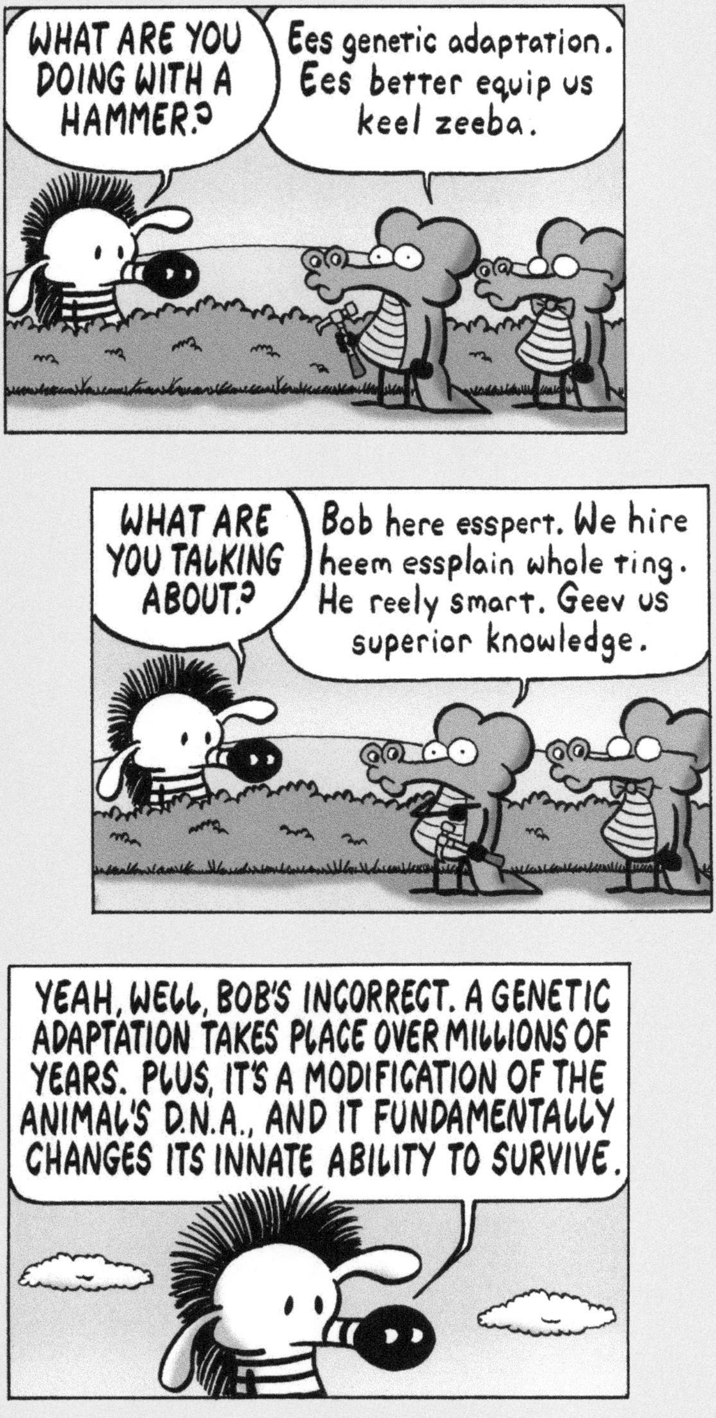
WHAT ARE YOU DOING WITH A HAMMER?
Ees genetic adaptation. Ees better equip us keel zeeba.
WHAT ARE YOU TALKING ABOUT?
Bob here esspert. We hire heem essplain whole ting. He reely smart. Geev us superior knowledge.
YEAH, WELL, BOB'S INCORRECT. A GENETIC ADAPTATION TAKES PLACE OVER MILLIONS OF YEARS. PLUS, IT'S A MODIFICATION OF THE ANIMAL'S D.N.A., AND IT FUNDAMENTALLY CHANGES ITS INNATE ABILITY TO SURVIVE.

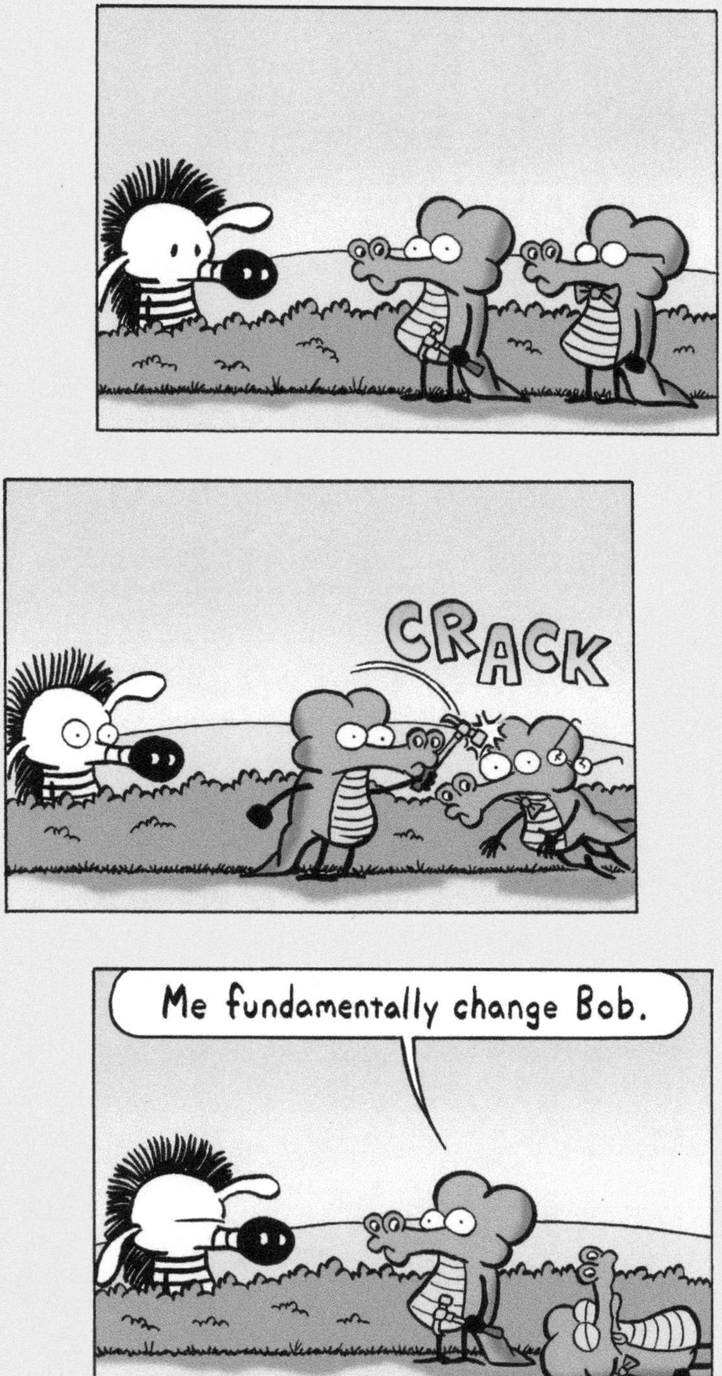
CRACK
Me fundamentally change Bob.

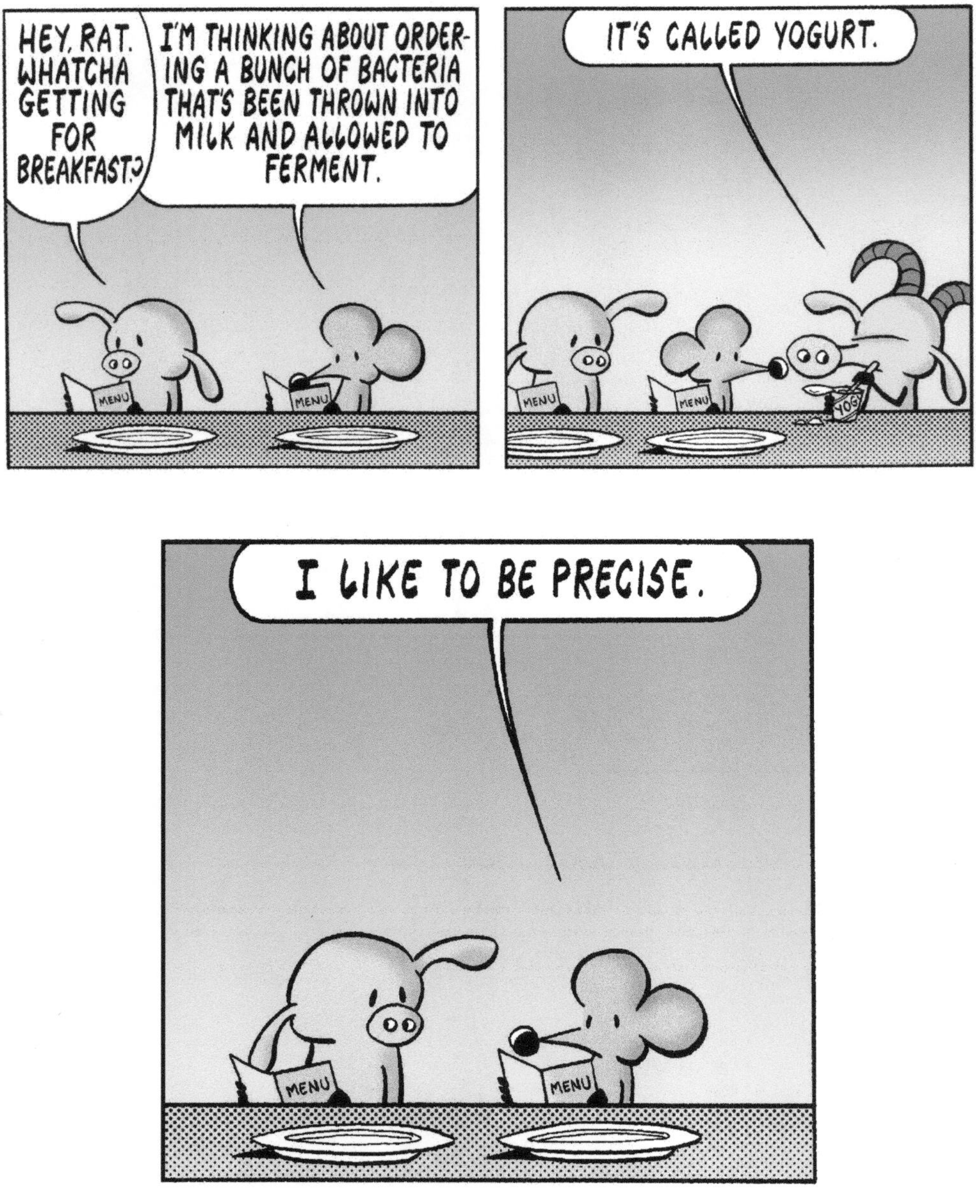
HEY, RAT. WHATCHA GETTING FOR BREAKFAST?
I'M THINKING ABOUT ORDERING A BUNCH OF BACTERIA THAT'S BEEN THROWN INTO MILK AND ALLOWED TO FERMENT.
MENU
MENU
IT'S CALLED YOGURT.
MENU
MENU
YOG
I LIKE TO BE PRECISE.
MENU
MENU

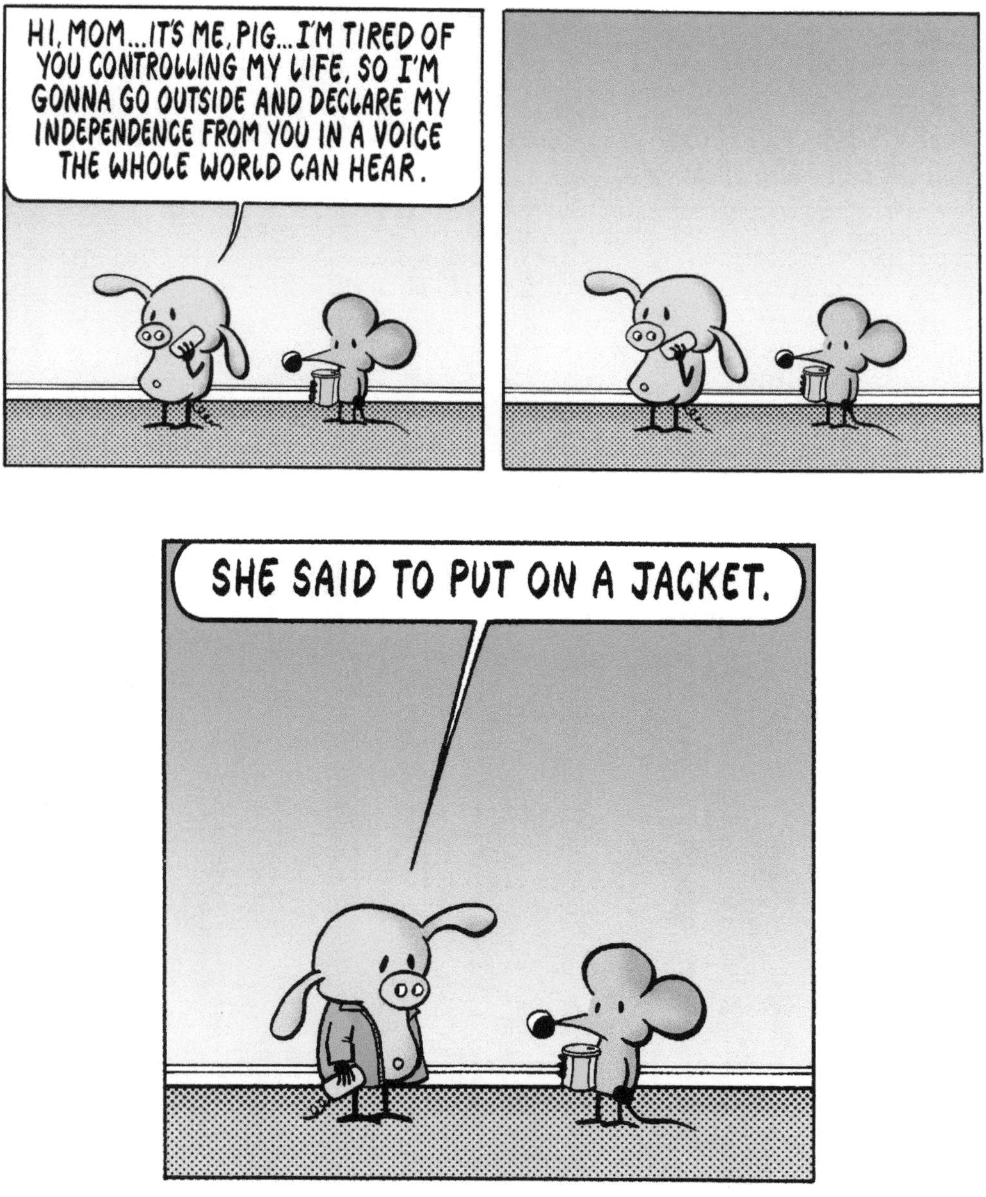
HI, MOM...IT'S ME, PIG...I'M TIRED OF YOU CONTROLLING MY LIFE, SO I'M GONNA GO OUTSIDE AND DECLARE MY INDEPENDENCE FROM YOU IN A VOICE THE WHOLE WORLD CAN HEAR.
SHE SAID TO PUT ON A JACKET.

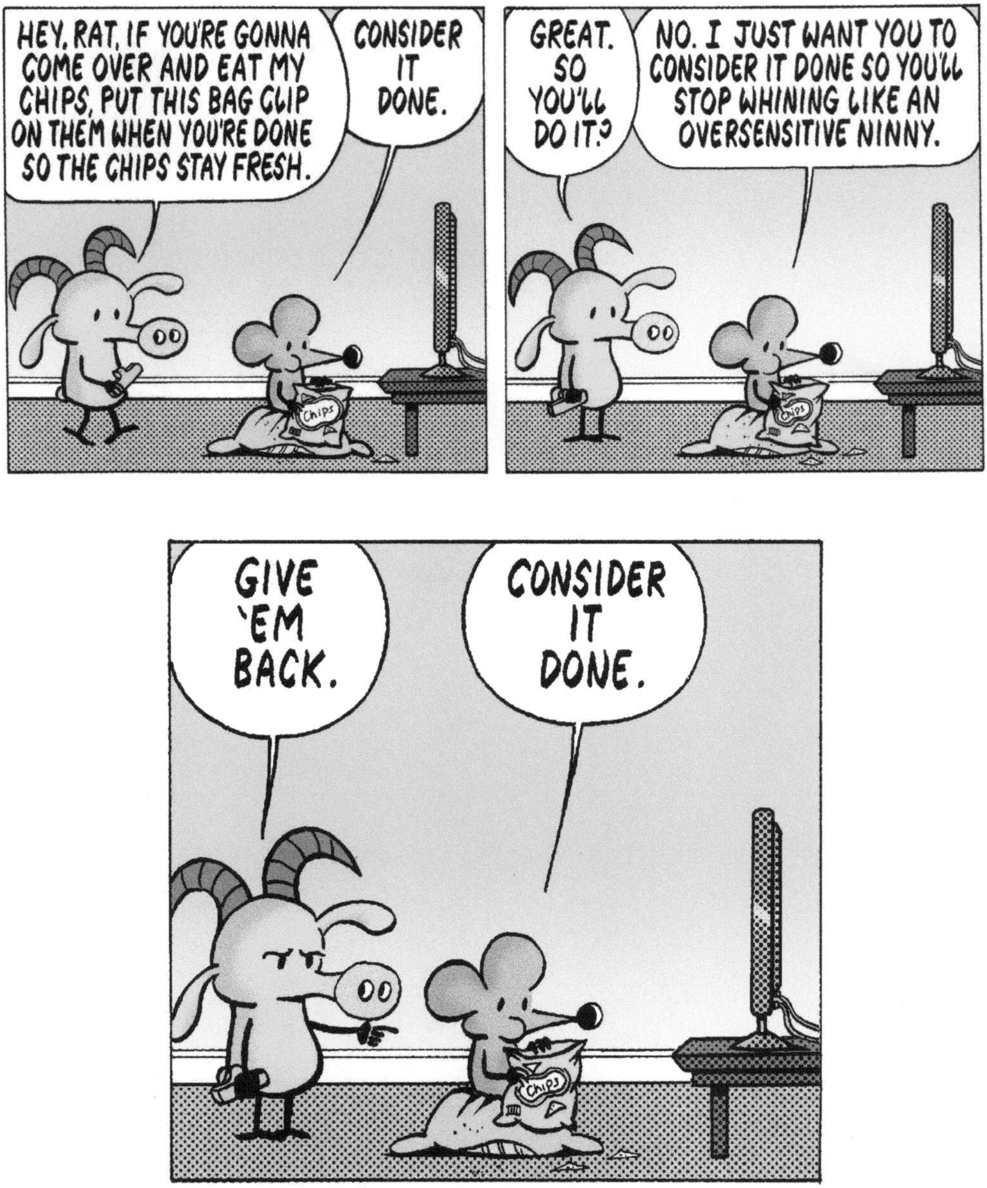
HEY, RAT, IF YOU'RE GONNA COME OVER AND EAT MY CHIPS, PUT THIS BAG CLIP ON THEM WHEN YOU'RE DONE SO THE CHIPS STAY FRESH.
CONSIDER IT DONE.
GREAT. SO YOU'LL DO IT?
NO. I JUST WANT YOU TO CONSIDER IT DONE SO YOU'LL STOP WHINING LIKE AN OVERSENSITIVE NINNY.
GIVE 'EM BACK.
CONSIDER IT DONE.
Chips

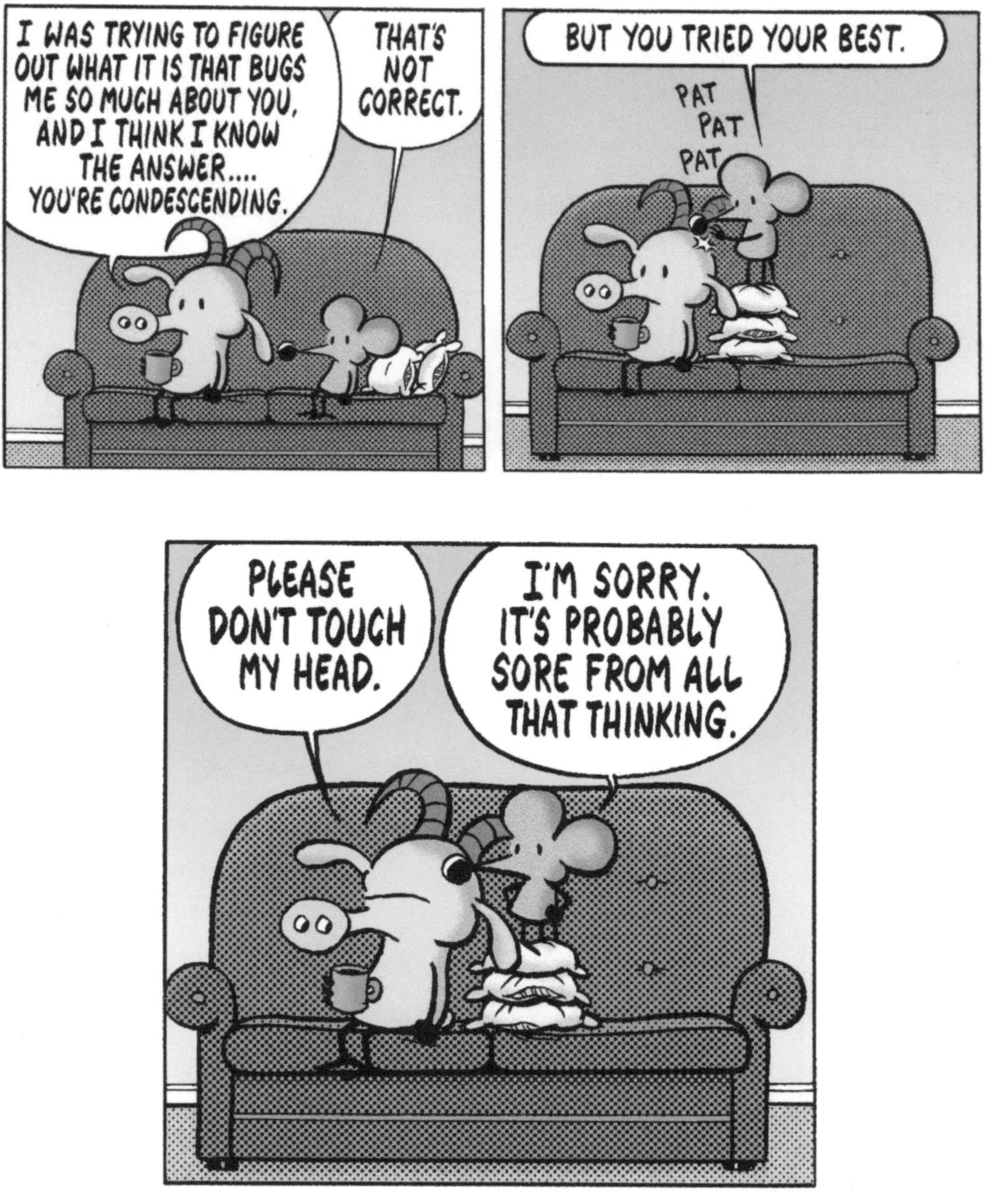
I WAS TRYING TO FIGURE OUT WHAT IT IS THAT BUGS ME SO MUCH ABOUT YOU, AND I THINK I KNOW THE ANSWER.... YOU'RE CONDESCENDING.
THAT'S NOT CORRECT.
BUT YOU TRIED YOUR BEST.
PAT PAT PAT
PLEASE DON'T TOUCH MY HEAD.
I'M SORRY. IT'S PROBABLY SORE FROM ALL THAT THINKING.

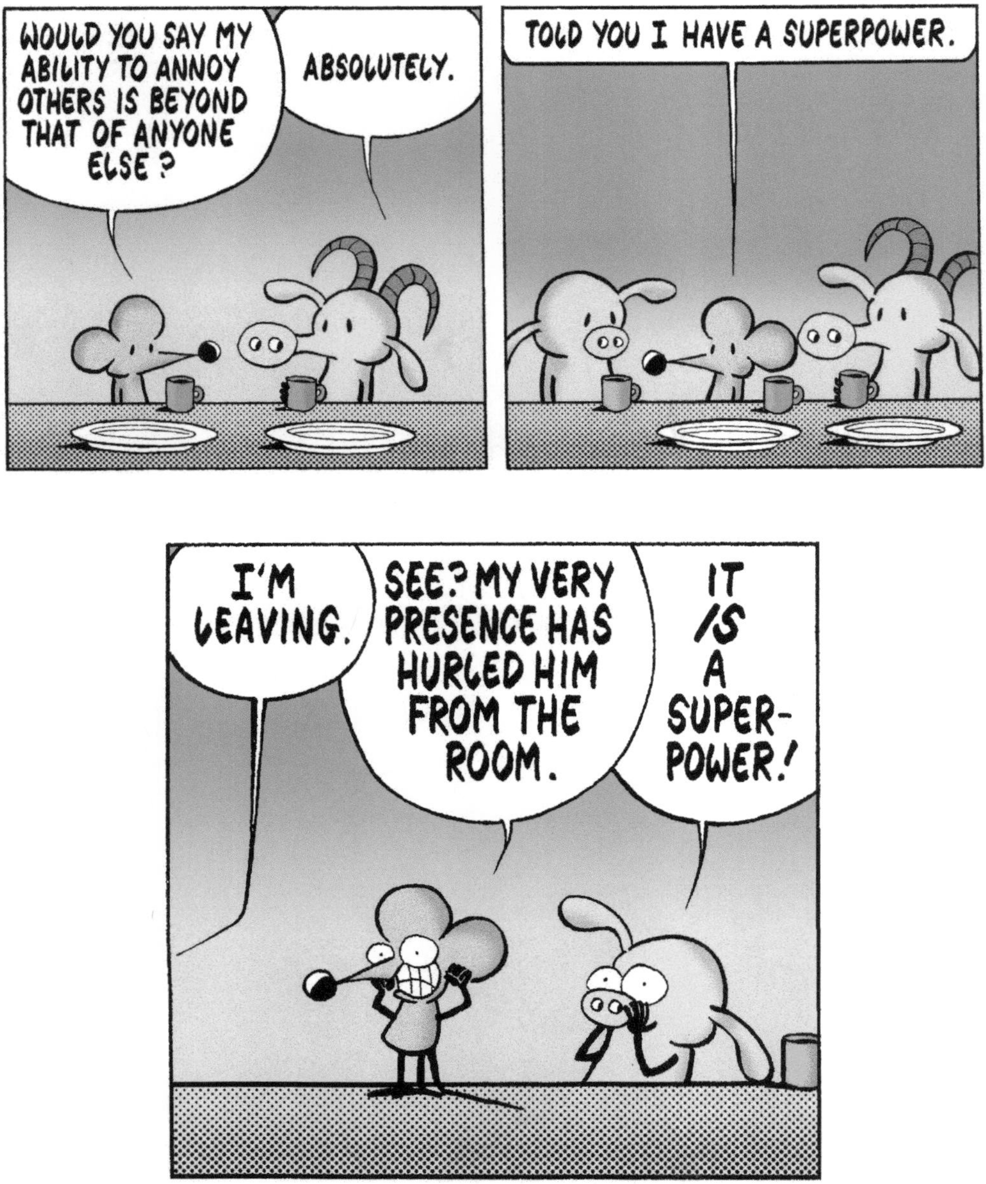
WOULD YOU SAY MY ABILITY TO ANNOY OTHERS IS BEYOND THAT OF ANYONE ELSE ?
ABSOLUTELY.
TOLD YOU I HAVE A SUPERPOWER.
I'M LEAVING.
SEE? MY VERY PRESENCE HAS HURLED HIM FROM THE ROOM.
IT IS A SUPER-POWER!

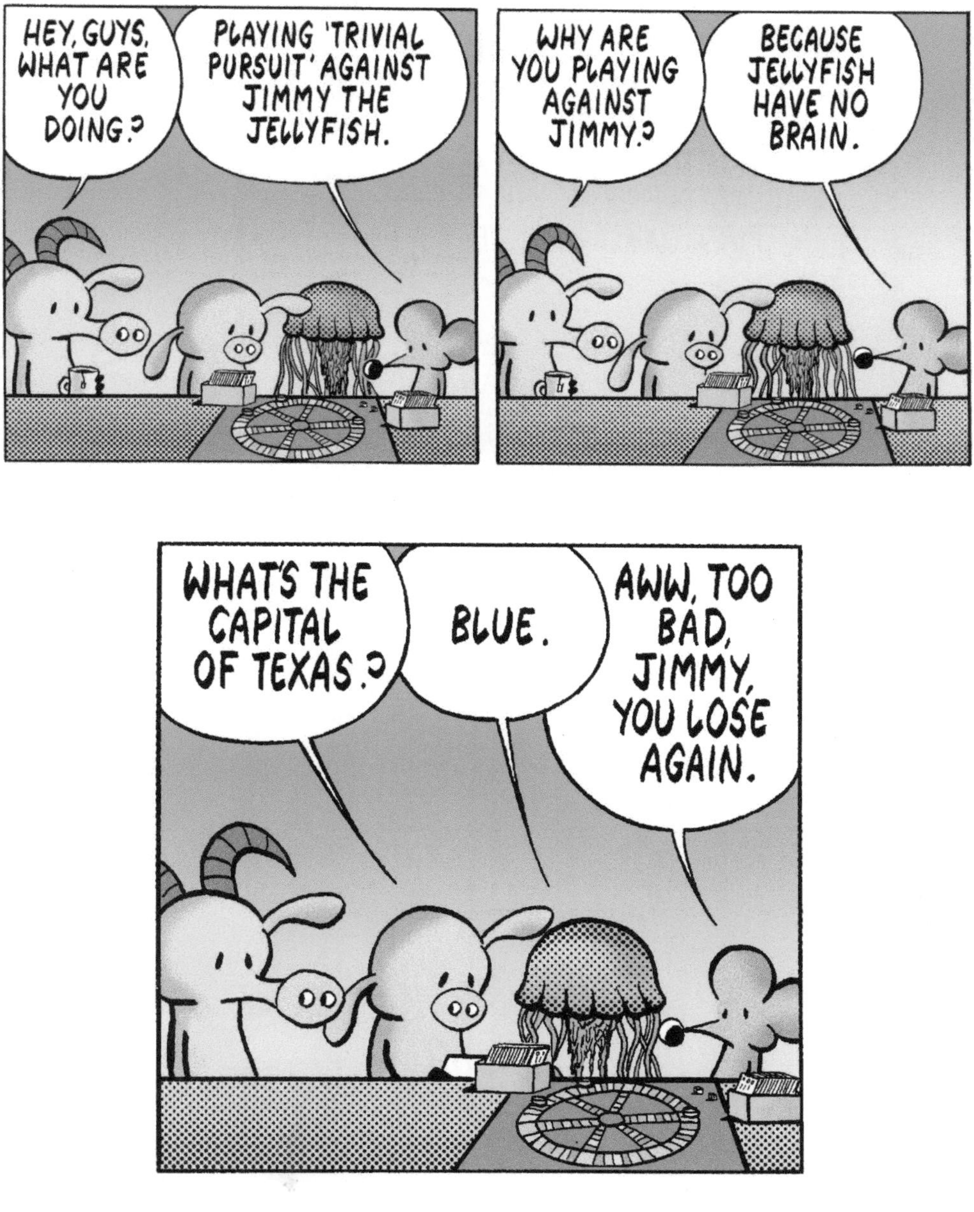
HEY, GUYS, WHAT ARE YOU DOING?
PLAYING 'TRIVIAL PURSUIT' AGAINST JIMMY THE JELLYFISH.
WHY ARE YOU PLAYING AGAINST JIMMY?
BECAUSE JELLYFISH HAVE NO BRAIN.
WHAT'S THE CAPITAL OF TEXAS?
BLUE.
AWW, TOO BAD, JIMMY, YOU LOSE AGAIN.

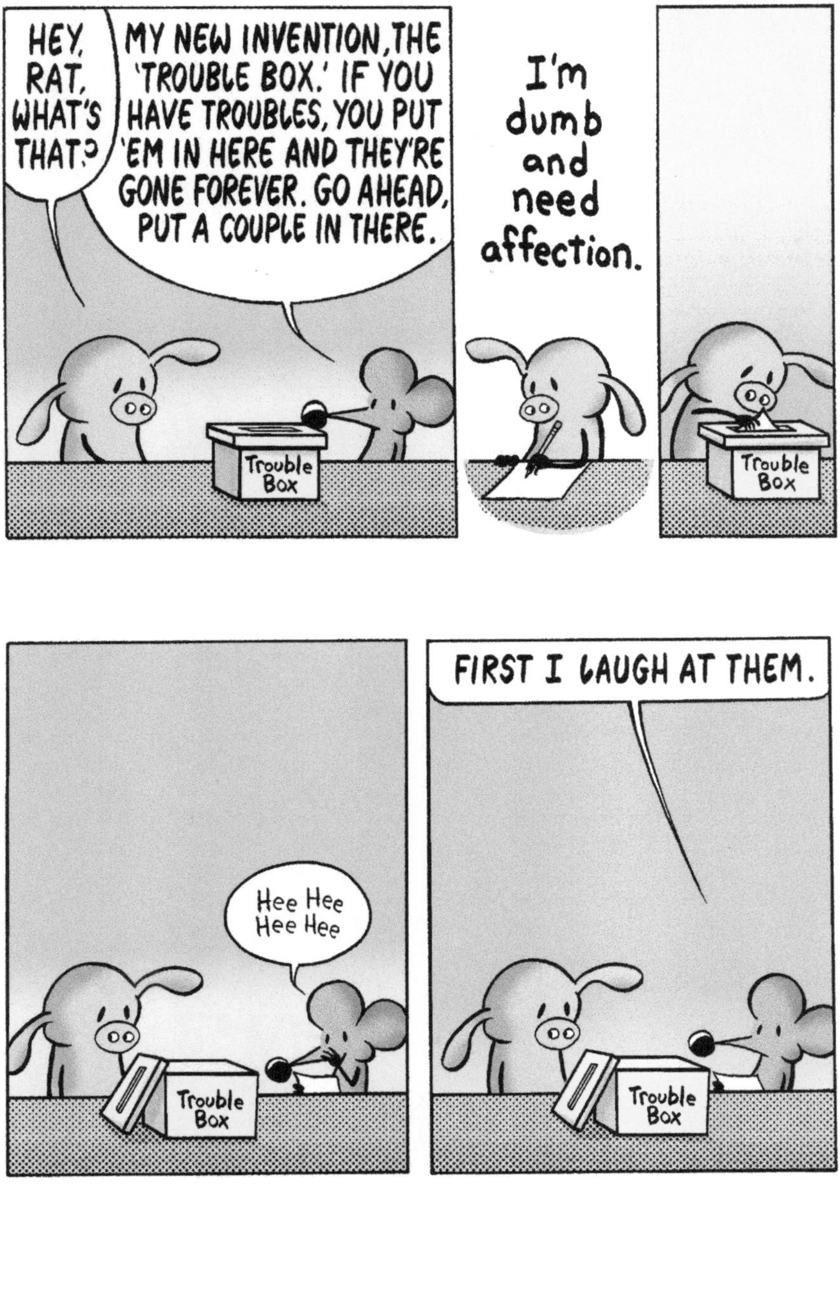
HEY, RAT, WHAT'S THAT?
MY NEW INVENTION, THE 'TROUBLE BOX.' IF YOU HAVE TROUBLES, YOU PUT 'EM IN HERE AND THEY'RE GONE FOREVER. GO AHEAD, PUT A COUPLE IN THERE.
Trouble Box
I'm dumb and need affection.
Trouble Box
Hee Hee Hee Hee
Trouble Box
FIRST I LAUGH AT THEM.
Trouble Box

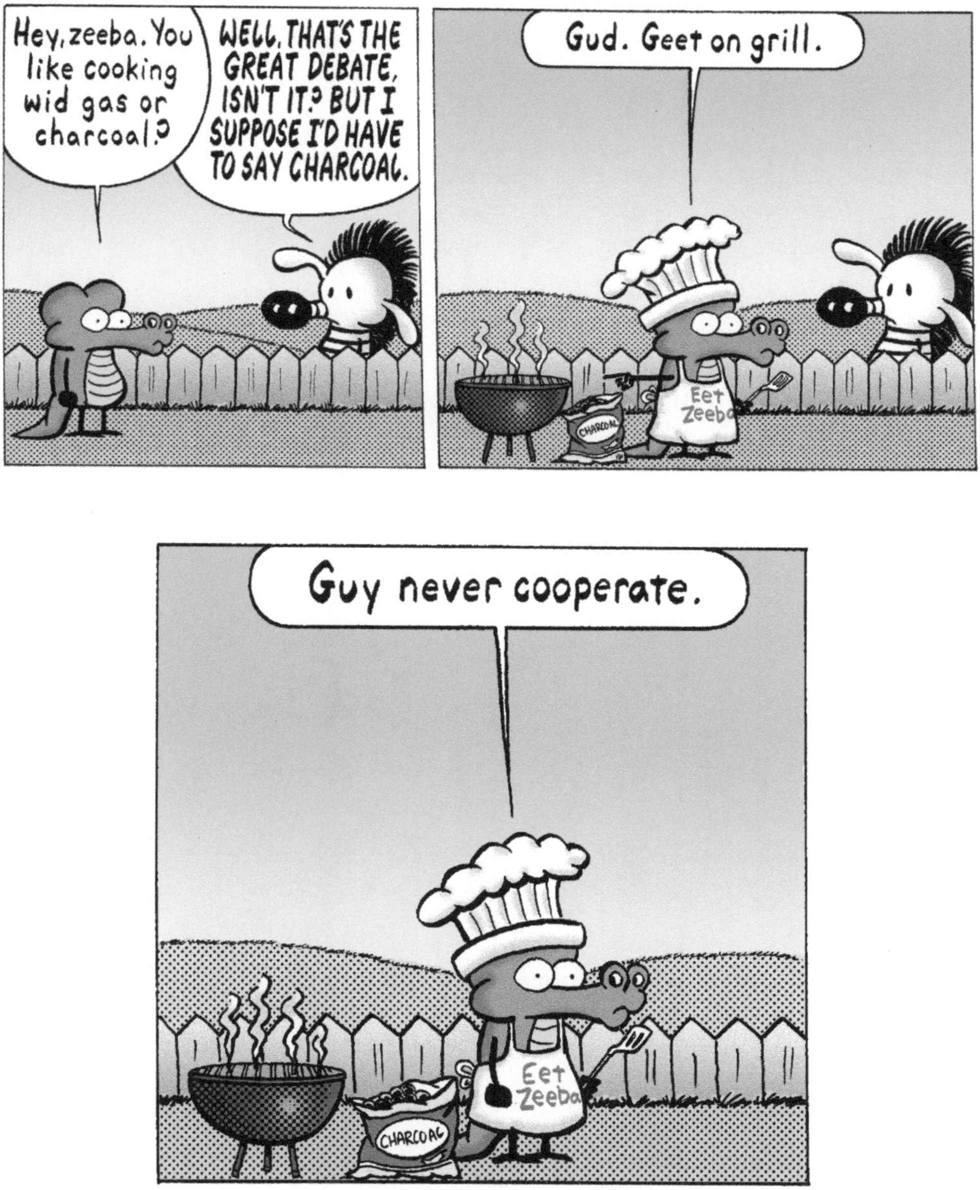
Hey, zeeba. You like cooking wid gas or charcoal?
WELL, THAT'S THE GREAT DEBATE, ISN'T IT? BUT I SUPPOSE I'D HAVE TO SAY CHARCOAL.
Gud. Geet on grill.
Eet Zeeba
CHARCOAL
Guy never cooperate.
Eet Zeeba
CHARCOAL

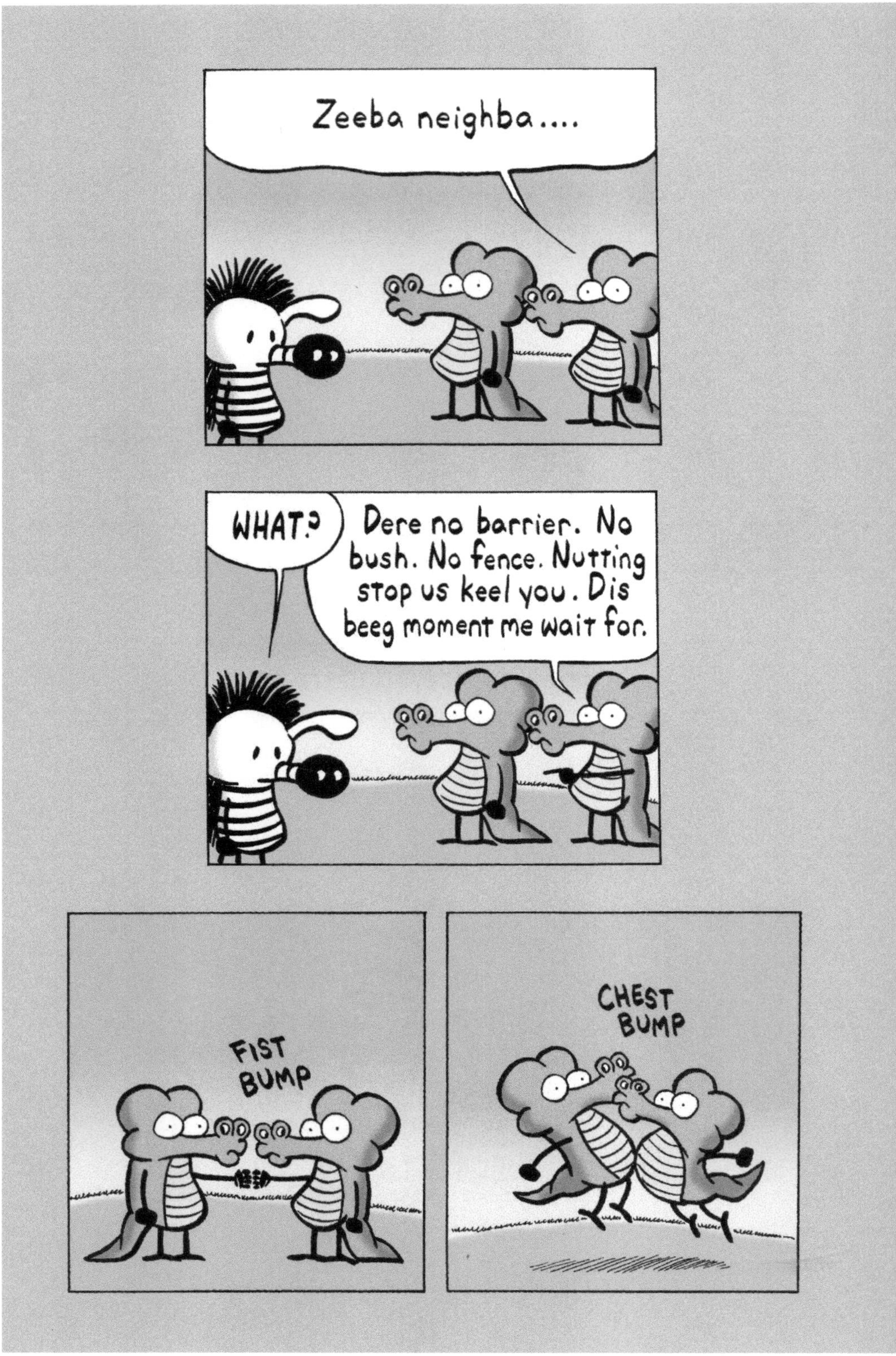
Zeeba neighba....
WHAT?
Dere no barrier. No bush. No fence. Nutting stop us keel you. Dis beeg moment me wait for.
FIST BUMP
CHEST BUMP

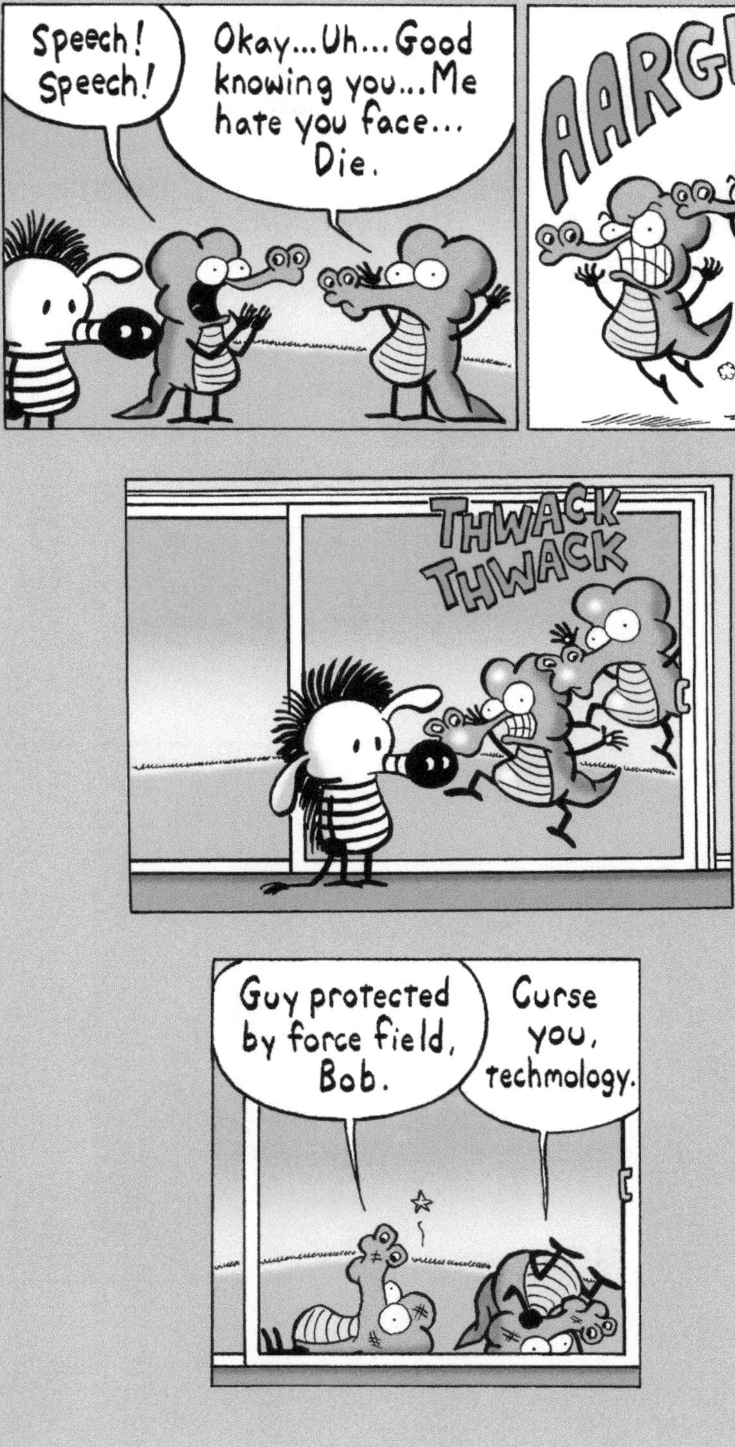
Speech! Speech!
Okay...Uh...Good knowing you...Me hate you face... Die.
AARGHHH
THWACK
THWACK
Guy protected by force field, Bob.
Curse you, techmology.

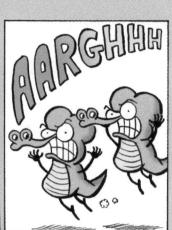

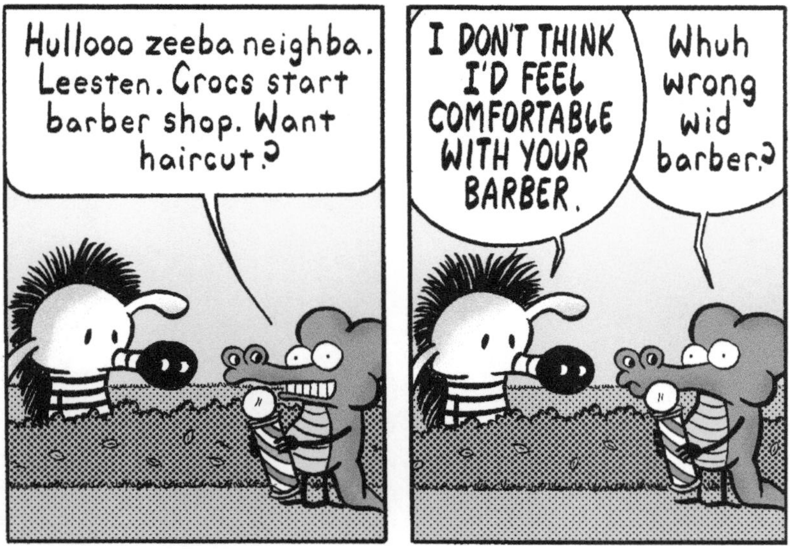
Hullooo zeeba neighba. Leesten. Crocs start barber shop. Want haircut?
I DON'T THINK I'D FEEL COMFORTABLE WITH YOUR BARBER.
Whuh wrong wid barber?

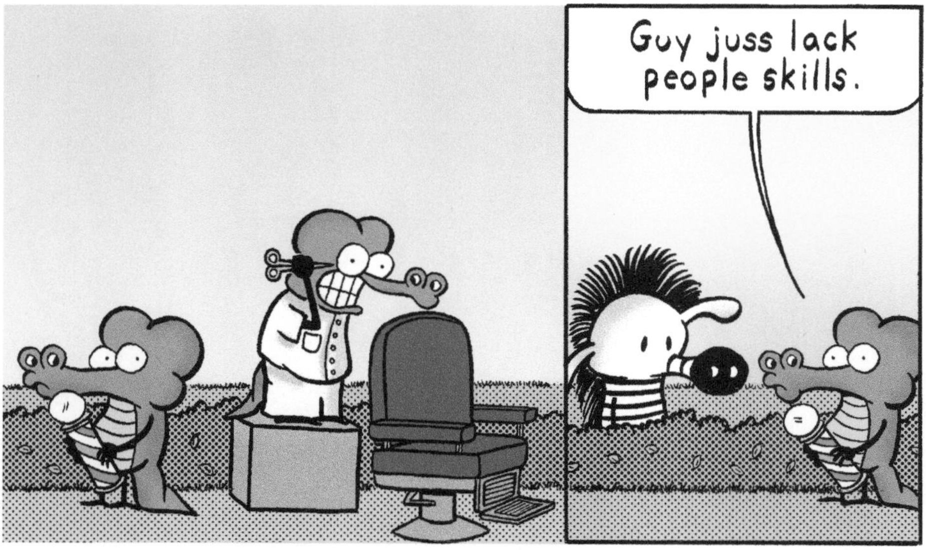
Guy juss lack people skills.

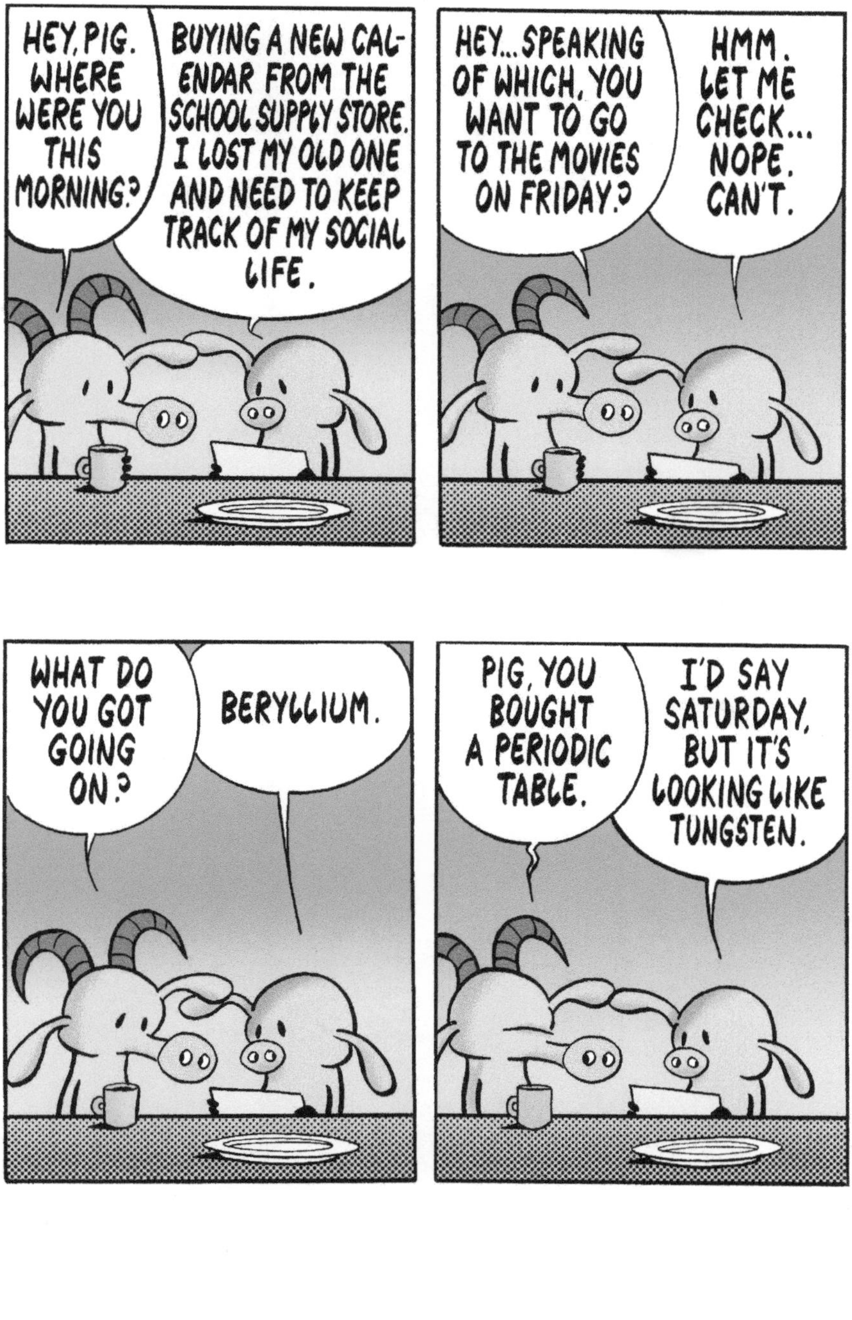
HEY, PIG. WHERE WERE YOU THIS MORNING?
BUYING A NEW CALENDAR FROM THE SCHOOL SUPPLY STORE. I LOST MY OLD ONE AND NEED TO KEEP TRACK OF MY SOCIAL LIFE.
HEY... SPEAKING OF WHICH, YOU WANT TO GO TO THE MOVIES ON FRIDAY?
HMM. LET ME CHECK... NOPE. CAN'T.
WHAT DO YOU GOT GOING ON?
BERYLLIUM.
PIG, YOU BOUGHT A PERIODIC TABLE.
I'D SAY SATURDAY, BUT IT'S LOOKING LIKE TUNGSTEN.

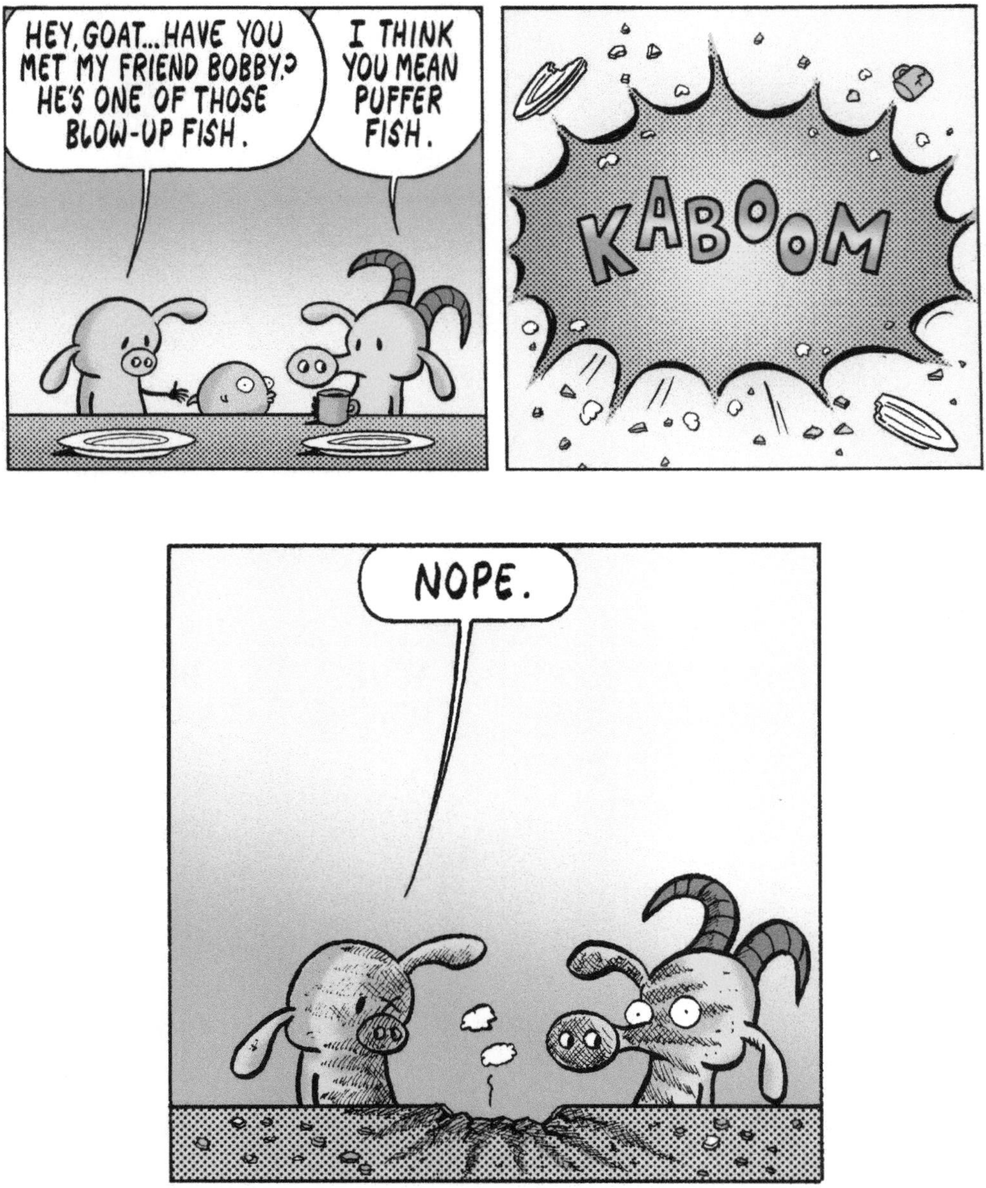
HEY, GOAT...HAVE YOU MET MY FRIEND BOBBY? HE'S ONE OF THOSE BLOW-UP FISH.
I THINK YOU MEAN PUFFER FISH.
KABOOM
NOPE.

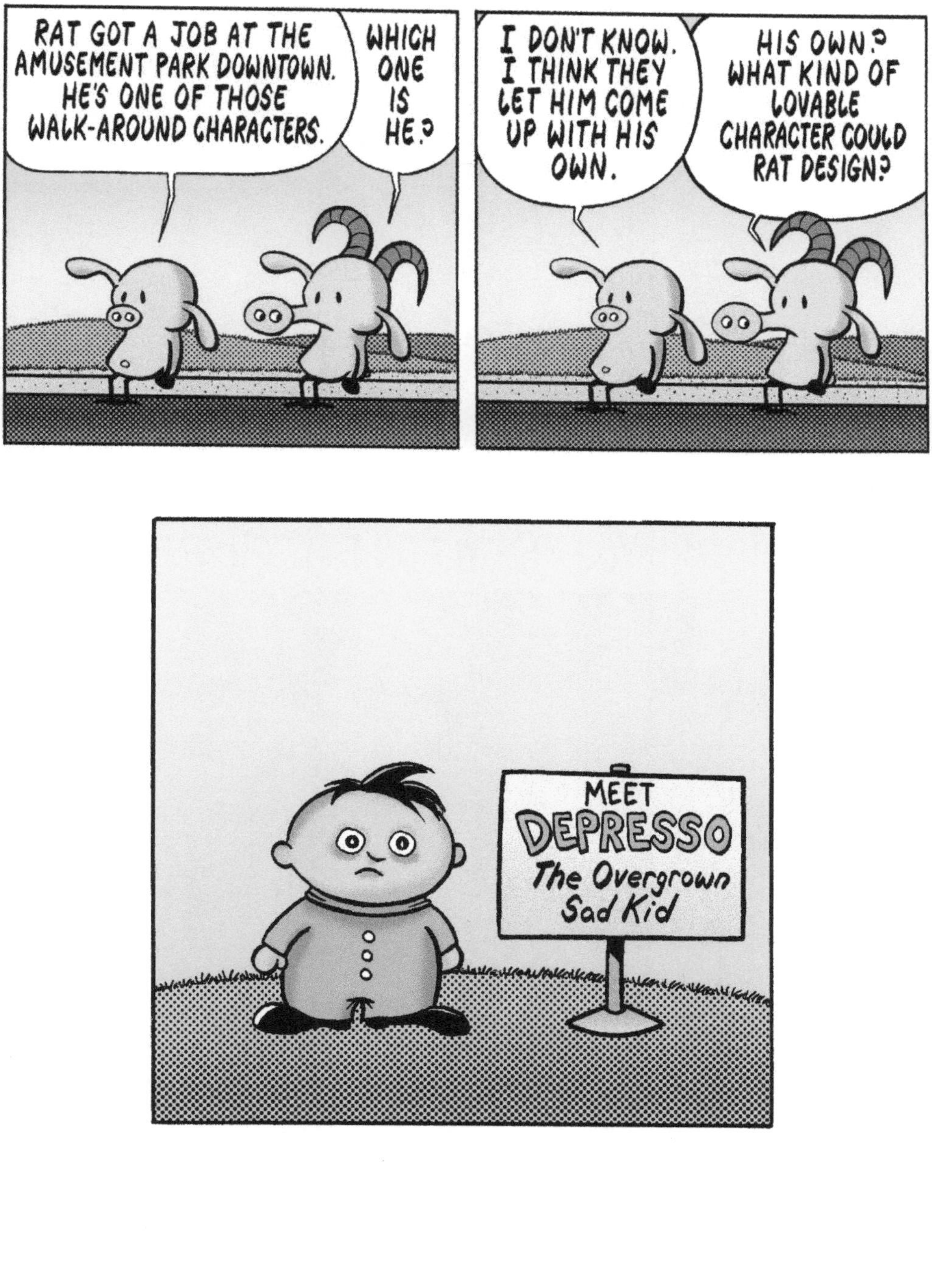
RAT GOT A JOB AT THE AMUSEMENT PARK DOWNTOWN. HE'S ONE OF THOSE WALK-AROUND CHARACTERS.
WHICH ONE IS HE?
I DON'T KNOW. I THINK THEY LET HIM COME UP WITH HIS OWN.
HIS OWN? WHAT KIND OF LOVABLE CHARACTER COULD RAT DESIGN?
MEET DEPRESSO The Overgrown Sad Kid

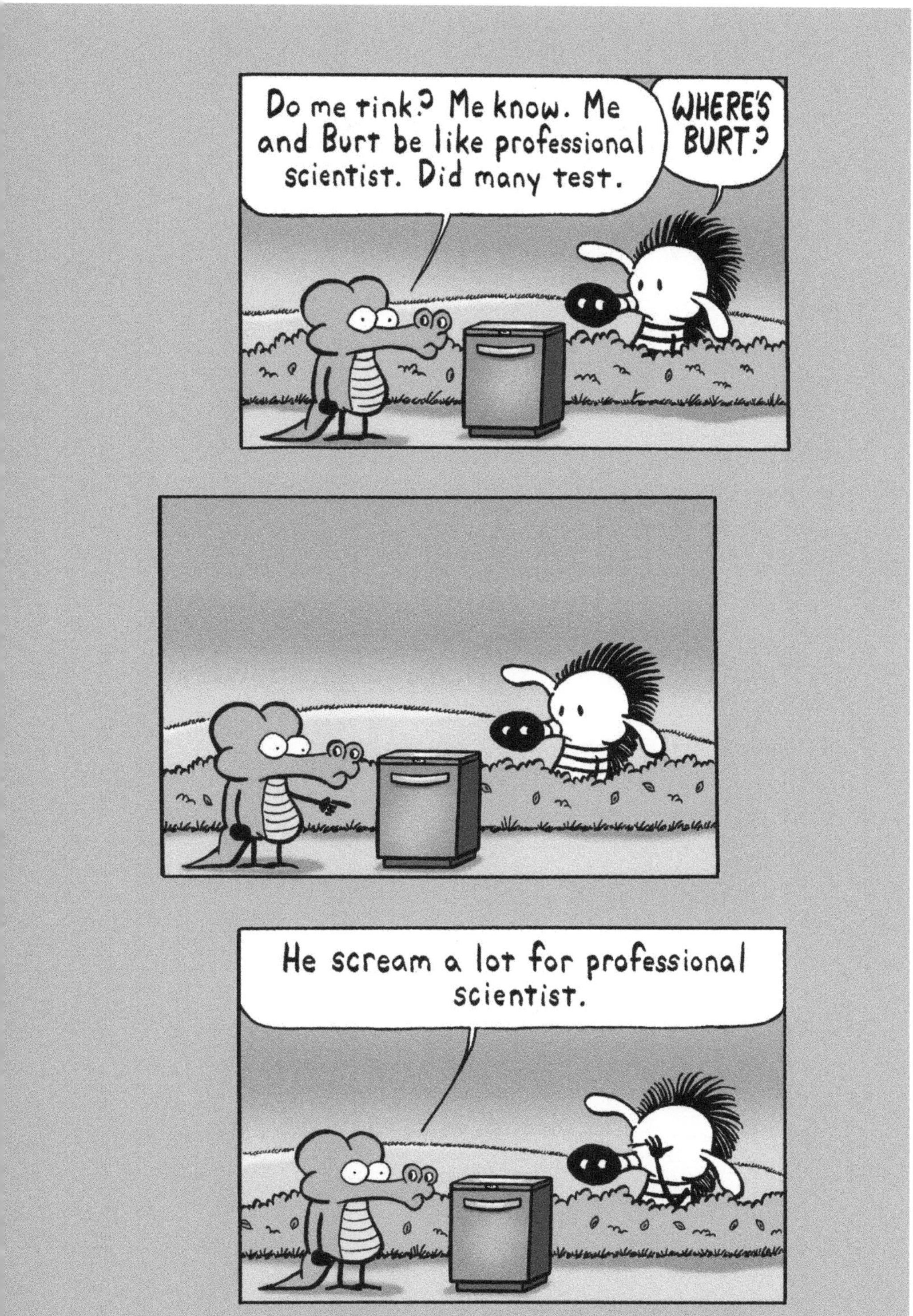
Do me tink? Me know. Me and Burt be like professional scientist. Did many test.
WHERE'S BURT?
He scream a lot for professional scientist.

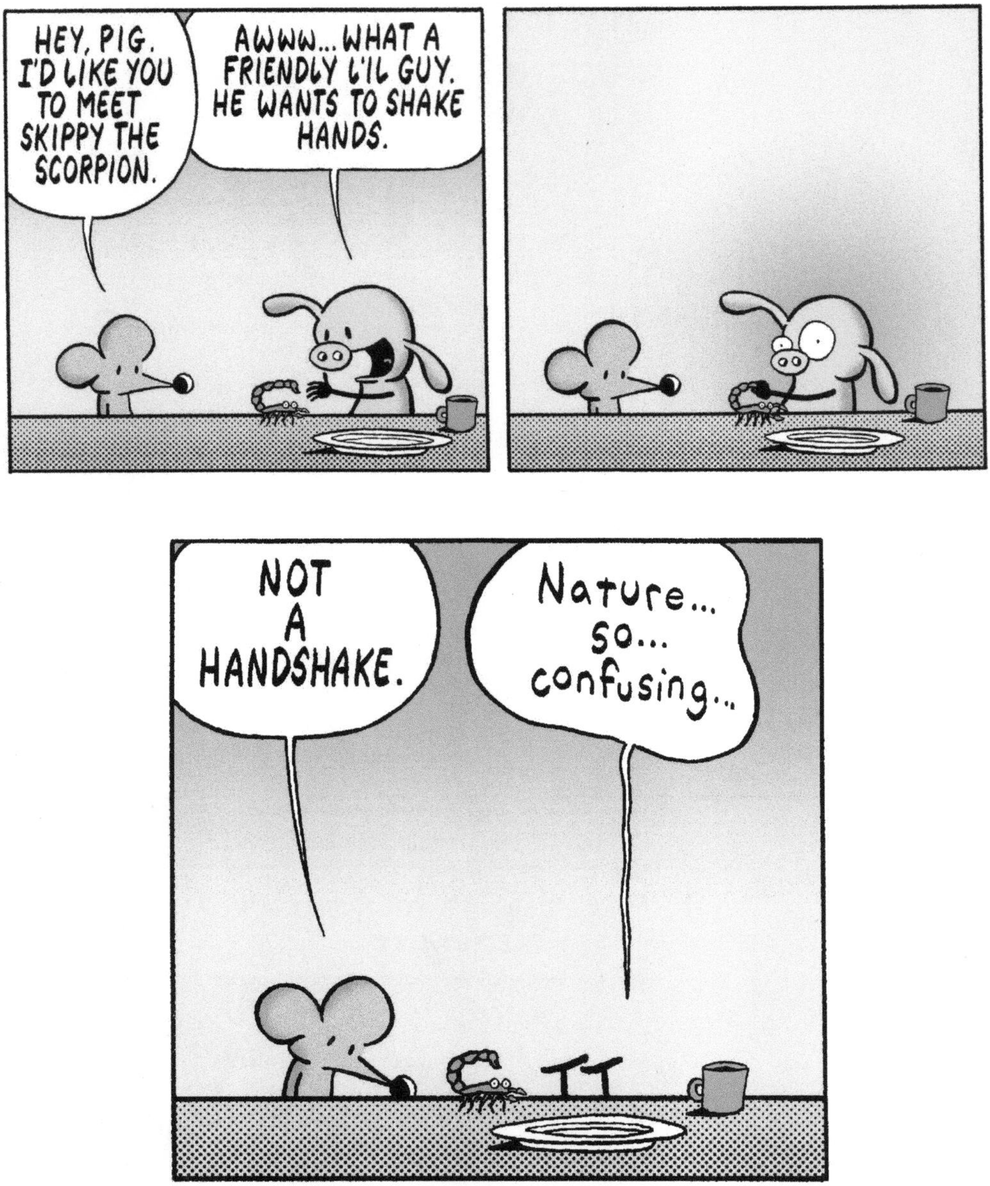
HEY, PIG. I'D LIKE YOU TO MEET SKIPPY THE SCORPION.
AWWW... WHAT A FRIENDLY L'IL GUY. HE WANTS TO SHAKE HANDS.
NOT A HANDSHAKE.
Nature... so... confusing...

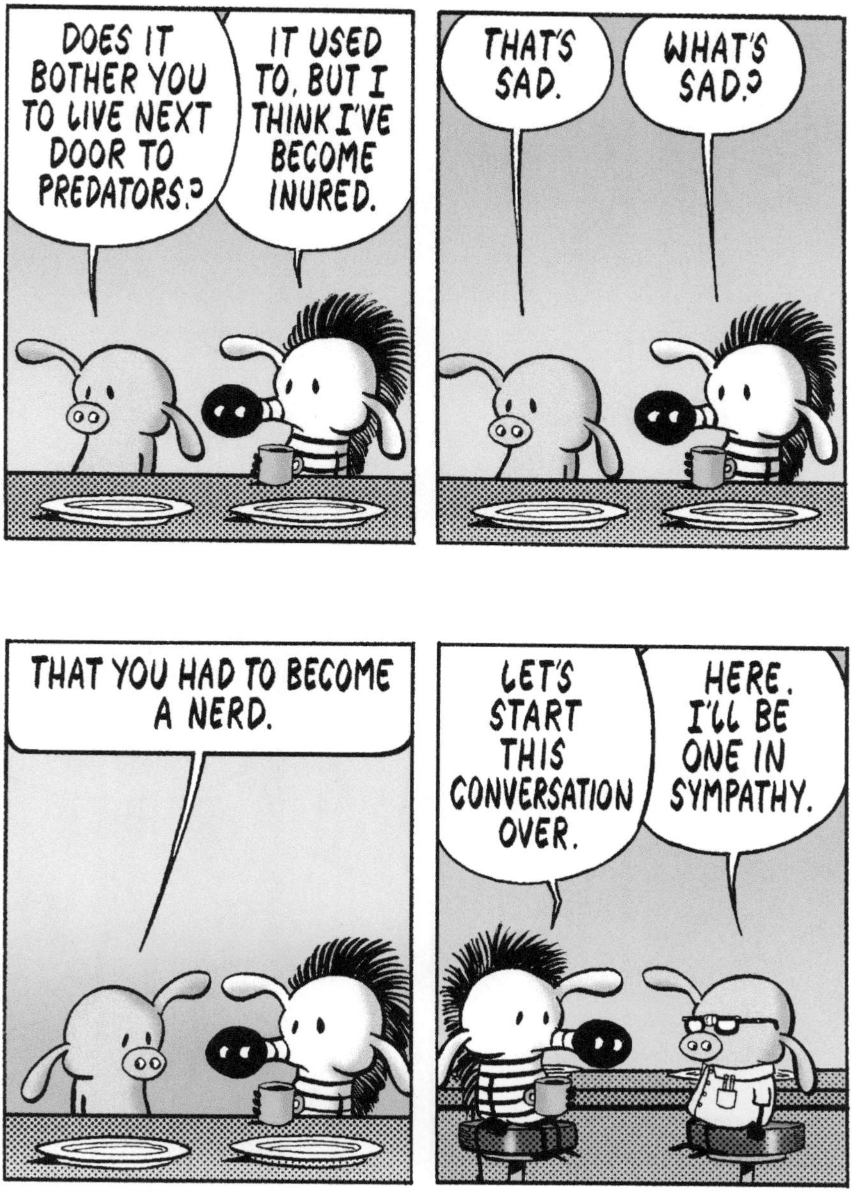
DOES IT BOTHER YOU TO LIVE NEXT DOOR TO PREDATORS?
IT USED TO, BUT I THINK I'VE BECOME INURED.
THAT'S SAD.
WHAT'S SAD?
THAT YOU HAD TO BECOME A NERD.
LET'S START THIS CONVERSATION OVER.
HERE. I'LL BE ONE IN SYMPATHY.

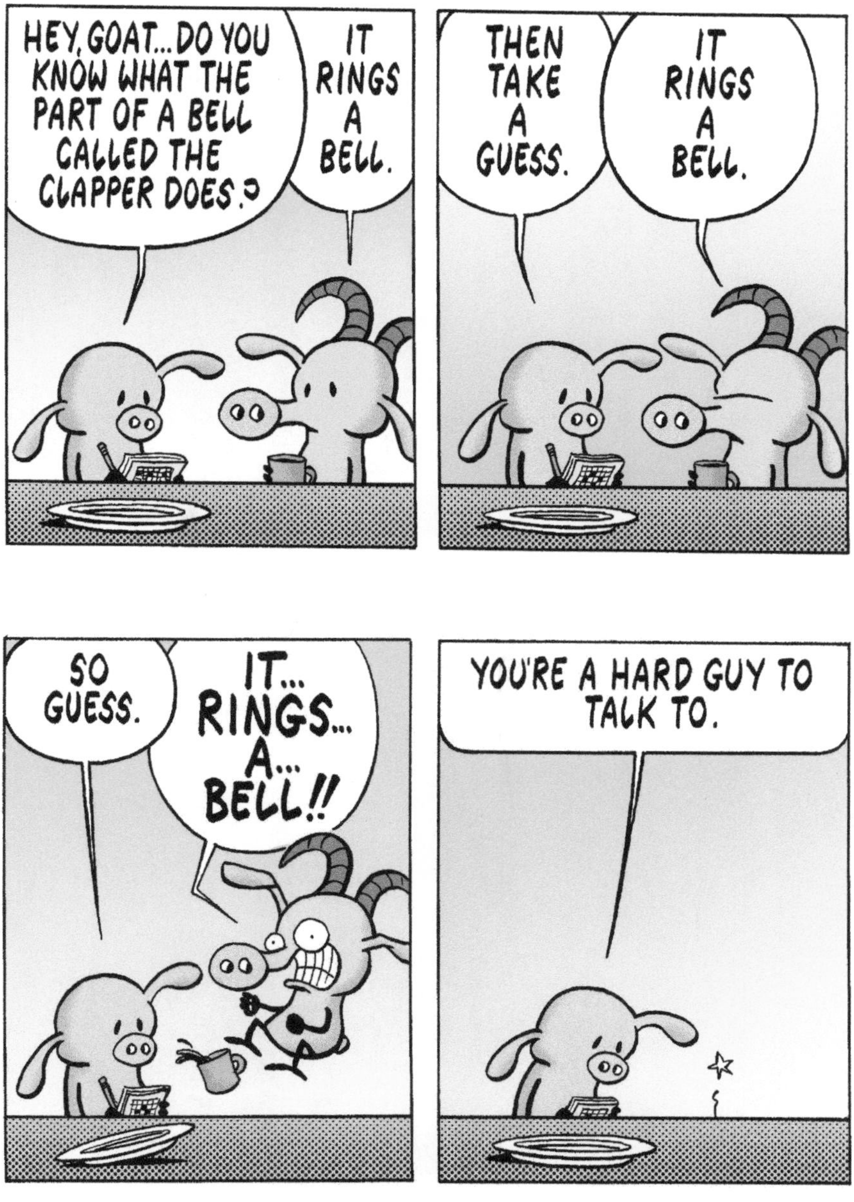
HEY, GOAT...DO YOU KNOW WHAT THE PART OF A BELL CALLED THE CLAPPER DOES?
IT RINGS A BELL.
THEN TAKE A GUESS.
IT RINGS A BELL.
SO GUESS.
IT... RINGS... A... BELL!!
YOU'RE A HARD GUY TO TALK TO.

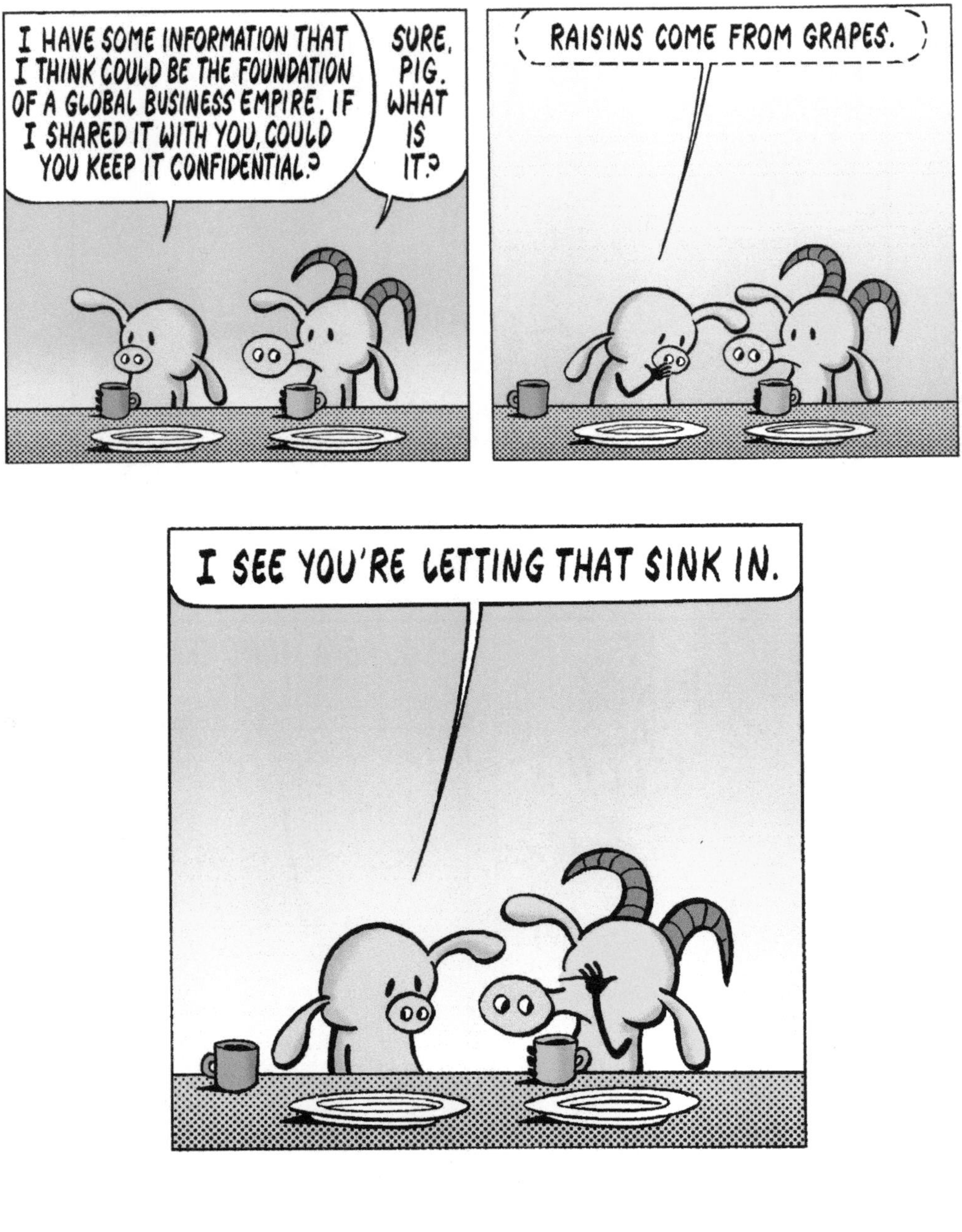
I HAVE SOME INFORMATION THAT I THINK COULD BE THE FOUNDATION OF A GLOBAL BUSINESS EMPIRE. IF I SHARED IT WITH YOU, COULD YOU KEEP IT CONFIDENTIAL?
SURE, PIG. WHAT IS IT?
RAISINS COME FROM GRAPES.
I SEE YOU'RE LETTING THAT SINK IN.

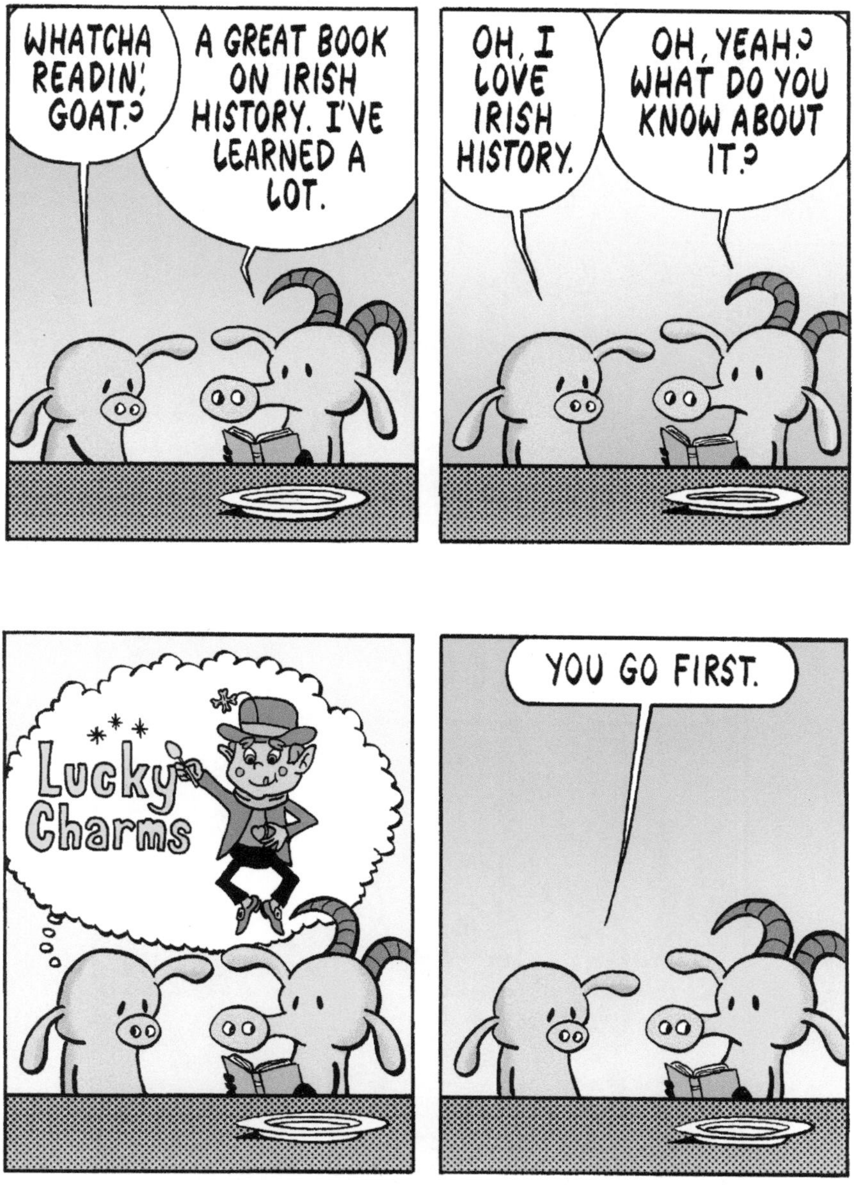
WHATCHA READIN', GOAT?
A GREAT BOOK ON IRISH HISTORY. I'VE LEARNED A LOT.
OH, I LOVE IRISH HISTORY.
OH, YEAH? WHAT DO YOU KNOW ABOUT IT?
Lucky Charms
YOU GO FIRST.

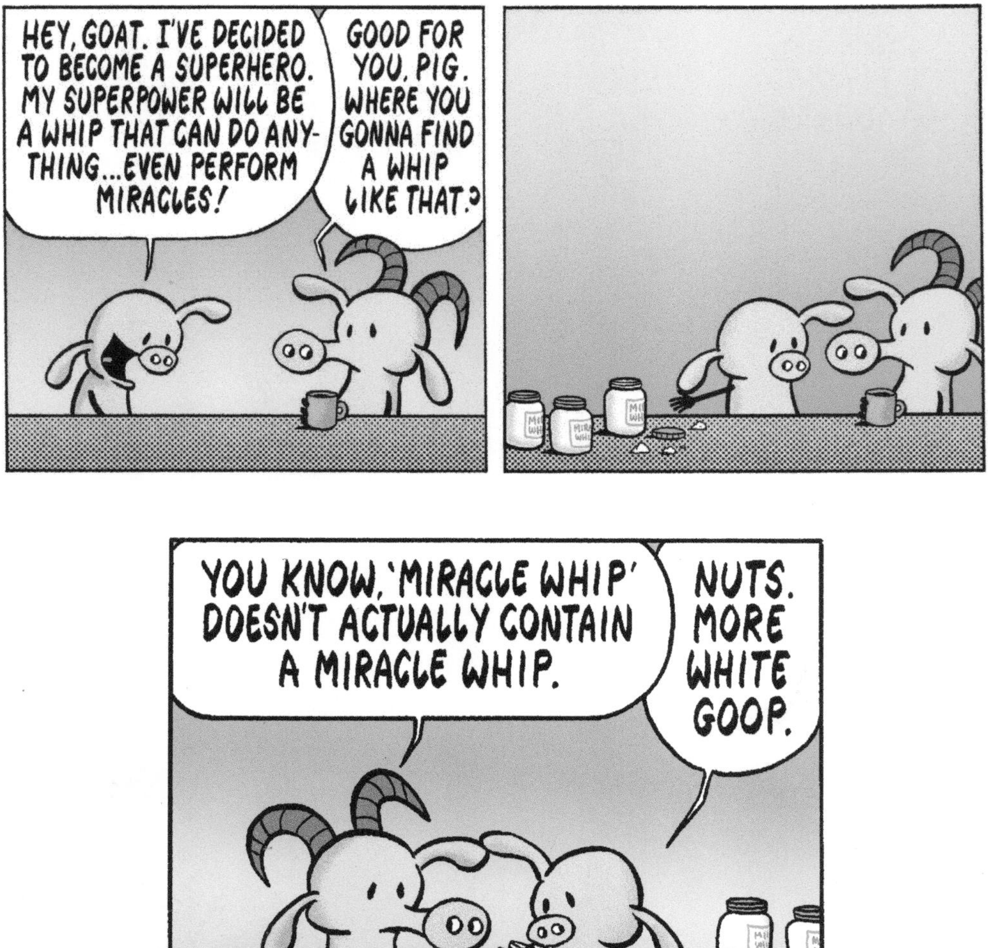
HEY, GOAT. I'VE DECIDED TO BECOME A SUPERHERO. MY SUPERPOWER WILL BE A WHIP THAT CAN DO ANYTHING...EVEN PERFORM MIRACLES!
GOOD FOR YOU, PIG. WHERE YOU GONNA FIND A WHIP LIKE THAT?
YOU KNOW, 'MIRACLE WHIP' DOESN'T ACTUALLY CONTAIN A MIRACLE WHIP.
NUTS. MORE WHITE GOOP.

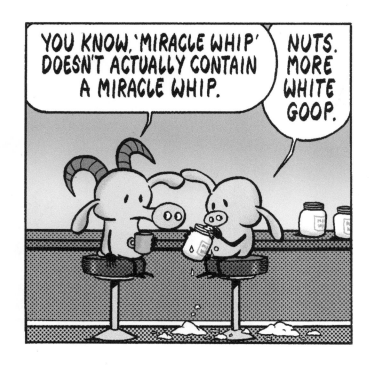

How 'bout YOU go run across highway, Bob?
GIMME BACK THE CART, PAL.
Peese no hit me, Man-Een-Funny-Pants.

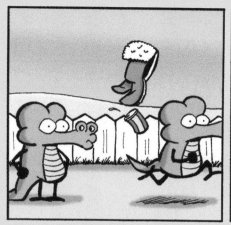

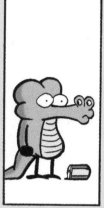

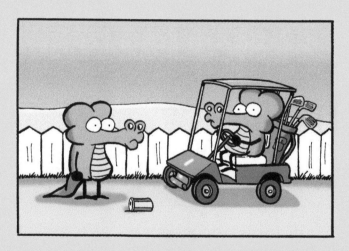

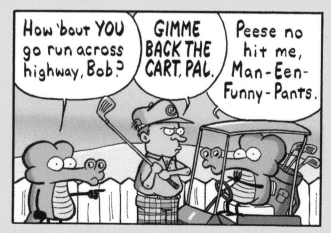

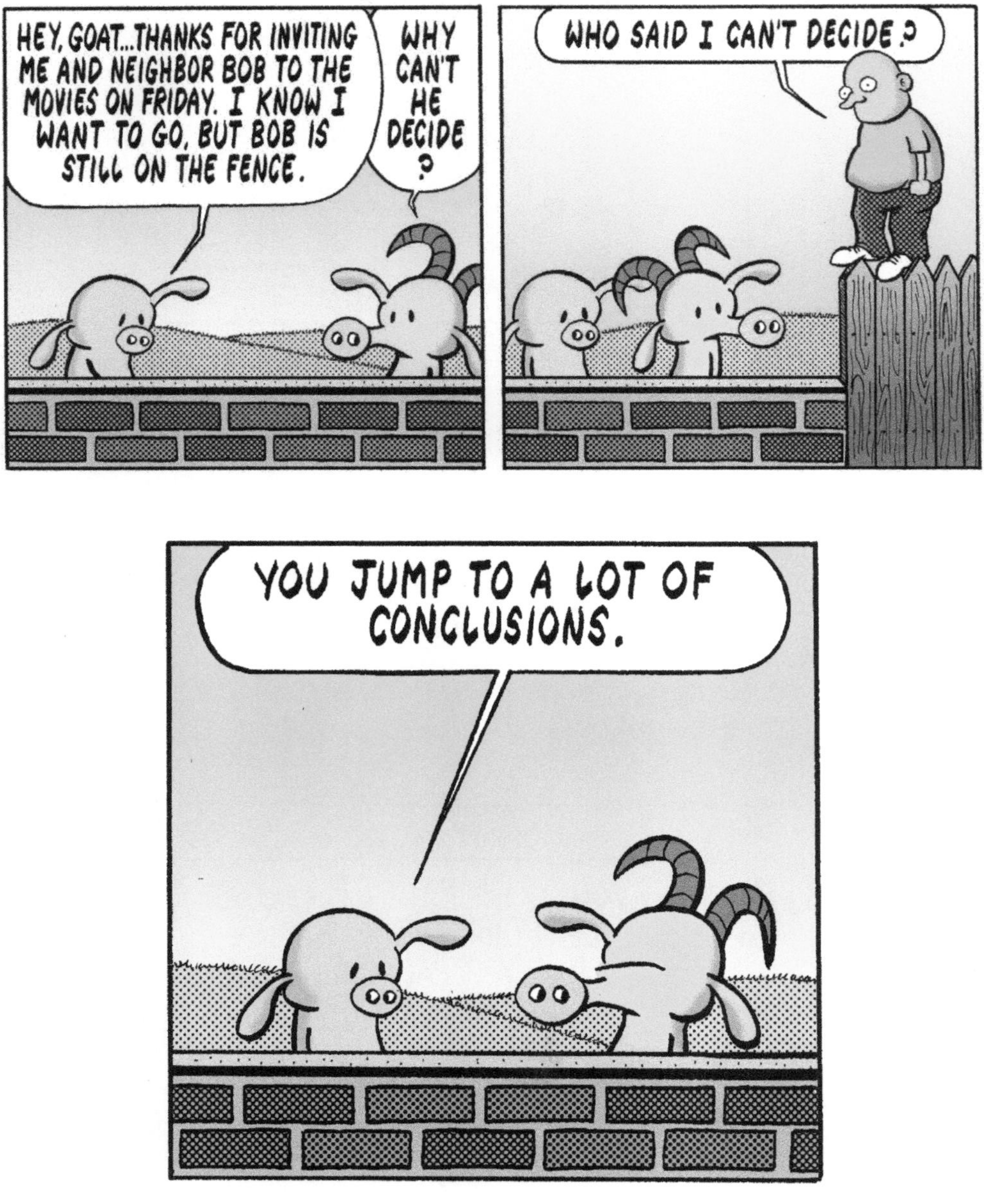
HEY, GOAT...THANKS FOR INVITING ME AND NEIGHBOR BOB TO THE MOVIES ON FRIDAY. I KNOW I WANT TO GO, BUT BOB IS STILL ON THE FENCE.
WHY CAN'T HE DECIDE?
WHO SAID I CAN'T DECIDE?
YOU JUMP TO A LOT OF CONCLUSIONS.

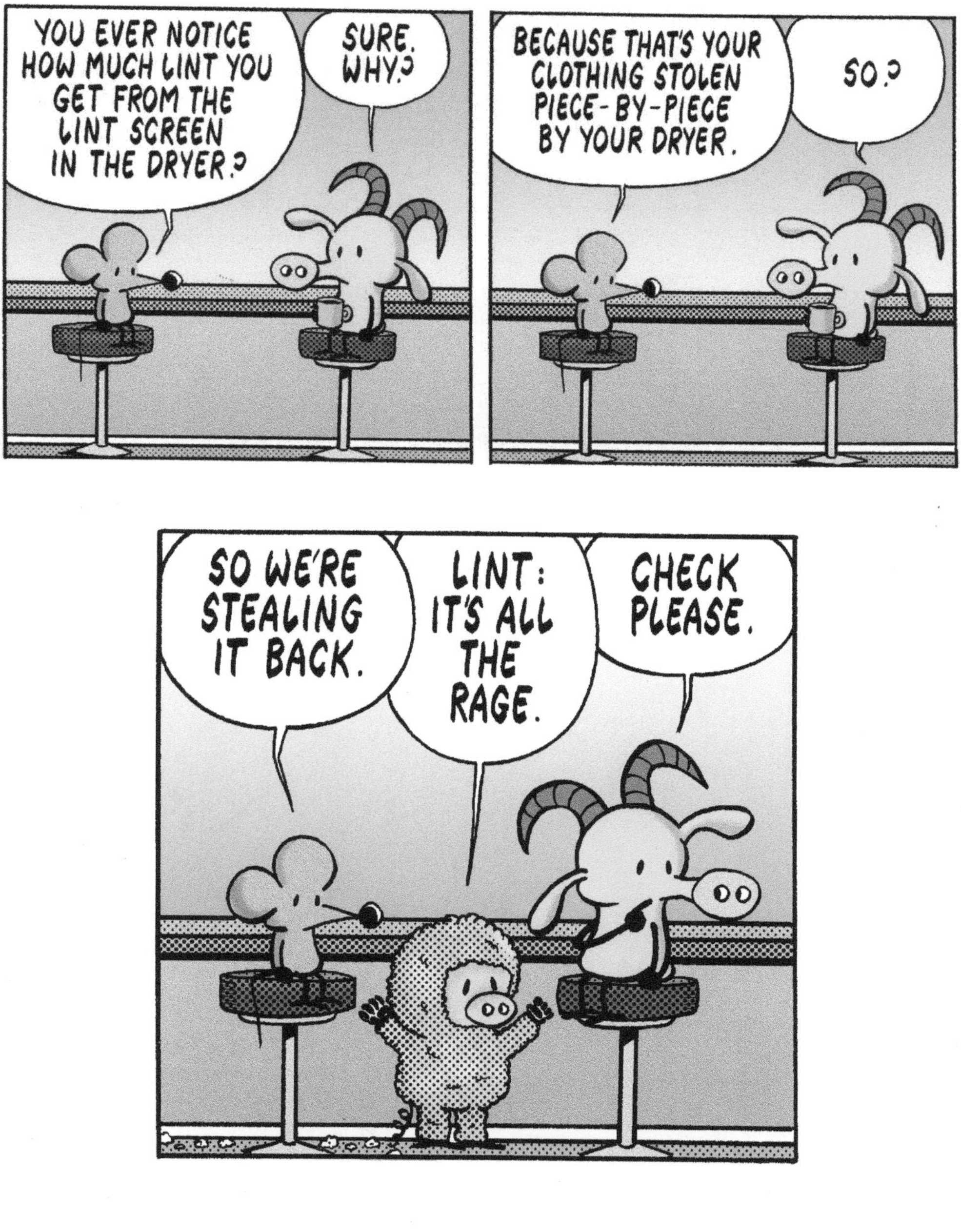
YOU EVER NOTICE HOW MUCH LINT YOU GET FROM THE LINT SCREEN IN THE DRYER?
SURE. WHY?
BECAUSE THAT'S YOUR CLOTHING STOLEN PIECE-BY-PIECE BY YOUR DRYER.
SO?
SO WE'RE STEALING IT BACK.
LINT: IT'S ALL THE RAGE.
CHECK PLEASE.

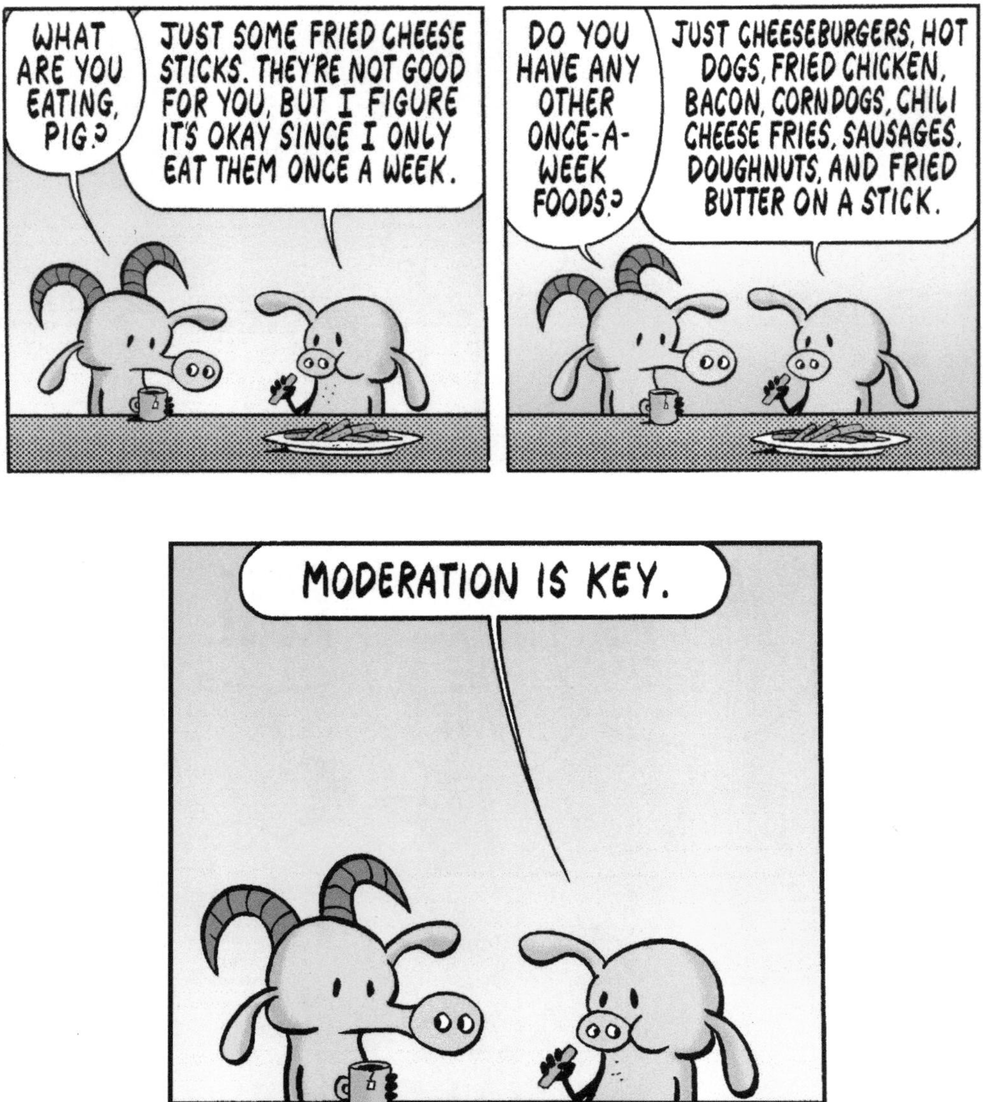
WHAT ARE YOU EATING, PIG?
JUST SOME FRIED CHEESE STICKS. THEY'RE NOT GOOD FOR YOU, BUT I FIGURE IT'S OKAY SINCE I ONLY EAT THEM ONCE A WEEK.
DO YOU HAVE ANY OTHER ONCE-A-WEEK FOODS?
JUST CHEESEBURGERS, HOT DOGS, FRIED CHICKEN, BACON, CORNDOGS, CHILI CHEESE FRIES, SAUSAGES, DOUGHNUTS, AND FRIED BUTTER ON A STICK.
MODERATION IS KEY.

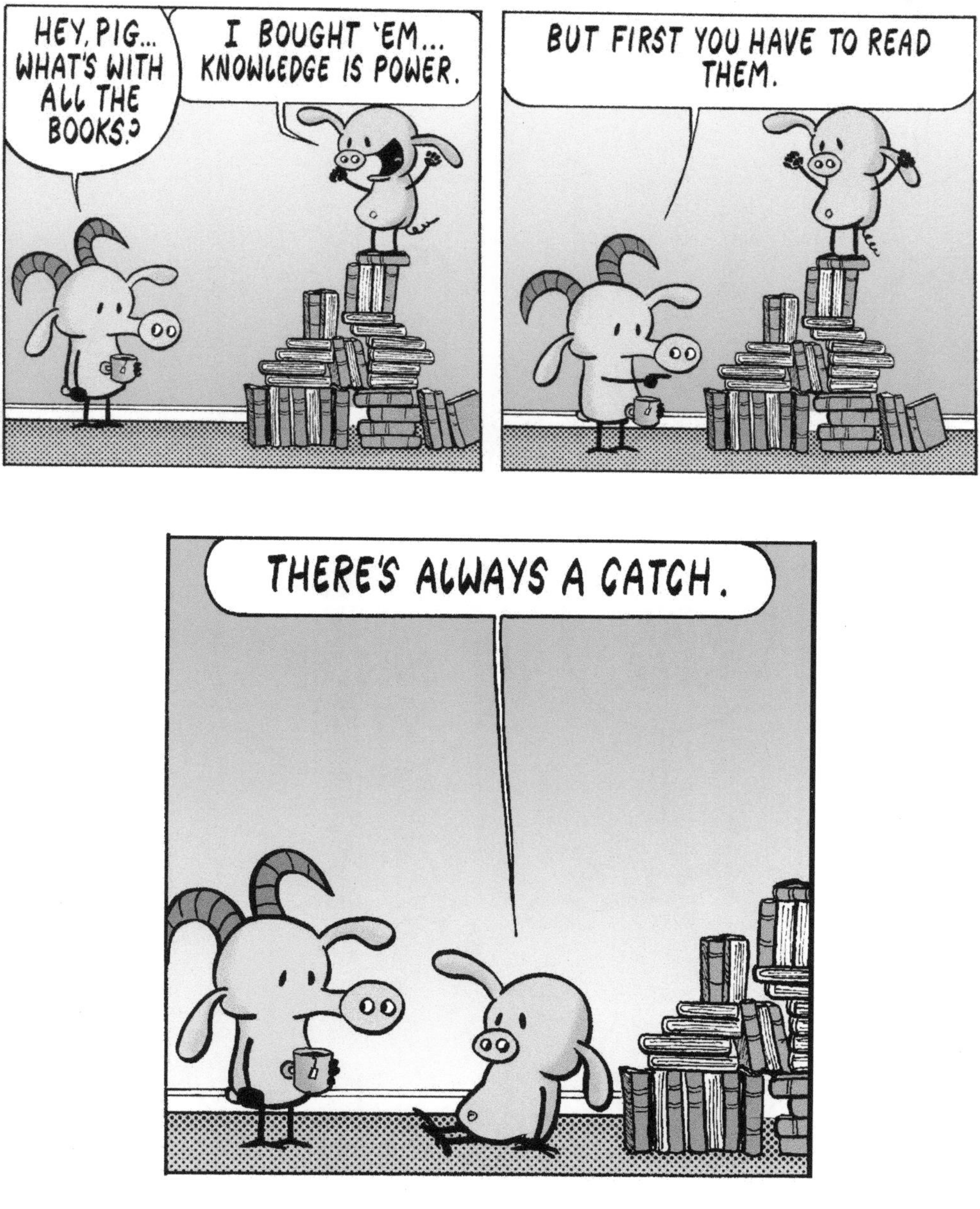
HEY, PIG... WHAT'S WITH ALL THE BOOKS?
I BOUGHT 'EM... KNOWLEDGE IS POWER.
BUT FIRST YOU HAVE TO READ THEM.
THERE'S ALWAYS A CATCH.

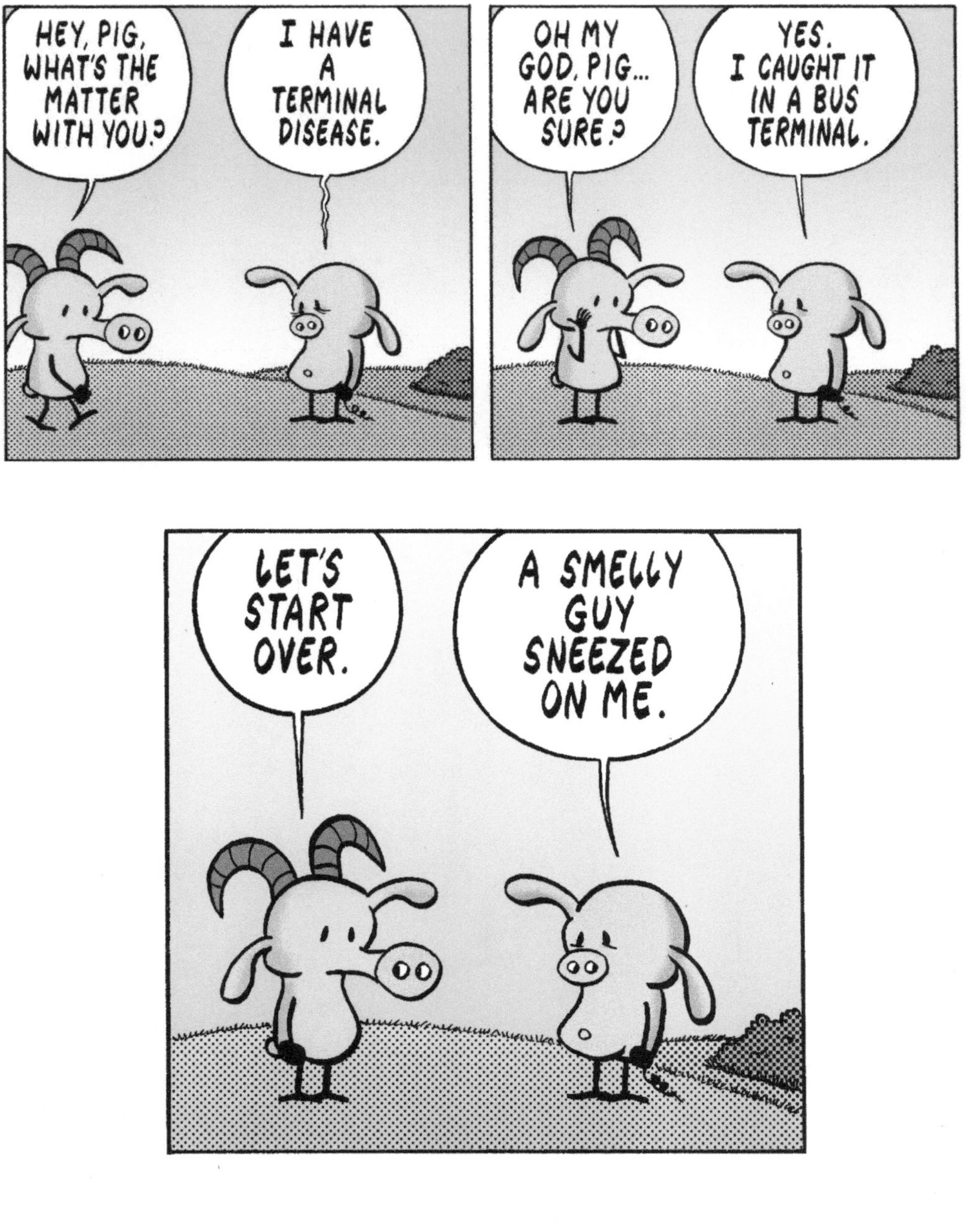
HEY, PIG, WHAT'S THE MATTER WITH YOU?
I HAVE A TERMINAL DISEASE.
OH MY GOD, PIG... ARE YOU SURE?
YES. I CAUGHT IT IN A BUS TERMINAL.
LET'S START OVER.
A SMELLY GUY SNEEZED ON ME.

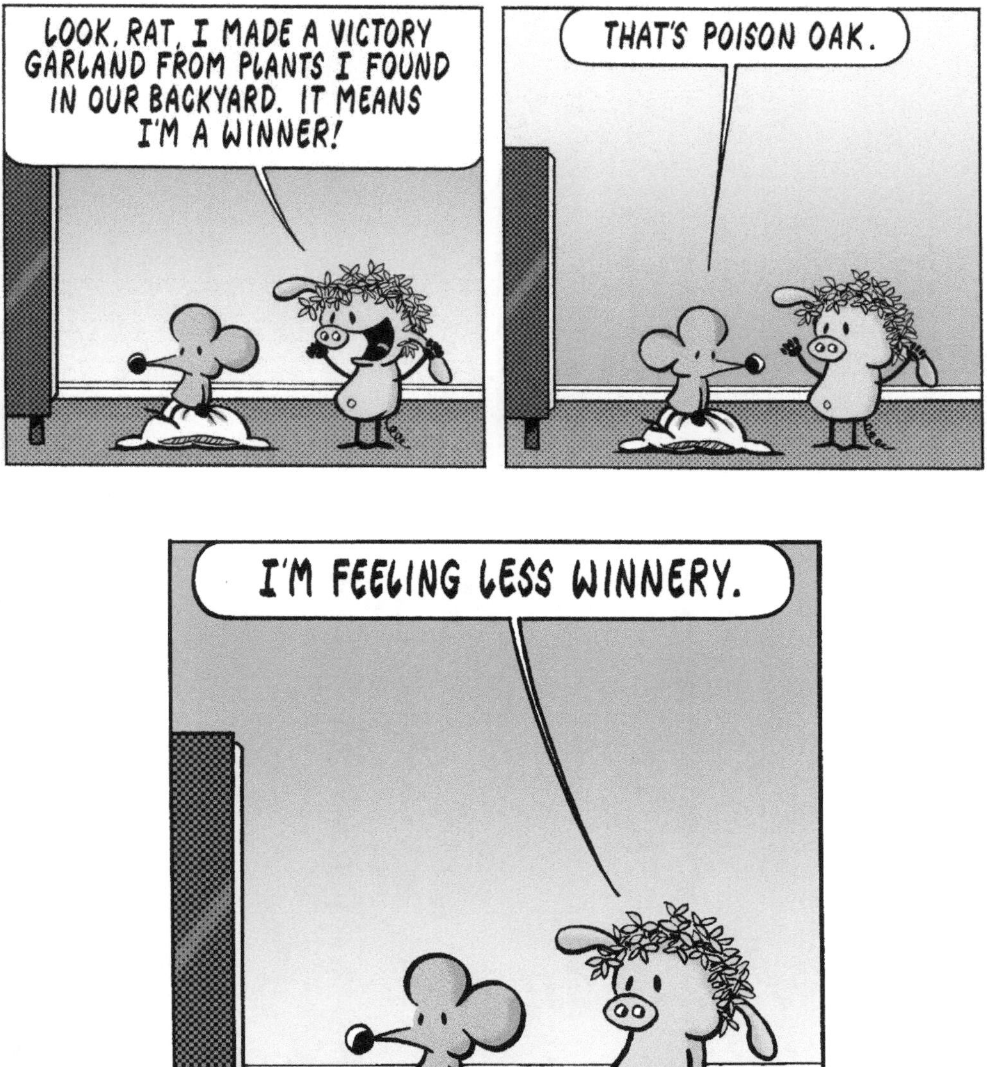
LOOK, RAT, I MADE A VICTORY GARLAND FROM PLANTS I FOUND IN OUR BACKYARD. IT MEANS I'M A WINNER!
THAT'S POISON OAK.
I'M FEELING LESS WINNERY.

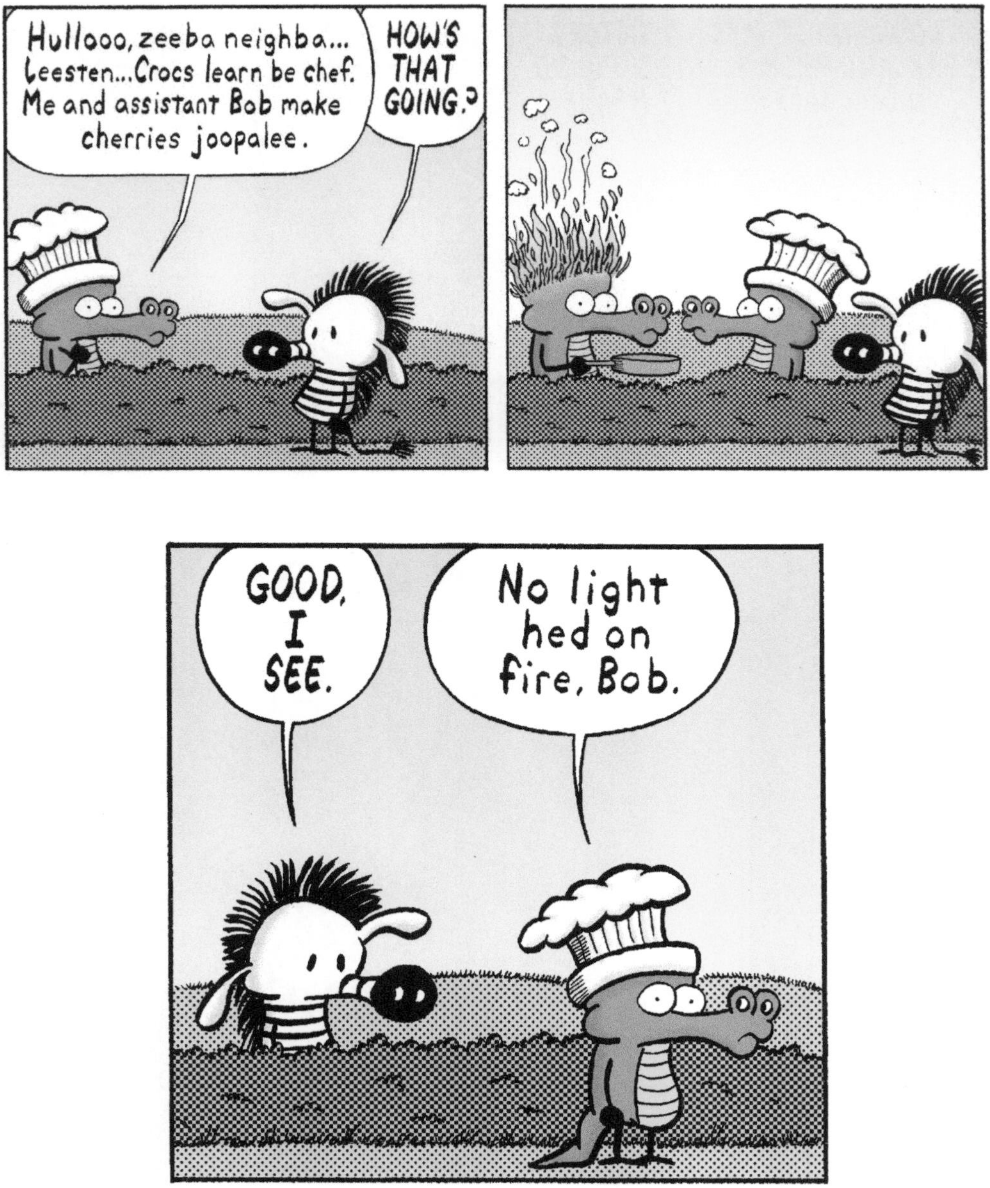
Hullooo, zeeba neighba... Leesten...Crocs learn be chef. Me and assistant Bob make cherries joopalee.
HOW'S THAT GOING?
GOOD, I SEE.
No light hed on fire, Bob.

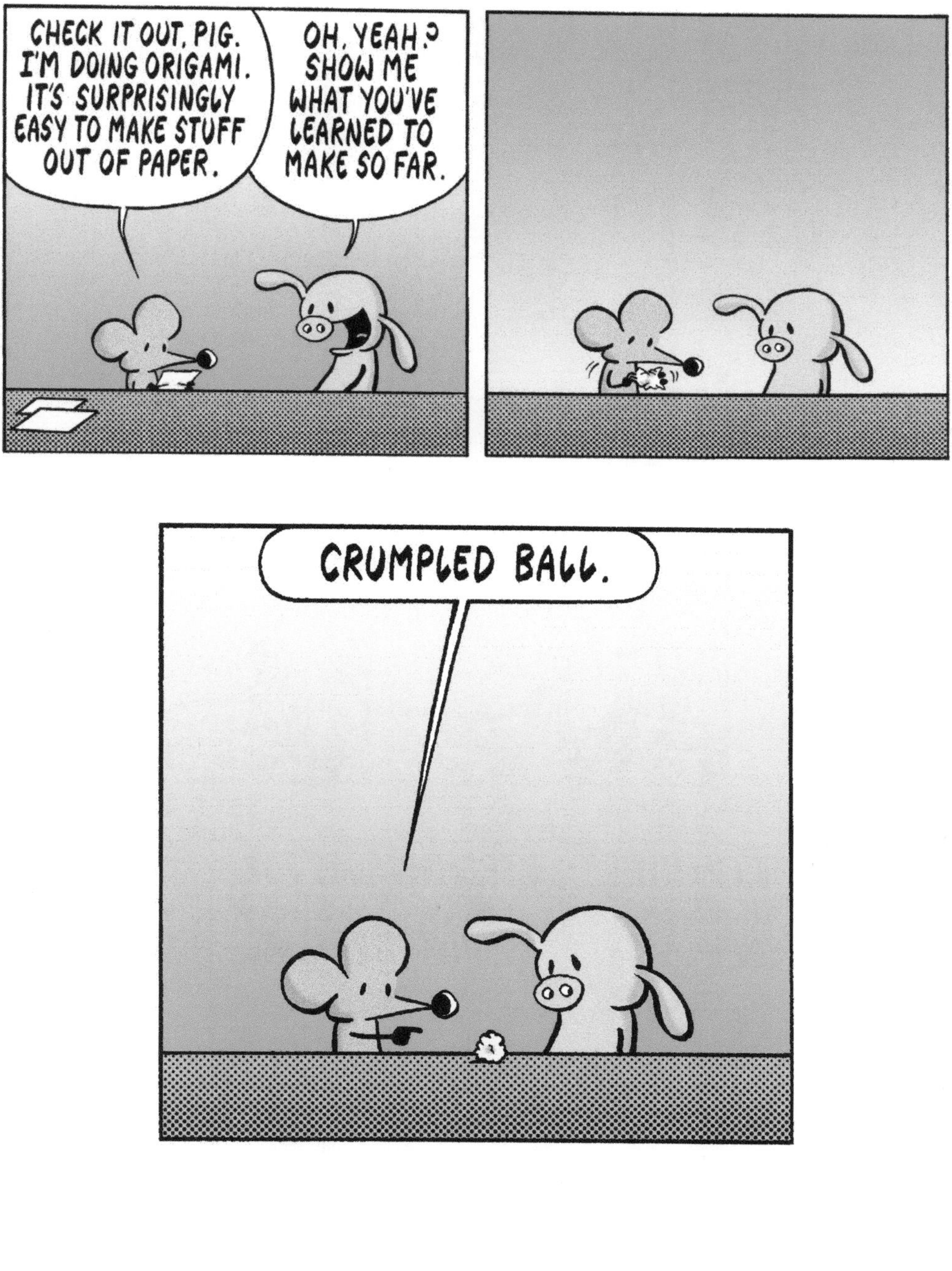
CHECK IT OUT, PIG. I'M DOING ORIGAMI. IT'S SURPRISINGLY EASY TO MAKE STUFF OUT OF PAPER.
OH, YEAH? SHOW ME WHAT YOU'VE LEARNED TO MAKE SO FAR.
CRUMPLED BALL.

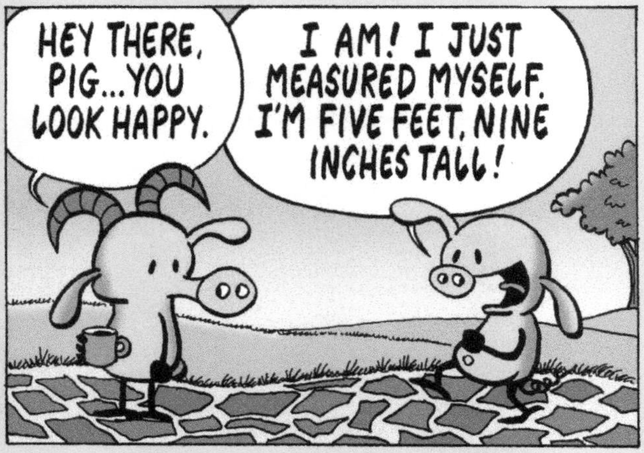
HEY THERE, PIG...YOU LOOK HAPPY.
I AM! I JUST MEASURED MYSELF. I'M FIVE FEET, NINE INCHES TALL!

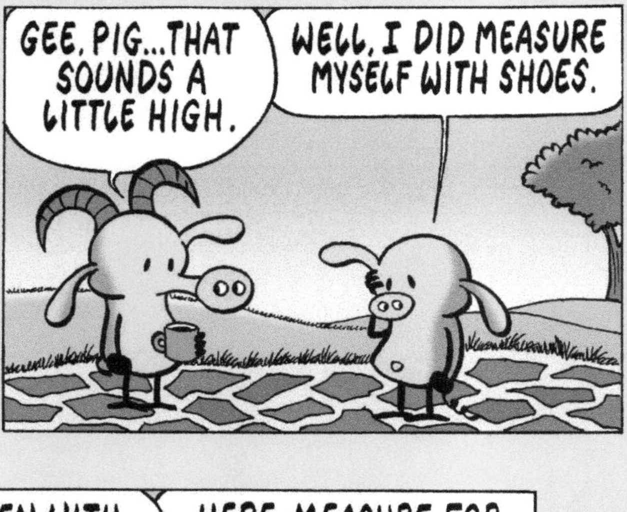
GEE, PIG...THAT SOUNDS A LITTLE HIGH.
WELL, I DID MEASURE MYSELF WITH SHOES.

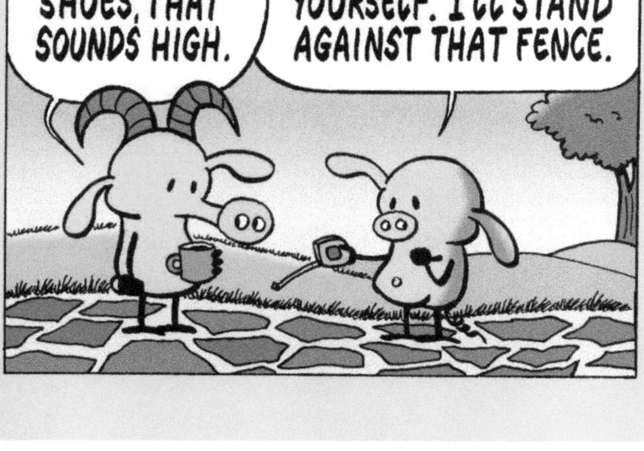
EVEN WITH SHOES, THAT SOUNDS HIGH.
HERE, MEASURE FOR YOURSELF. I'LL STAND AGAINST THAT FENCE.

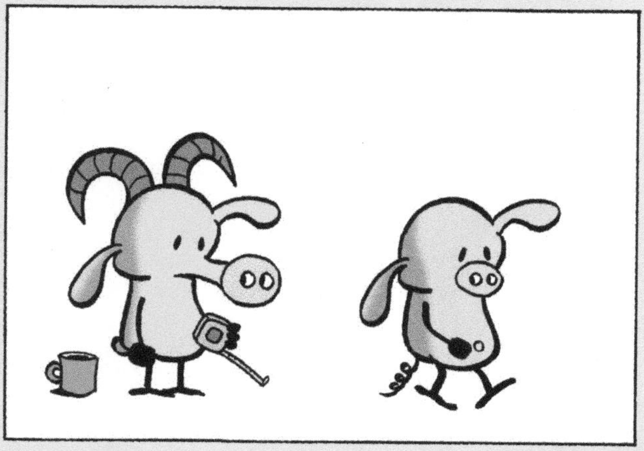

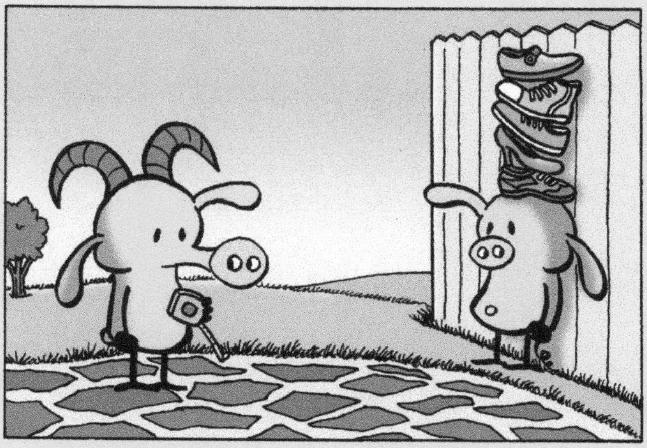

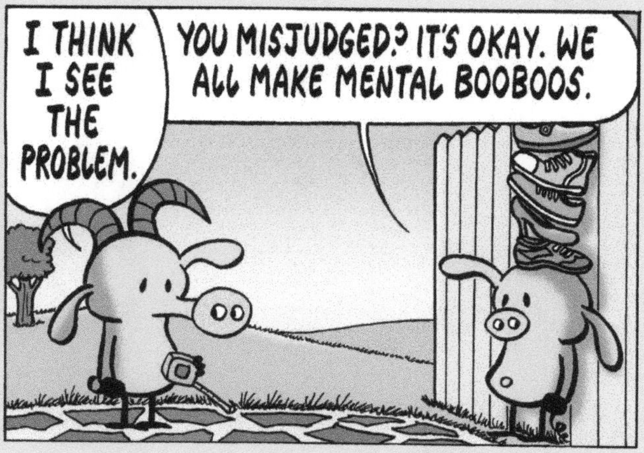
I THINK I SEE THE PROBLEM.
YOU MISJUDGED? IT'S OKAY. WE ALL MAKE MENTAL BOOBOOS.

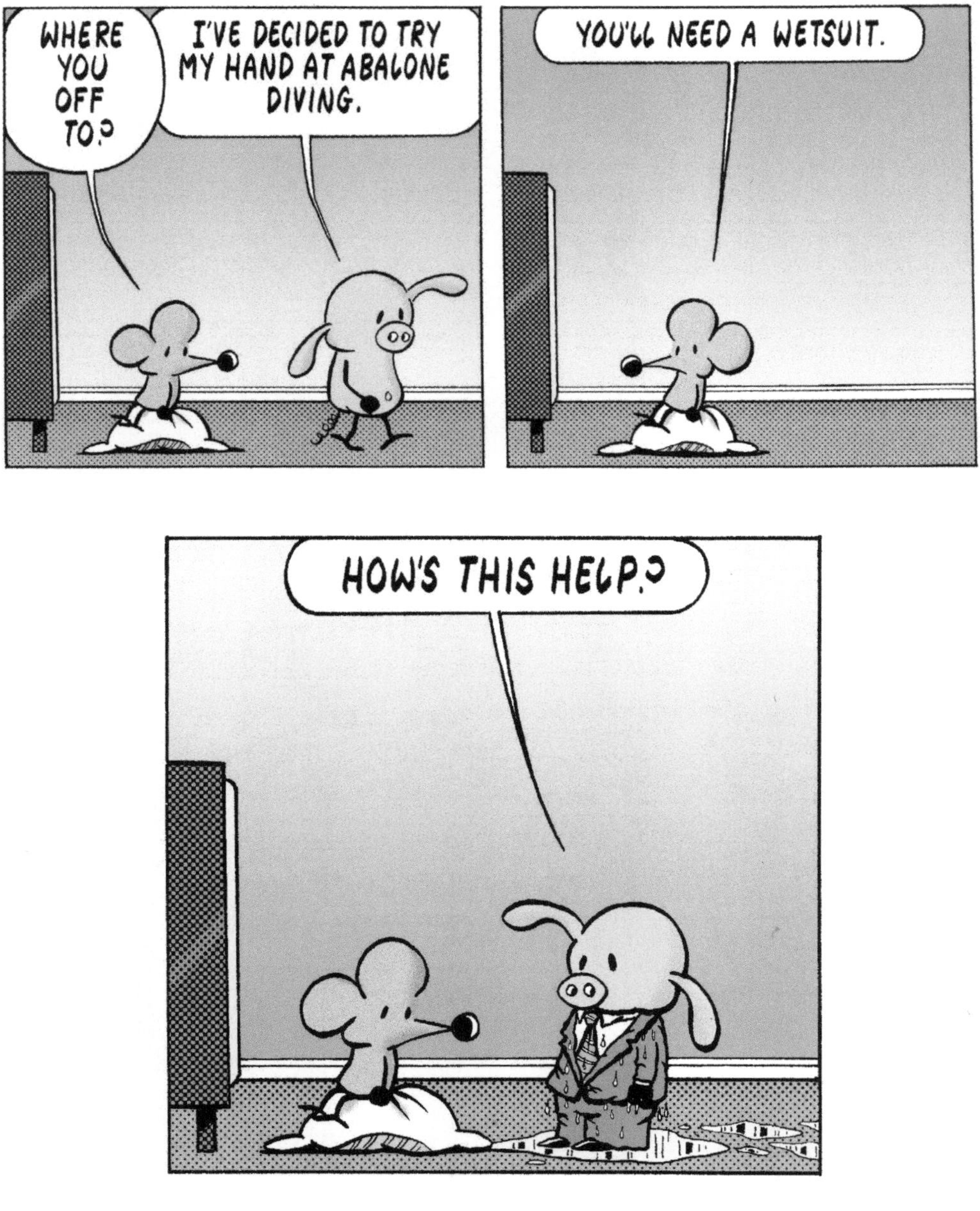
WHERE YOU OFF TO?
I'VE DECIDED TO TRY MY HAND AT ABALONE DIVING.
YOU'LL NEED A WETSUIT.
HOW'S THIS HELP?

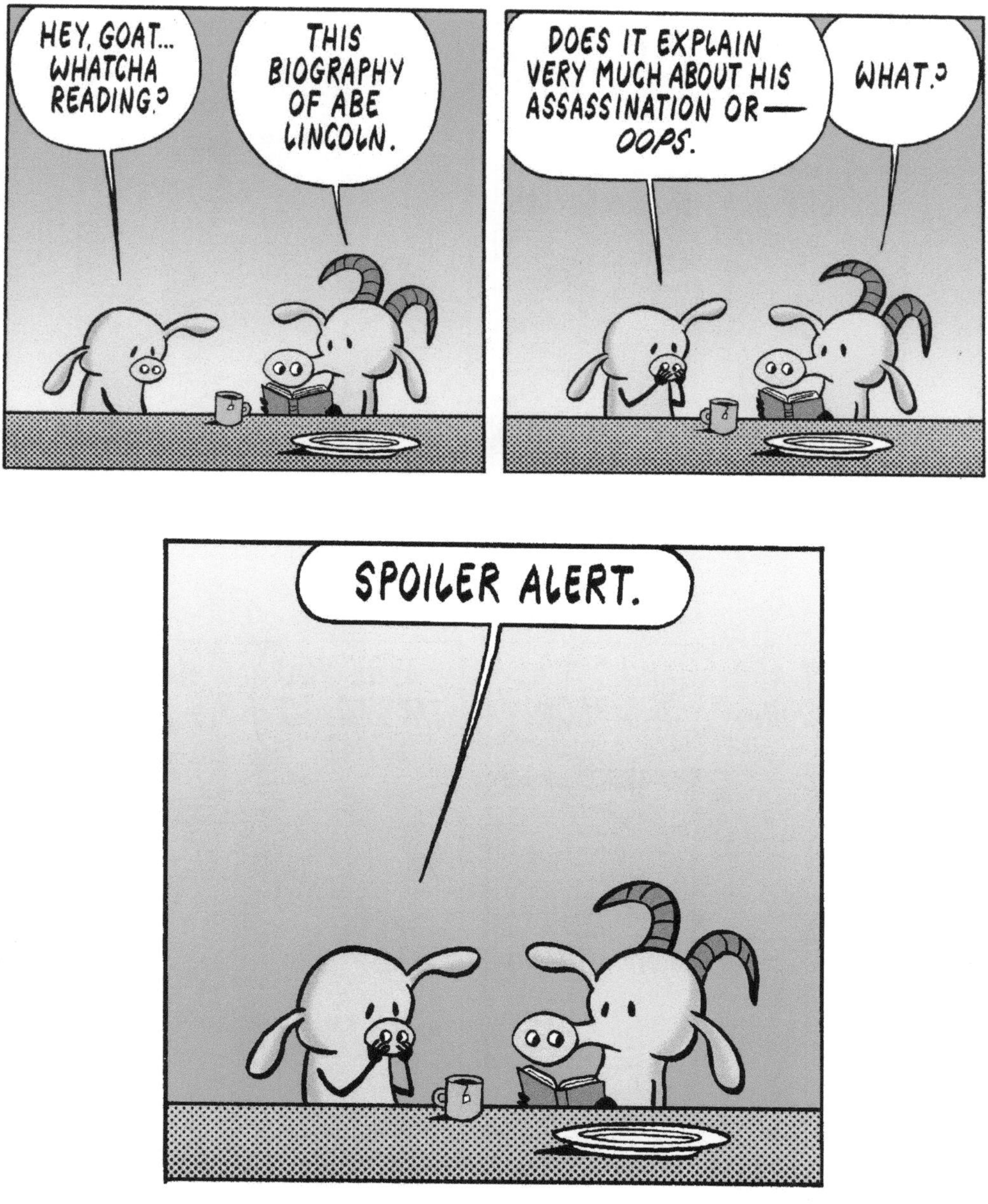
HEY, GOAT... WHATCHA READING?
THIS BIOGRAPHY OF ABE LINCOLN.
DOES IT EXPLAIN VERY MUCH ABOUT HIS ASSASSINATION OR— OOPS.
WHAT?
SPOILER ALERT.

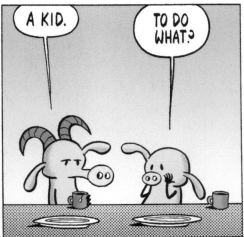

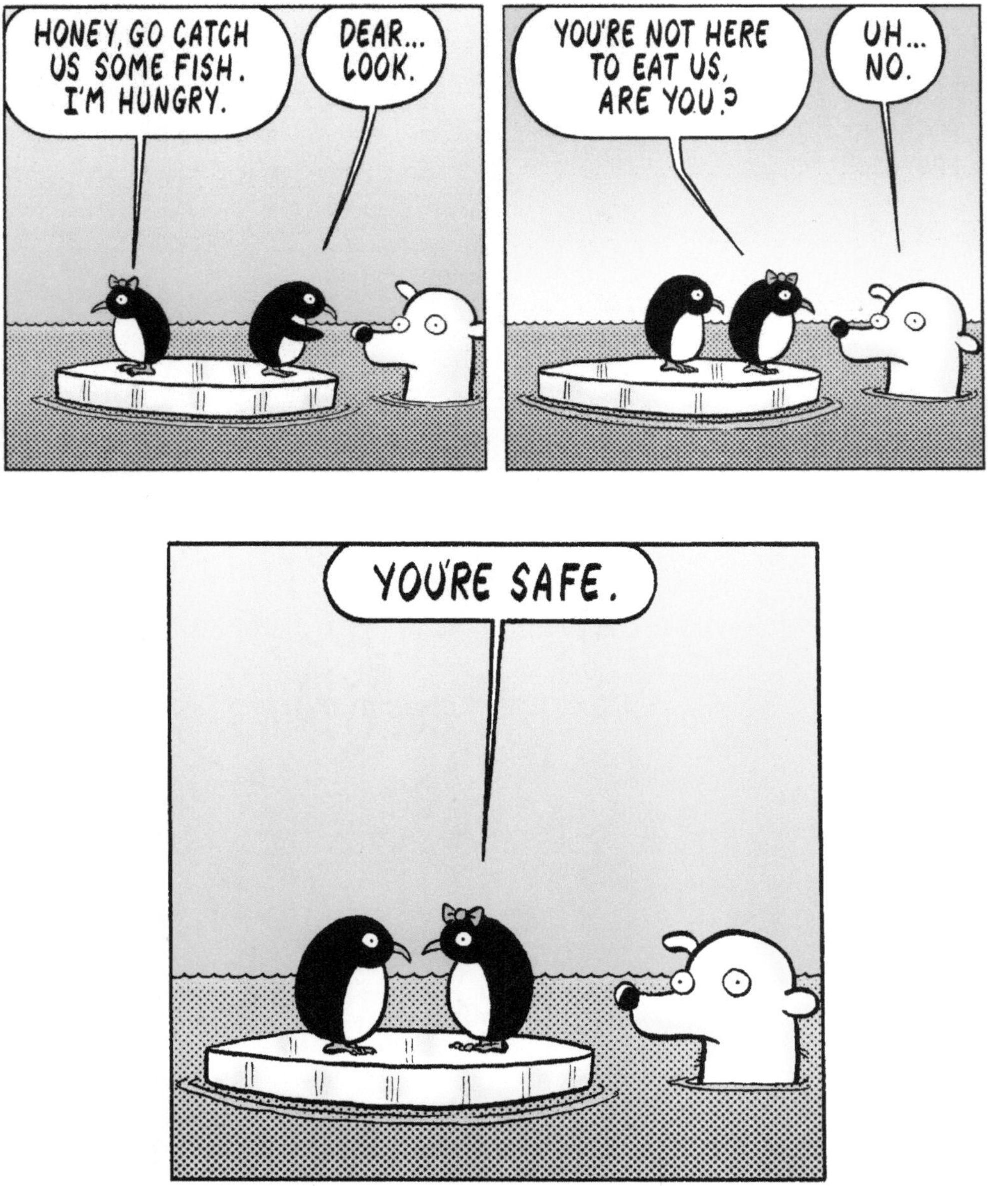
HONEY, GO CATCH US SOME FISH. I'M HUNGRY.
DEAR... LOOK.
YOU'RE NOT HERE TO EAT US, ARE YOU?
UH... NO.
YOU'RE SAFE.

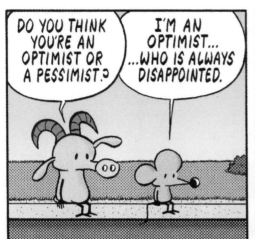

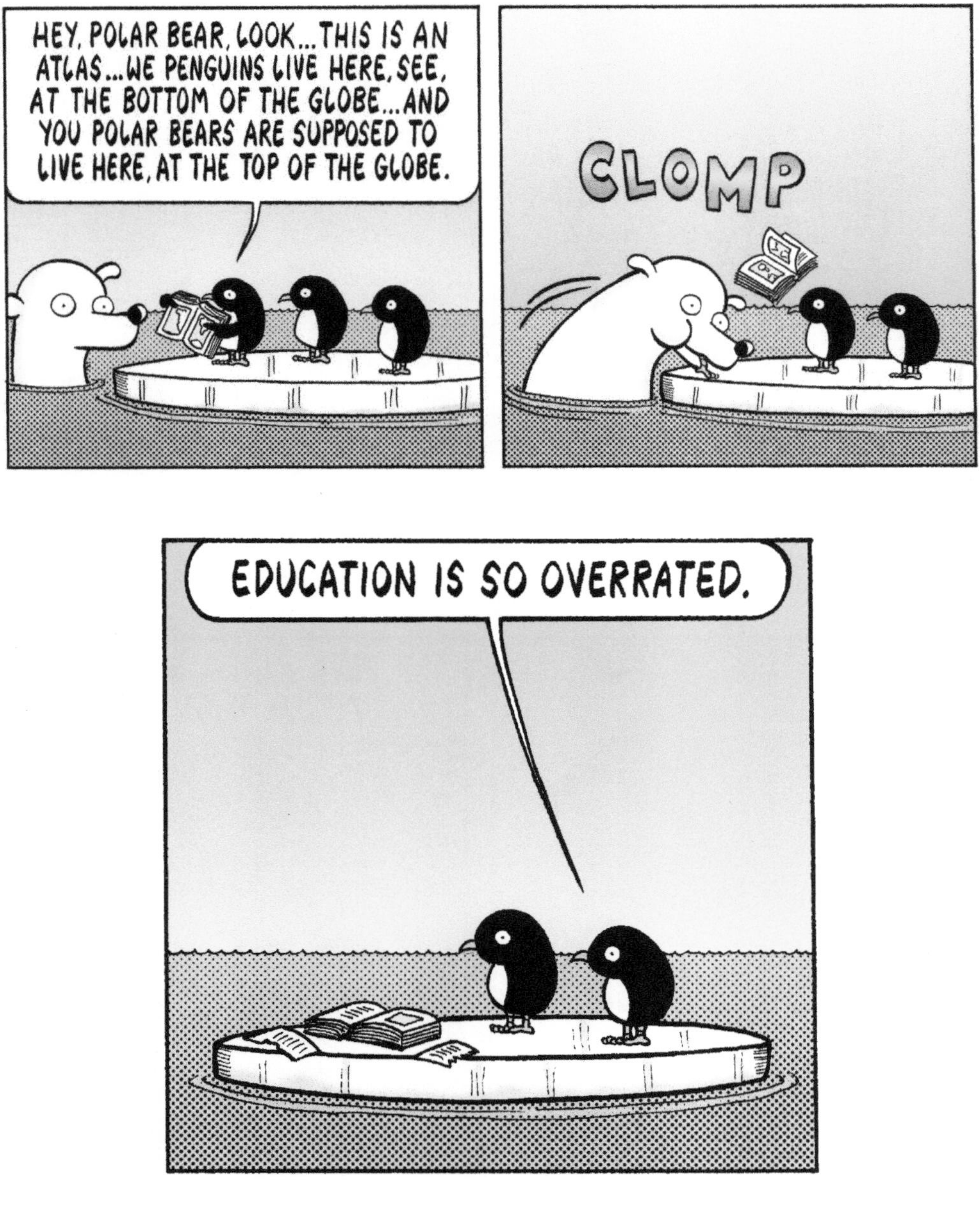
HEY, POLAR BEAR, LOOK...THIS IS AN ATLAS...WE PENGUINS LIVE HERE, SEE, AT THE BOTTOM OF THE GLOBE...AND YOU POLAR BEARS ARE SUPPOSED TO LIVE HERE, AT THE TOP OF THE GLOBE.
CLOMP
EDUCATION IS SO OVERRATED.

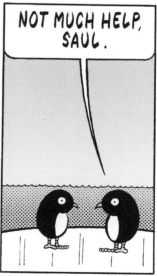

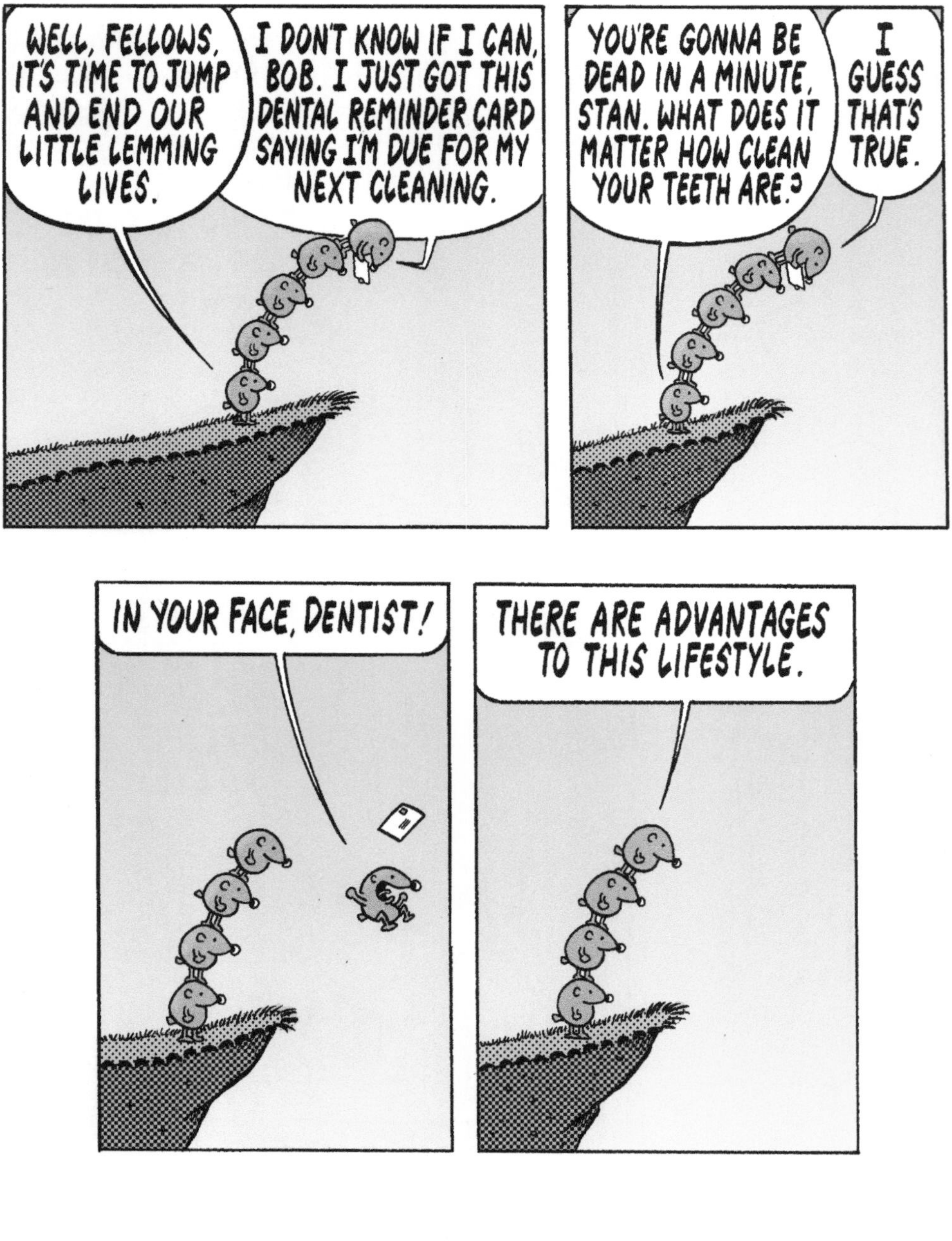
WELL, FELLOWS, IT'S TIME TO JUMP AND END OUR LITTLE LEMMING LIVES.
I DON'T KNOW IF I CAN, BOB. I JUST GOT THIS DENTAL REMINDER CARD SAYING I'M DUE FOR MY NEXT CLEANING.
YOU'RE GONNA BE DEAD IN A MINUTE, STAN. WHAT DOES IT MATTER HOW CLEAN YOUR TEETH ARE?
I GUESS THAT'S TRUE.
IN YOUR FACE, DENTIST!
THERE ARE ADVANTAGES TO THIS LIFESTYLE.

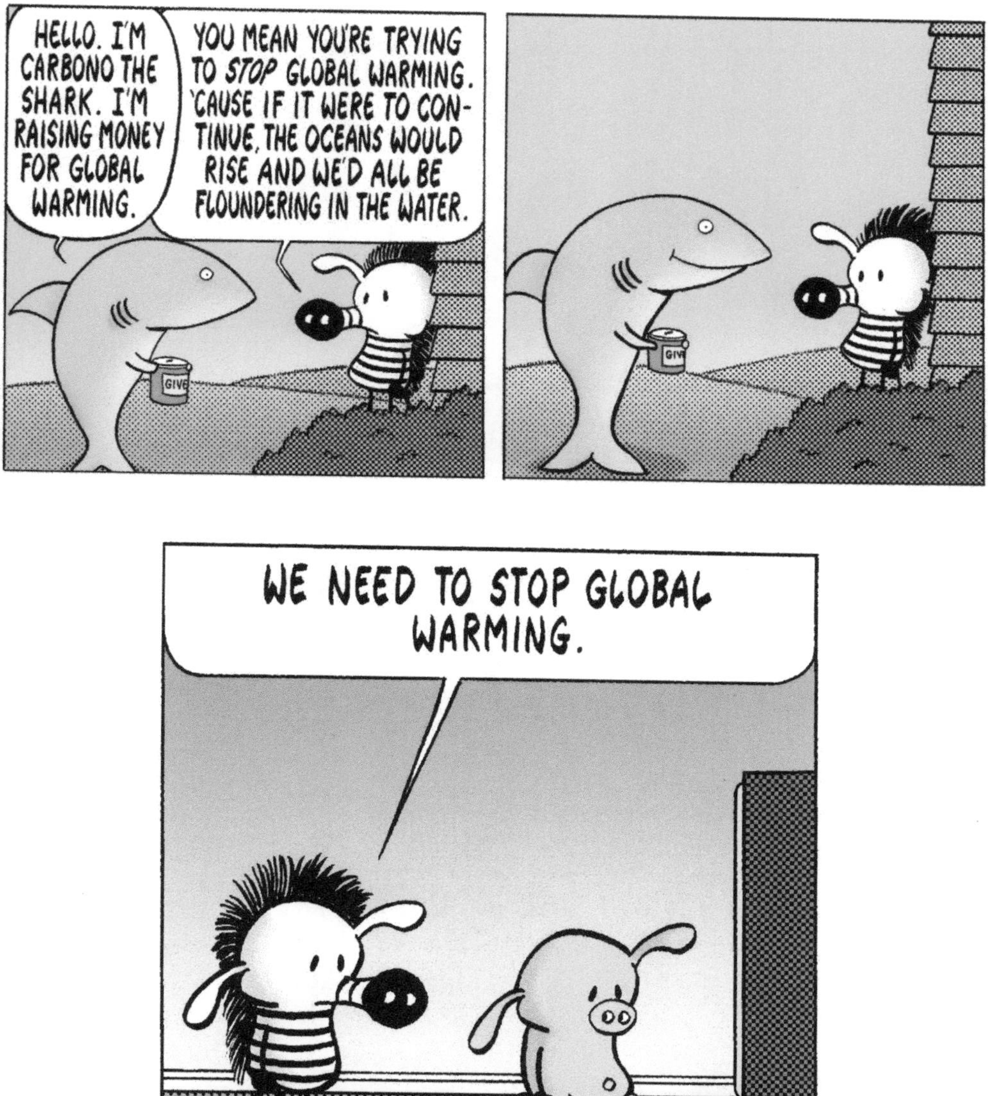
HELLO. I'M CARBONO THE SHARK. I'M RAISING MONEY FOR GLOBAL WARMING.
YOU MEAN YOU'RE TRYING TO *STOP* GLOBAL WARMING. 'CAUSE IF IT WERE TO CONTINUE, THE OCEANS WOULD RISE AND WE'D ALL BE FLOUNDERING IN THE WATER.
GIVE
WE NEED TO STOP GLOBAL WARMING.

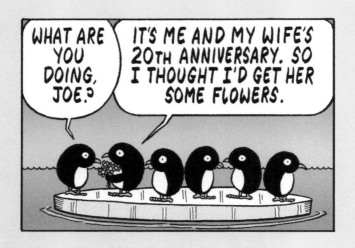

Andrews McMeel Publishing
a division of Andrews McMeel Universal
1130 Walnut Street, Kansas City, Missouri 64106

www.andrewsmcmeel.com

ISBN: 978-1-4494-8495-8

Library of Congress Control Number: 2015955642

*Pearls Before Swine* can be viewed on the Internet at www.pearlscomic.com.

---

**ATTENTION: SCHOOLS AND BUSINESSES**

Andrews McMeel books are available at quantity discounts with bulk purchase for educational, business, or sales promotional use. For information, please e-mail the Andrews McMeel Publishing Special Sales Department:
specialsales@amuniversal.com.

**Be sure to check out other *Pearls Before Swine* AMP! Comics for Kids books and others at ampkids.com.**

amp! COMICS for kids

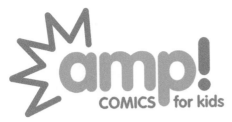

# Check out these and other books at ampkids.com

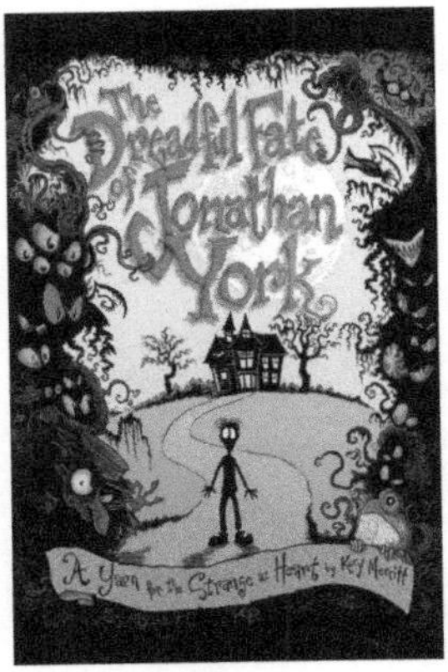
The Dreadful Fate of Jonathan York

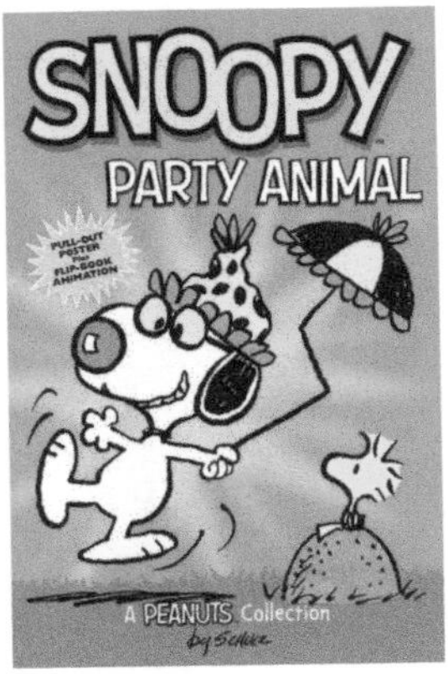
SNOOPY
PARTY ANIMAL
A PEANUTS Collection

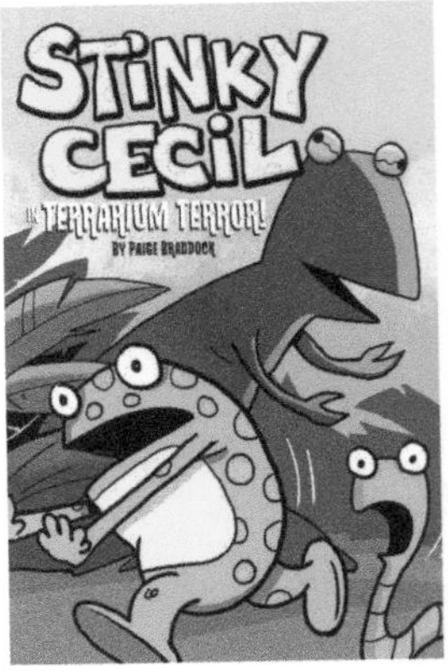
STINKY CECIL
IN TERRARIUM TERROR!

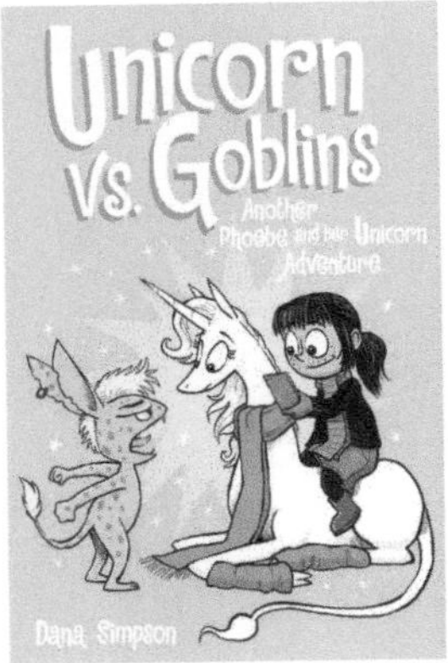
Unicorn vs. Goblins
Another Phoebe and her Unicorn Adventure
Dana Simpson

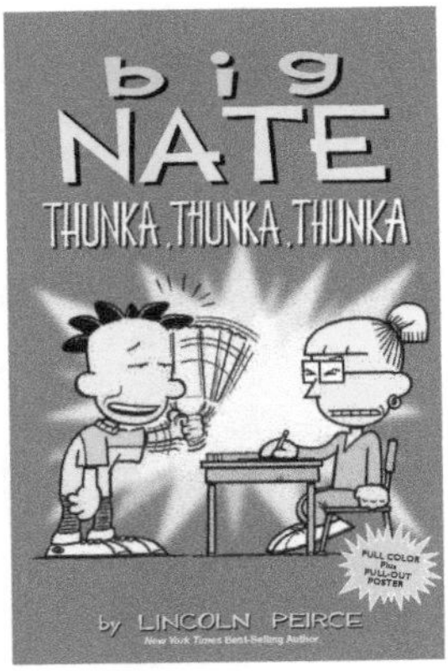
big NATE
THUNKA, THUNKA, THUNKA
by LINCOLN PEIRCE

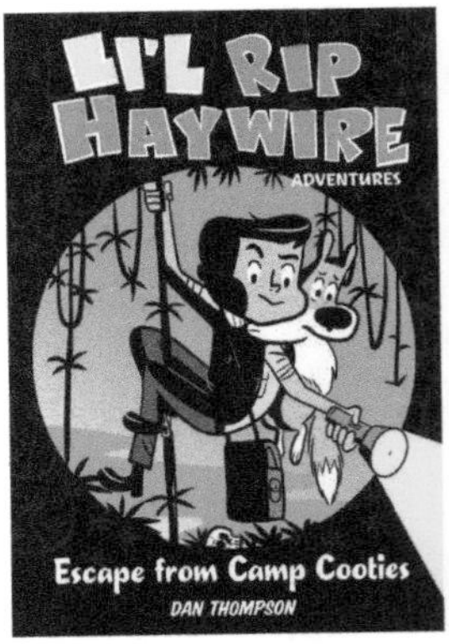
LI'L RIP HAYWIRE
ADVENTURES
Escape from Camp Cooties
DAN THOMPSON

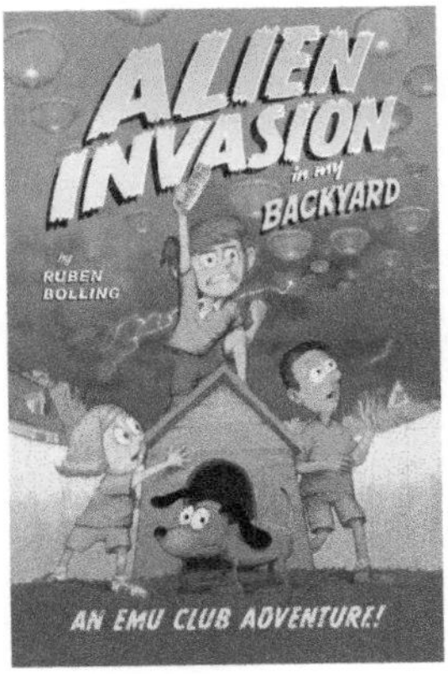
ALIEN INVASION in my BACKYARD
by RUBEN BOLLING
AN EMU CLUB ADVENTURE!

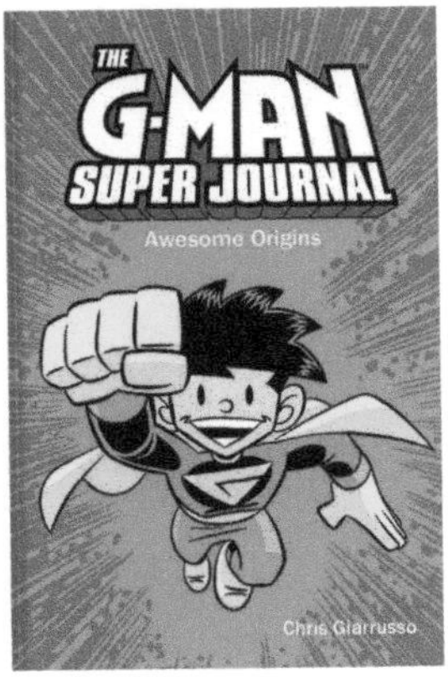
THE G-MAN SUPER JOURNAL
Awesome Origins
Chris Giarrusso

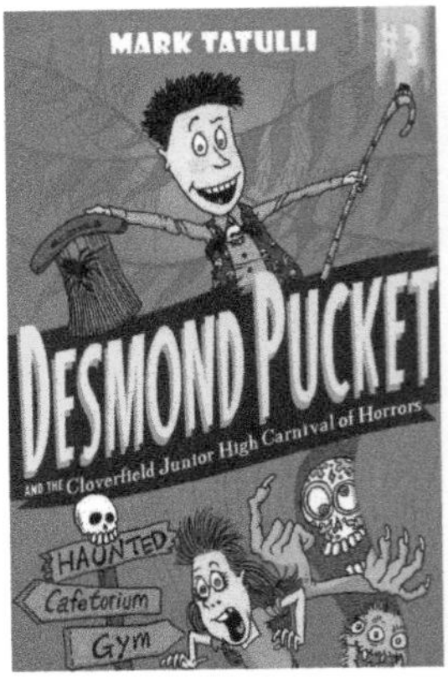
MARK TATULLI
DESMOND PUCKET
AND THE Cloverfield Junior High Carnival of Horrors
HAUNTED
Cafetorium
Gym

**Also available:**
**Teaching and activity guides for each title.**

AMP! Comics for Kids books make reading FUN!

CPSIA information can be obtained
at www.ICGtesting.com
Printed in the USA
LVHW071449100121
676153LV00012B/443